THE ARTIST AND THE FEAST

THE ARTIST AND THE FEAST

Lucy Steeds

UNION
SQUARE
& CO.

NEW YORK

UNION SQUARE & CO.

NEW YORK

ISBN 978-1-4549-6052-2
ISBN 978-1-4549-6054-6 (Paperback)
ISBN 978-1-4549-6053-9 (e-book)

For information about custom editions, special sales, and premium purchases,
please contact specialsales@unionsquareandco.com.

Printed in the United States of America

2 4 6 8 10 9 7 5 3 1

unionsquareandco.com

Cover design by Patrick Sullivan
Cover art: Bridgeman images: Private Collection/Christie's Images (fruit and shellfish);
Rijksmuseum, Amsterdam, The Netherlands (cheese and nuts);
Shutterstock.com: arteria.lab (paint), BERNATSKAIA OKSANA (fire),
CHIRAPHAN (burnt wood), JayPierstorff (palette)
Interior design by Kevin Ullrich

For my father, who gave me a love of language, and my mother, who taught me to go further than I dared.

We only see what we look at. To look is an act of choice.

John Berger, *Ways of Seeing*

I mislead him and do not tell him the truth because, by lying, I can dance in and out of the prison bars.

Celia Paul, *Self-Portrait*

...aptitude. The scent of growing up, of a friend.

...woman has traveled a long way, to stand here, in a tavern
...part of the Maximus Gallery. Crowds ebb like shoals of fish
...heels clicking against the polished wooden floor, but
...does not move. She stands straight and still, a [fork]
over one arm.

...does not take her eyes from the painting,
a large canvas, wide and tall, with an ornate golden frame.
...are vivid. The paint is thick like glue. She could reach
...and run her fingertip over the ragged surface if she
...but she does not.

...eyes shift to a plaque affixed to the wall.

Edouard Tartuffe, 1859–1921
Le Festin (The Feast), 1920
Oil on canvas

The Feast depicts a table laden with food, some half-eaten, some
rotting, but nobody present. The colours are characteristic of
Tartuffe's bright, luminous palette, and the painting showcases the
distinctive brushwork which earned him the name "Master of Light."
Particular skill is shown in the reflections in the wineglasses and
the smear of butter on a silver knife. The table is laid for thirteen,
which has led some to suggest it is an allegory of the Last Supper.
The uneaten feast can be seen to represent the futility of decadence
at the First World War, as well as lives interrupted and pleasure
... The Feast is the only painting to survive the fire that
...

LONDON, 1957

A woman. A painting. The sense of greeting an old friend.

The woman has traveled a long way to stand here, in a cavernous room of the National Gallery. Crowds ebb like shoals of fish around her, heels flitting against the polished wooden floor, but the woman does not move. She stands straight and still, a folded raincoat over one arm.

She does not take her eyes from the painting.

It is a large canvas, wide and tall, with an ornate golden frame. The colours are vivid. The paint is thick like glue. She could reach out a hand and run her fingertip over the cragged surface if she wanted, but she does not.

Her eyes shift to a plaque affixed to the wall.

Edouard Tartuffe, 1859–1921
Le Festin (*The Feast*), 1920
Oil on canvas

The Feast depicts a table laden with food, some half-eaten, some rotting, but nobody present. The colours are characteristic of Tartuffe's bright, luminous palette, and the painting showcases the distinctive brushwork which earned him the name "Master of Light." Particular skill is shown in the reflections in the wineglasses and the smear of butter on a silver knife. The table is laid for thirteen, which has led some to suggest it is an allegory of the Last Supper. The uneaten feast can be seen to represent the futility of decadence after the First World War, as well as lives interrupted and pleasure wasted. *The Feast* is the only painting to survive the fire that destroyed Tartuffe's studio in 1920.

A smile flickers across the woman's face. She remembers the fire. She remembers the stacks of paintings buckling among dancing amber flames. She remembers the acrid smell of smoke and melting varnish. A wall of heat. Paint evaporating into fumes.

She remembers this painting too. She remembers *The Feast* cracking down the middle, fire lapping at its edges. She remembers orange tongues eating at the canvas until wineglasses and melon halves and slices of ham were reduced to nothing but dry black curlicues on the studio floor. She remembers the fire swallowing the feast whole.

And most of all, she remembers setting the blaze.

PART I

THE PAINTER

SAINT-AUGUSTE-DE-PROVENCE, 1920
JOSEPH

A stranger comes to town. He walks along a dusty road, fields of lavender on one side, a placid green river on the other. The sun beats down on his bare head and he carries only a battered knapsack over one shoulder. He is young, barely twenty, and walks tall and straight like a ballet dancer, or a soldier who has never seen war. The town is a sleepy hamlet in the south of France. The stranger is Joseph Adelaide.

He clutches a letter in his hand. He has read it over and over but it contains only one word:

Venez. Come.

Beneath that is a signature. The letter is from somebody Joseph has never met but he knows the signature intimately. It is a signature most often found in the corner of paintings. It is scrawled in the corner of Joseph's favourite painting in the National Gallery, *Bathers at Arles*. It appears on paintings in gilded frames at Sotheby's and the Knoedler. And it is at the bottom of a letter addressed to him.

Joseph had been apprehensive about sending his request at first. He had reworked and rewritten it, crossing out his puny phrases and feeble wording. He had gone through draft after draft until one day, after months of agonising, his sister had snatched the letter from his hand and taken it to the post office herself.

There had followed months of silence. Joseph put the letter out of his mind; he had been foolish to think he would get a response. Arrogant, even. He buried his head in his hands whenever he thought of it.

But then . . . this. In early June a single sheet of paper had arrived.

He had not needed the return address to know who the letter was from. He had not needed the cluster of foreign stamps or the blue ink of the French postal service. The signature had told him everything. He had packed his bags that very morning, sent a telegram to his editor to let him know that yes, it was happening, yes, he had received a reply, and yes, he was going. He did not know when he would be back.

Joseph had caught a crowded train to Charing Cross, then another to Dover and talked his way onto a steamer bound for Calais. A further train had taken him to Paris where he had spent an uncomfortable night in a rickety boardinghouse before catching the morning train to Avignon. It was late when he arrived, too late to go on, and so he took a room in the hostel by the station. The next morning he wandered the pale stone streets, knapsack over his shoulder. There were no trains to where he needed to go next. No public transportation at all. He eventually managed to flag down a trundling milk cart and hitch a ride to Saint-Auguste, where he has just been deposited on the side of the road.

He is dusty. He is sweaty, and nearly blinded by the hot, white light of the Mediterranean sun.

A crinkled woman in the village tobacconist has given him directions: go down the empty road, keeping the river on your left.

Go past the tumbledown church until you come to a donkey track. If you reach the caves you have gone too far. Turn left off the road and follow the donkey track. You will see no one. Keep walking past the ruined buildings, and just when you think you have gone the wrong way you will come to an old farmhouse. Good luck.

Joseph looks about himself now, at the dry, shimmering fields and the trees that rise like columns of smoke. He rubs a lavender stalk between finger and thumb, staining them with its tangy scent. He does not know what he will find at the end of this path. His feet are ungainly in his brother's too-big boots, and he tries to focus on the steady in and out of his breath. He has his letter of introduction: a telegram from his editor, hastily sent to the Paris boardinghouse where he had tossed and turned. And most importantly, he has that one scribbled word: *Come.*

He passes what looks like a sheep pen, and beyond that a dilapidated structure that could be a shepherd's hut. Or an ice store? He knows nothing of life in the countryside. He is used to the horizonless vistas of a grey city, not this fresh expanse of clear air and buttery light. He steps beneath the dappled shadows of peeling plane trees, weaves through a twisted olive grove, and then, finally, he sees it: a low, rambling farmhouse. It is made of soft yellow stones turned golden in the afternoon sun. The roof is encased in a lattice of vines. The windows are small to keep out the heat.

Joseph takes a deep breath and steps up to the front door. Its blue paint is flaking and the handle is browned with rust. He knocks.

No answer.

He knocks again, pressing his ear to the door, but there is no sound from within. "Hello?" he calls, his voice dry and crackling, but the only response is the dull hum of crickets, and the steady thump of his heart.

Something twinges in his stomach. He feels glaringly at odds with his surroundings: too pale, too foreign to be here. He takes off his glasses and wipes them on the corner of his shirt. Perhaps this is a sign. The empty road, the deserted house: perhaps it is a warning that he should turn around, hurry back up the lonely path, go home with his tail between his legs.

He has the curious sensation that he is being watched.

Joseph steps back, shielding his eyes and taking in the hazy landscape. Sunlight radiates from the yellow fields and dust sticks to the olive trees, dark and fragrant in their arthritic twists. This is a place he knows well, though he has never been here before. He recognises it from paintings of hay bales and wheat fields, from sketches of green, snaking rivers and purple dusks over distant hills.

He shifts the knapsack onto his shoulder and walks around the edge of the house, stumbling over a fallen roof tile. Loose stones are scattered about as if the house is dissolving into the ground. Sun-bleached grass grows right up to the walls, but Joseph notices there are footstep-trodden paths winding this way and that. A wheelbarrow lies rusting in the sun, but its belly is full of freshly cut flowers.

Somebody is here.

Joseph rounds the back of the house and comes to a stone terrace, which gives way to a long, undulating field. Down at the bottom he can see a copse of trees and what might be a river, slipping darkly through green bushes.

As Joseph steps onto the terrace, his heart stutters in his chest. There is a man in an old wicker chair. He is leaning back with a cigar in one hand, the index finger of the other resting in a jar of honey. Joseph watches as he takes his finger from the honey and sucks it, slowly, before returning it to the jar. He takes a long drag of the cigar.

Here is the man Joseph has traveled days and miles to see. The man who answered his letter with a single command. The Master. Edouard Tartuffe.

Joseph's knapsack falls to the ground with a thunk. Tartuffe looks up. He is about sixty or so. Robust, full-faced and wide about the middle, with a frothy grey beard spreading down his front as if he has spilt it. He has one milky eye. The other is quite sharp, but the one he turns on Joseph now is clouded and ghostly.

He removes his finger from the honey. "Who," he asks in thick, gravelly French, "are you?"

Joseph steps forward, fumbling for the telegram of introduction in his knapsack. "My name is Joseph Adelaide," he says hastily, pulling out the sheet of paper from his editor. "I am a journalist. I wrote to you several months ago and you did me the kindness of replying." Joseph's French is good but it still feels strange to him, like he is wearing another man's clothes. "You invited me here." He holds out the telegram. "You invited me here . . . and now I have come."

The old man sucks honey from his finger and stares at Joseph with his mismatched eyes. He is wearing a loose smock stained like a butcher's apron and his fingers are rimed with paint. With a grunt, he holds out a hand for the telegram. Joseph stumbles forward and gives it to him.

Tartuffe squints. Then frowns. "I cannot read this," he says gruffly, and tosses the paper to the ground.

Joseph is startled for a moment. Then he realises: the telegram is in English. "I . . . I'm sorry," he stammers, the sweat beneath his armpits growing warm and sour. "It is a letter from my editor, thanking you for welcoming me. For allowing me to come here." He stoops to pick up the crumpled telegram. "You see, I have come to write an article about you."

Tartuffe gives no sign of recognition so Joseph fumbles about himself once more. "I have come . . . to profile you. Here . . ." He holds out a second piece of paper, which Tartuffe takes with a look of distrust. It is the letter in the painter's own hand, bearing only the word: *Come.*

Tartuffe frowns again, his sticky hand trembling as he looks at the letter's front and back. Then up at Joseph. "I do not know what this is."

"But . . . you wrote it."

Suddenly it is as if a blood vessel has burst. As if a dam has broken and the old man's patience can be tested no longer. "I do not have time to write my own letters!" he barks, waving his cigar in the air. "I do not know what this is! Sylvette!" he shouts. "Sylvette!" He is agitated, twisting in his chair and calling over his shoulder. "Sylvette! I cannot have strange men coming to the house on a Tuesday! I cannot be disturbed when I am working!"

Joseph takes a step back, tripping over his knapsack. He has been warned about this. He has heard the stories. The woman's eyes in the tobacconist had widened when he told her where he was going. She had asked him to repeat the name of the person he sought, as if giving him a chance to provide a different answer. But he had said the name again and her lips had tightened. When she gave him directions it had been with a small, warning shake of her head as if to say: do not disturb the slumbering bear.

"A recluse," is what Joseph's editor had called Tartuffe. "Misanthrope" was one word murmured in art circles, as was "hermit" and even "tyrant."

But so was "genius." Here was the man who could create beauty from nothing. Here was an artist who had dined with Van Gogh and argued with Cézanne. Who had expanded the boundaries of paint and colour and light itself. And so Joseph was prepared to expose himself to all the slings and arrows, the tirades and the tempests, the bursts of anger and the wild swings of mood. He would face all of it, just for a chance to meet the man sitting in front of him now. The man who had made him see the world anew.

"Sylvette!" Tartuffe bellows again. "Sylvette!"

And suddenly a young woman is there. She appears at the end of the terrace, wiping her hands on a thin cotton apron.

"My niece," Tartuffe grumbles by way of introduction, not looking at her. The woman has large brown eyes and her skin is smattered with freckles. Her hair is cropped short in the latest fashion, but here it looks more practical than chic. Tartuffe hands her the letter over his shoulder. "Explain."

Sylvette unsticks the paper and inspects it. She has a girlish face but her hands are rough and work-worn. Her brown hair glows like copper in the afternoon sun, and she has a slim cigarette tucked behind one ear.

Joseph itches in the long, hot silence as Sylvette reads the only word on that piece of paper. Then she looks up, and says simply,

"Here is your Young Man with Orange."

Joseph glances from Sylvette to Tartuffe. Either he has misunderstood or mistranslated, but the old man shows no confusion. Instead he stares at Joseph as if seeing him for the first time. He gets up, wiping his honeyed finger on his trousers and walks around him. Appraising him. He tucks a thumb under Joseph's chin and turns his head this way and that.

"Ettie, fetch me an orange," he says without taking his eyes from Joseph's face. Sylvette disappears into the house and returns a moment later clutching a small waxy orange.

Tartuffe holds it up to Joseph's cheek, as if to see how the colour works against the pale English face. "Yes," he murmurs. "Yes."

He puts the orange into Joseph's palm and takes a step back to see the effect: the weary, dust-shrouded traveler and the bright burst of fruit. Then he inches forward and, gently, with both hands, slides the glasses from Joseph's face. He looks at him for a long moment, then slides them back. "All right." He wipes his hands on the corner of his smock. "All right. Listen to me very carefully," he says as he sits back down. "I have no interest in your work, Monsieur Adelaide. I do not wish to be the subject of any article or feature. I do not give interviews. I do not care what you are writing . . . But I am in need of a model."

The hum of crickets dies down. The twitch of a breeze that was troubling the terrace wraps itself up into nothing. "A model?" Joseph asks, and his voice is a croak.

"Can you sit very still?" Tartuffe presses. "Can you be absolutely silent? Can you promise not to interrupt me, not to touch anything, not distract me? Can you live as a shadow except when I need you to be the Young Man with Orange?"

Joseph's mouth is dry as parchment. A tightness comes over his body. This is not how the scene was meant to go. He has promised his editor an interview. He has gathered all the money he owns, he has slammed the door in his father's face. He has traveled for days through dust and smog and heat. He came here to write an article that no one has written before. "I . . . I'm not a model," he says. "I am here to write about you. To—"

"If you will not sit for me then you can turn around and leave right now," Tartuffe says briskly, taking a drag of his cigar. "But if you sit for me and let me paint you . . . then you may stay. Write whatever you want. I do not care. I will not read it. I just need you to be silent and still. Can you do that?"

Joseph watches the cigar tip glow and then dim. Two halves of himself strain in opposite directions. He is no model, no muse. He is too self-conscious for that. But then again . . . he is here. He is standing before the greatest painter of the age, closer than anyone has come in many years.

Joseph feels the balance of the scales hanging on his answer. On one side is the admission that *no, this was a mistake*. A quick shuffle home and an apology to his father, a note to his editor explaining his error. Another thing at which he has failed. But on the other side of the scales . . . a hazy, golden opportunity. The chance to stare into those marble eyes and unlock the man behind them. To work his way into the mind of this fabled, mysterious painter.

Joseph meets Tartuffe's gaze. He squares his shoulders, and, with a voice that comes from somewhere deep in his chest, he says, "Yes. I can do that."

"Good." Tartuffe claps his hands together, a grin emerging within his beard. "You may stay until I complete the painting. When I am finished, you leave."

"Yes." Joseph nods. "Yes, all right, thank you." But Tartuffe waves his hand. He is already turning to his niece again. "Ettie," he says, "find the boy somewhere to sleep." The deal is struck. The stage is set.

Up a winding staircase, across a dimly lit landing, under a low-slung beam and over to a solitary door. Ettie heaves it open with a shove of her shoulder and stands back to let Joseph enter. The room is small. It squats beneath the eaves of the house where the heat of the day has collected.

Joseph puts his knapsack down carefully. Letting his eyes adjust to the dimness, he sees that the room is filled not with furniture, but with props. A cluster of china vases occupies one corner. There is a butterfly net, a broken drum, a rusting pitchfork. Metal teapots, coils of rope, an old birdcage. There is a dried-out bouquet of flowers, now brittle and faded, the ghost of a still-life arrangement. Empty picture frames are stacked along one wall and a roll of canvas has been kicked against another. The room is suffused with an air of neglect; it is where every unwanted object has been ushered.

Joseph steps forward. He has left his boots in the hall and the floor is grainy under his bare feet. The wooden boards are furred with dust. There is one small window in the corner, round like a porthole, and he crosses over to it, stooping to avoid hitting his head on the low ceiling. Through the glass he can see the rolling field at the back of the house, and in the distance the glint of the river, black and glossy in the evening light. He tries to open the window but the handle has been painted over. It is sealed shut.

Joseph turns and tries to smile at Ettie. She is standing in the corner, hands behind her back, watching him closely. "This is very kind of you," he says. "Thank you." She does not reply.

An iron-frame bed has been pushed against one wall. The mattress looks lumpy and the bedding must once have been white but is now a stale yellow. This is not the house of a man who welcomes guests. The only other furniture in the room is a desk hidden under a pile of plates, and beside it a large oval mirror. "This . . . this is the mirror from *Empty Room*," Joseph exclaims. "It is the mirror from the painting, I recognise it!" Ettie looks at him blankly.

Joseph crosses the room excitedly and runs a hand along the mirror's wooden frame. He had first seen a copy of *Empty Room* in a page of *The Burlington Magazine*. It was a dodgy halftone reproduction but even in scratchy black and white the painting had transfixed him. *Empty Room* shows a shadowy bedroom: the vague corner of a mattress, rumpled sheets, an oval mirror. It is this mirror that reveals the rest of the room: an unmade bed. A gold wedding band on a dressing table. An open window, curtains gently blowing towards a field of poppies.

Joseph had rushed to see the painting at the Royal Academy where it had hung in pride of place at last year's Summer Exhibition. He had marveled at its size and its scale, at the liveliness of the brushwork and the bloodred spray of the poppies. He had brought his nose close to the canvas. He had stood far away. He had come upon the painting sideways, trying to trick his brain into seeing it again for the first time. He had stood with his mouth agape, taking in the light, the texture, and the way the reflected world seemed brighter than the real one.

Joseph had known that he was standing in front of a masterpiece. It was the first great painting of the war that had recently cracked the continent apart. But this was a war painting from the perspective of someone who had been left behind. Destruction seen through an open window; in the pale reflection of a mirror. In the emptiness of a wedding ring. It was dazzling. It was overwhelming. It was like nothing he had seen before.

He turns to remark upon all of this to Ettie, but she has gone.

That night they eat dinner on the terrace beneath a creaking pergola hung with grapes. Ettie has spread the long wooden table with plates of tomatoes and artichokes, rows of neat white asparagus, and a basket of crusty bread. Wine is poured into small green-glass tumblers.

"So, Joseph," says Tartuffe, roughly tackling the asparagus with his fingers. "Tell me about your training."

Joseph is flattered by the light of attention, by the milky eye turning on him like a search beam. "My training, sir?"

"Where did you learn about art? What is your background?" There is a slippery sound as Tartuffe sucks a vinegary asparagus stalk.

Joseph shifts in his chair. "I went to art school for a year," he says. "The Slade, in London?" A grunt.

"I know the basics," Joseph continues. "I can sketch a figure and mix paints. I know about perspective and how to arrange a composition. I can use pastels and oils and chalk. I can . . . well, that's about it really. I left after a year." He takes a hasty sip of wine. "It was . . . it wasn't for me, in the end." His mind twitches at the memory of his hushed-up departure from the prestigious school. "I am trying to make my name as an art writer instead."

Tartuffe takes a slurp of wine. Drips catch in his beard like jewels.

"I wrote an article about Schiele's etchings recently?" Joseph tries again. He is not sure why he is asking it as a question. It is as if he is seeking the old man's approval, asking for his affirmation, *Yes, you did write an article! Well done!*

But Tartuffe only grunts. He is scraping the flesh from an artichoke petal with his small, square teeth.

"I don't know if you read *The Inkling*?" Joseph asks. "It is the magazine I write for in London. Only founded last year. Harry, my editor, used to be at—"

"Stop!" The movement is so sudden Joseph upends the bread-basket. Tartuffe has stood up and is leaning heavily over the table. He points at Ettie's plate. "Give it here!" he barks.

Mutely, Ettie slides her plate towards him. A stack of tomatoes seeps into a half-eaten hunk of bread. Tartuffe takes it roughly from her and marches inside the house. A moment later, the front door slams.

"Has he . . . has he left the house?" Joseph asks.

Ettie looks at him but does not answer. An uncomfortable silence warps the air. Ettie looks down at the empty place where her food had sat a moment before.

Tartuffe reemerges a few minutes later and sits back down, tucking a napkin into his collar. "I am preparing some studies," he explains gruffly to Joseph, ripping more petals from the artichoke. "Studies of food. Food on plates . . . food being eaten. The colours and shapes on Ettie's plate just then . . . the texture . . ." He sucks a deep purple petal. "I needed it."

Joseph nods and glances over at Ettie. She stares into the empty darkness, does not meet his eye, does not reach for any more food.

"Now." Tartuffe takes another gulp of wine. "Tell me, how did you come to speak French so well? I do not expect such things from the English."

Joseph has eaten nothing so far, so nervous is he of having a mouth full of food while Tartuffe is questioning him. He leans forward now, sitting on his hands and looking very carefully at his fork. "I learned French as a child," he says. "My father is English but my mother was Swiss."

"I'm sorry," says a soft voice.

Joseph looks up. It is Ettie who has spoken. She is staring at him with wide, searching eyes and her face is pale in the moonlight. There is a short silence, and then Tartuffe erupts with laughter.

"Sorry . . . for being . . . Swiss!" he chortles. Tears bead the corners of his eyes and he bangs his fist on the table. "I'd be sorry too if I were Swiss! Ha!" He lets out a hoarse laugh. "Ha!"

"No, no," Ettie says quickly, her cheeks flushing. "You said 'was Swiss.' *Was.*" She looks imploringly at Joseph. "I am sorry she is dead."

There is a sharp pause. Joseph had not even thought about it. He had said it instinctively: *was Swiss.* But now his mother's death has joined the table, sat down like an uninvited guest and leaned forward as if to say, *Here I am. Why don't you acknowledge me?*

Joseph clears his throat and picks up a piece of bread to have something to do with his hands. "She died of the Spanish flu," he says. "Two years ago now."

It had been his father who brought the news. He dragged it home with him along with the evening newspaper and a letter from the Front. At first Joseph had thought it must be news of his brother, stationed far away in a Belgian trench, that had cast the shadow across his father's face. It must be news from the war that had conjured the black cloud that followed his father into the house and knocked over the umbrella stand. It must be that which had slammed the study door and smashed a decanter of port.

But it was not Rupert. The letter from the Front contained no shocking news, and nor did the evening paper tossed onto the hallway floor. No, it was a one-line telegram from the hospital that brought death into their house. Joseph's mother had died with the abruptness of a candle being blown out. One moment she was there and the next . . . nothing. She was gone.

The flu had taken her within three days. She was a volunteer at the local hospital and from there it had been easy to contain her in a ward with the rest of the sick: the coughing, the spluttering, the feverish. Joseph had not been allowed to visit her but he knew she would get better. She was hale and hearty; she had survived measles and mumps and scarlet fever. This was the woman who hiked up the Alps in the summer and went on marches without an overcoat. She pinned suffragist banners to trees in the local park and was once arrested for stealing a policeman's helmet. She was full of life. She would come home. Of course she would.

The telegram from the hospital confirmed only the date and time of her death, and the fact that her lungs had filled with fluid and she had most likely suffocated to death. With those scant words, Joseph's world had become darker and more strange than he had ever known.

His mother's death leans back and looks around the candlelit dinner table. *There*, it seems to say. *Enjoy your food.*

Tartuffe blows his nose on a napkin. He has pushed back his chair and is staring off into the distance. The night is ink black. A constellation of fireflies shifts across the field, spreading and regrouping like a net of stars.

Joseph stands up. He is suddenly weary, exhausted from his journey and the tense energy that has knotted his muscles since he arrived. "Thank you for the dinner," he says, making an awkward sort of bow to Tartuffe. "And for your hospitality, sir. I will see you in the morning."

Tartuffe wafts a hand in his direction but does not look at him. "Enough of this 'sir' business," he grumbles. "If you are in my house, you call me Tata."

ETTIE

Strange to have somebody in the house again. Strange to have another chair at the table. Another heart beating softly in one of the beds.

Strange, strange, strange, after all this time.

Ettie treads the unlit corridors, trailing her hands along the rough plaster walls. She moves from room to room, tidying away loose paintbrushes, returning stray corks to bottles of wine. She opens the back door and strikes a match. Lights a cigarette.

It is strange to have somebody look at her again.

She is used to slipping in and out like a minnow, barely perceived before she is gone again. She is here one moment, gone the next.

This is how she likes it.

But tonight at dinner Joseph had looked at her, really *looked* at her. Not at what she was holding or what was behind her. He had looked at her, and he had asked her a question.

She inhales. Exhales. A thin stream of smoke pools into the night.

Ettie has learned to be patient. She has spent her life waiting just out of sight, out of reach. She will wait to see how this tale unfolds, how the pieces fall into place. She will wait to see what happens.

JOSEPH

Edouard Tartuffe is a recluse. Once the most celebrated painter of his day, the golden boy of the Paris art scene has not been glimpsed outside his home for nearly thirty years. At the height of his success Tartuffe exiled himself to the south of France and has remained there ever since. He gave no warning, no explanation. Now he is known only by the paintings which emerge from his Provence farmhouse each year: a steady stream of work which appears without announcement and without fanfare. There are no exhibitions, no public events, no interviews and no engagement with the unanswered question: Why did one of the greatest painters of our age turn his back on the world?

Apprenticed under Cézanne, Tartuffe's stride soon overtook his master's and he displayed his first solo exhibition at the age of nineteen. Genius, paired with the formal training of the Académie des Beaux-Arts in Paris, begat some of the greatest experiments in painting of the last half-century. Tartuffe was a leading proponent of mixing his colours straight onto canvas rather than preparing them on the palette. His style is distinctive, instantly recognisable for its thick brushwork and heavy buildup of paint. It has been called explosive, even violent. But Tartuffe's real artistry lies in his instinctive understanding of colour. His paintings are light-filled, and while his themes are dark the execution is luminous.

Many movements have tried to claim Tartuffe as one of their own but he has never allied himself with a particular group or style. His work is experimental, defying identification with Impressionism, Fauvism, Cubism or any other -ism that tries to embrace him. Tartuffe belongs to no tribe. Yet while his paintings reject categorisation, critics are united on one thing: Edouard Tartuffe is a trailblazer in every sense of the word. He is the Master of Light.

Joseph pauses on that last sentence, then scratches it out. It is a bit much to declare that someone is the Master of Light. He needs to remain levelheaded. Objective.

He is up early, awake with the hum of crickets in the field below. He is sitting up in bed, a thin grey notebook on his knees, pencil in hand. The air is full of lazily drifting dust motes. A fly throws itself again and again at the sealed window. Joseph breathes in the smell of the attic bedroom where he has been sequestered, tingling with nervous disbelief that he is *here*. Here, in the very farmhouse in which Tartuffe—Tata, he reminds himself—hid himself away all those years ago.

But why? Why did he exile himself to this beautiful but lonely spot?

It is an unsolved puzzle. A mystery waiting to be cracked. Joseph riffles through his notebook. His research material has been scant: he could find no profile of Tartuffe in the stacks of *Burlington* and *Connoisseur* magazines he has collected over the years. No photographs beyond 1890. There is no self-penned autobiography. No manifesto. No artist's statement. There is only a hole: a great, gaping lacuna in the written record. And now Joseph is here to fill it.

Something in Tata's art changed when he left Paris. Where his paintings were once full of people, now they show only empty spaces. His recent work has a lonely quality. It is not just that his paintings have no people in them, it's that they show an *absence* of people. Tata's subjects are a rumpled bed. Wet footprints on a hot garden path. A pile of clothes shed on the bare floor. His paintings depict a world in which people have always just left the scene: someone was here but now they have gone.

But why has everyone disappeared? Why did Tata banish people from his life and his work?

Joseph chews the end of his pencil.

There is a name hovering on the tip of his tongue. The name of a man who might be a clue to all these answers: Tata's one-time tutor, his mentor and his friend, Cézanne. The rumours that swirled around the art world latched on to a supposed feud between the two painters. An irreconcilable rift. Something scandalous. But now Cézanne is dead and Tartuffe has not spoken to the outside world for thirty years.

How much weight should Joseph give these glimmers of gossip? Would it be possible, all these years later, to piece together what happened? He shifts in the uncomfortable bed and goes back to his notebook.

Away from the easel, Tartuffe is equally elusive. He rarely leaves his house and does not welcome visitors. He refuses to give interviews and once, famously, ripped up a reporter's notebook in the street. Word has it that he has fallen out with everybody except his wine merchant. His reputed feud with Céz—

There is a knock at the door and Joseph hurls the notebook under his bed. He had not heard anyone approach. He pulls the fraying bedsheet up to his chin and calls, "Come in?"

The door opens and it is Ettie. She is standing in the milky sunlight, an earthenware jug in her arms. She casts around for somewhere to put it but the desk is covered in Joseph's papers and so she opts for the floor, stowing it beside an old birdcage.

"Are you ready?" she asks, straightening up.

"Ready for what?"

"Ready to be painted."

Tata's studio is a converted stable block. It sits removed from the main house, a short stomp away through the long grass. Light pours in through wide, open windows. The walls are whitewashed and the floor is a patchwork of bare bricks spattered with paint. It is bright and light and airy, a welcome change from the cramped squatness of the house. Tata is already there when Joseph arrives, a cigar clamped between his teeth as he rummages in a jar of paint-brushes. He grunts a welcome but does not look up.

Stacks of canvases are propped against the walls. Joseph takes a slow walk around them: an exhibition of unfinished work. Some paintings contain only a few lines but others are filled with colour. There is a study of lemons in a porcelain bowl. A grapefruit, a plate of sardines, a half-eaten nectarine. Joseph can almost taste the fleshiness of the food in the thick gumminess of the paint.

There are some older paintings here too. Joseph can see that the style is different, more formal. The shapes have not yet broken apart. There are beach scenes, a city street, and a couple of brightly coloured paintings from a trip Joseph knows Tata once made to Morocco. He turns his head to look at a canvas propped on its side: a little boy clutching a monkey to his chest.

Joseph makes a mental note of everything. The banks of clut-ter, the eruptions of colour around the walls. It is like being inside the great man's mind. He notes the smells of the studio: linseed oil for loosening paint (warm, nutty), turpentine for cleaning brushes (sharp, acidic), and through the windows, the dry scent of olive trees baking in the sun. Joseph walks over to a table at the back of the studio that has been spread with plates. There is a platter with a crab shell and a dish of shriveled grapes. There is an empty wine-glass, a rotten plum, a delicate fish spine, pale folds of flesh still clinging to the bones. And there is Ettie's plate with its abandoned tomatoes from the night before.

"Don't!" barks a voice as Joseph reaches out a hand. "Do not . . . touch . . . the food!" Tata comes up behind Joseph and yanks him roughly away. "I told you! I told you not to touch anything!" His face is red and he gives a snort like a bull, then turns and strides back to his paintbrushes. "Come!"

Joseph rubs his shoulder where Tata grabbed it, then follows him to the end of the room where a canvas is waiting on an easel.

In front of it is a three-legged stool.

"Sit!" Tata barks.

Joseph perches awkwardly on the stool. He tries to get com-fortable as Tata scrutinises him. He has placed Joseph next to a window, a square of light that looks out onto a parched field. The sky is unblemished by clouds. "Put this on," Tata says, throwing something at him. It is a billowing piece of white cloth, rather large. Joseph removes his shirt and pulls on this oversized smock, old-fashioned in style and with a gaping neck. He folds his shirt carefully and places it beneath the stool.

"Good," Tata says. "Good." Then he reaches into the pocket of his trousers and pulls out an orange. He weighs it in his hand for a moment, then comes forward and places it in Joseph's palm. He lifts Joseph's chin. Lowers his shoulder. As Joseph is being positioned he is vaguely aware of movement out of the corner of his eye. He senses, rather than sees, that it is Ettie, quietly clearing some of the plates away. He did not hear her enter.

Finally, Tata slides Joseph's glasses from his face and the world blurs. He feels vulnerable, like a newborn animal. He blinks a few times and tries to get used to this softened version of the studio.

The fuzzy outline of Tata steps back. He nods, content with his composition, wraps an apron around his midriff, and retreats behind the wide square of the canvas. There is the sound of shuffling, of a brush being rubbed into paint, and then a throat being cleared. "Today I am outlining, so it is important you hold this position," Tata says. "Do not move unless I tell you to. Do not speak. Do not let me see you breathing."

Joseph itches in the coarse white smock. The day is already thick with heat and his skin pearls with sweat. He wants to wipe the moisture from his upper lip but does not dare move a muscle. He tries to commit this pose to memory, willing his body to remember exactly how Tata wants it.

Time passes very slowly.

Is Ettie still here? Is she watching them? He wants to twist around and look for her but he must remain as immobile as stone.

He tries not to blink too frequently.

Tata shuffles backwards and forwards as he plots his coordinates onto canvas. Joseph imagines him placing a shoulder here, a hand there. He grunts as he works, standing an arm's length from the canvas and making wide, brisk strokes with a long-handled brush. Occasionally he bustles over from behind the easel to arrange Joseph's body, to shift the angle of his jaw or the direction of his gaze.

Joseph breathes everything in. He does not want to forget a second of this. He longs to see the other side of the canvas, to watch the painting emerge. After his mother died, art became his salvation. It was the only thing that could occupy his mind for more than a minute and hold back the dark clouds that bloomed at the edges of his thoughts.

The greatest lesson his mother taught him was not to worry about *understanding* art. "Just let it wash over you," she used to say. "Don't worry about what it means. Just look, and take whatever you need from it."

It was she who introduced him to the work of Tartuffe.

"This man is doing something different," she said as they stood side by side in the National Gallery. This was a man who could paint light because he understood darkness. His images were loose, experimental, because he knew that life did not hold its shape. Tartuffe's paintings told the truth about the world in all its shattered, rippling complexity. "How does it make you feel?" his mother used to ask as they stared at a painting together. Not "What do you think it means?" *How does it make you feel?*

After she died Joseph repeated these pilgrimages, this time alone. He would pick a painting at random and stare at it. He removed his glasses, letting the paint blur, losing himself in the shapes and the colours. The anxious judder of his heart slowed. Over time, his mind calmed.

It was during these lonely visits that his thoughts turned to the man who created the paintings his mother had loved so much. Where was Edouard Tartuffe now? Who was the man who knew exactly how complicated the world was? Perhaps in finding Tartuffe, Joseph could find a way back to his mother. Back to those golden days when they stood hand in hand in front of the paintings. Back when Tata's canvases and Joseph's life were both filled with light.

Back when everything was different.

A citrusy tang seeps into the air. Joseph has squeezed the orange so hard he has pierced the skin. He tries to steady himself. Breathes as slowly as possible. He has eaten nothing all morning and his stomach gurgles but Tata pays him no notice. He is only a shape. A living collection of lines which will one day transform into the image of a man. He keeps his nostrils unflared, his hands relaxed, just the way Tata wants them. He lets his mouth go soft. He sinks into himself, feeling Joseph Adelaide recede. He wants to fade away, to become someone else. He will let Tata transform him into someone new.

He will become the Young Man with Orange. And perhaps, if he is lucky, he will also be the young man who cracks Tartuffe; who brings back a piece of the giant to show the world.

Let me in, Joseph thinks. *Just let me in and tell me all your secrets.*

ETTIE

Ettie picks through the papers on Joseph's desk. He has few possessions but he has arranged them neatly: envelopes in one pile, blank paper in another, written correspondence in a third. He has lined up his pencils along the edge of the desk. There is a pair of notebooks, an India rubber, and a knife for sharpening pencils. In the centre of this arrangement sits a small clunky typewriter. Ettie runs her fingertips over the keys, feeling the indents where Joseph's fingers fit. *He brought one bag*, she thinks, *and this is what he filled it with.*

The page in the typewriter is blank. He has not written anything yet.

She sifts through the papers, careful not to disturb the precise alignment of their corners. There is an official-looking telegram from a man named Harry, and a letter in handwriting so wild she can barely decipher it. It looks like the scribblings of a madman.

There is one book on the desk. *The Odyssey* by Homer.

Her head twitches to one side, ears alert for any sound in the house. But Tata and Joseph are still in the studio. She is alone. She picks up a soft grey notebook and flicks through it. Joseph's handwriting is cramped and his pages are slashed with arrows and crossings-out, as if he is continually doubting himself. *Not this word*, the lines seem to say. *This one, no . . . wait . . . this one.*

To the left of the typewriter is a note dashed off on a scrap of paper. *Talk to Ettie?* it says. *Ask her questions.*

She runs her fingertip over Joseph's handwriting, dark and spiky as a bramble. She likes the way he has spelled out her name, committing it to paper in sharp black lines. She lets her fingers rest on it for a moment, then leaves the note where it is. She must not linger. She casts her eyes over the desk to confirm everything is as she found it and then slips from the room, easing the door silently into its frame.

JOSEPH

The days fall into a steady rhythm. Mornings are spent in the sunlit studio, Joseph perched atop the wooden stool, Tata surveying him with his mismatched eyes. Ettie, Joseph is always vaguely aware, moves like a shadow beyond them: cleaning, tidying, making sure Tata has everything he needs before he knows he needs it. She lays out his brushes. She sweeps the dust that creeps in under the door. She pores over his notes, his sketches, his preparatory studies, and spirits them all away, priming the studio each day for the master to work.

Joseph grows accustomed to staying still. He bristles at how his father would scoff at what he is doing. *Loafing*, he would call it. *Idling, slacking, languishing.* But it is physical work, Joseph wants to retort in these imaginary arguments. It is agonising, bodily work, and he must train himself to fix his gaze on a faraway point, to detach his mind from his muscles and ignore the creeping pain in his limbs. The sun that burns the nape of his neck. The sweat that glides over his body.

At noon each day Tata throws down his brush and declares that his work is done. He will only paint Joseph in the morning, he explains, when the light is right. Ettie appears, like a spirit summoned, to collect Tata's apron, his dirty brushes, his paint-stained rags. She bows her head to inspect his palette. She counts the colours, looking at what has been used and what has not, glancing between the paints and the canvas. Then she turns, and disappears out the studio door.

For the rest of the day Joseph is left to his leisure, to wander the yellow fields, to hover awkwardly about the house, to try to write. For just as Tata is painting a portrait of Joseph, so Joseph is creating a portrait of Tata. He needs to extract some information from this closed-up man, some alchemical formula which he can write about and say, *Here. I have solved the riddle of the recluse. I have found the equation to his genius and I lay it out for you now.*

It is a hunger he has not felt in a long time. His senses have become blunted over the last few years; dulled by death and despair. But here, in this remote, ramshackle farmhouse, something inside him is coming alive.

To send or receive letters, Joseph must go to the village tobacconist which doubles as the post office, as well as the general store and source of all local gossip. Salomé, the crinkled woman behind the counter, always has a smile for Joseph, a gummy grin which splits her face like a rotten apple. The shop is dry and earthy, like the tobacco she chews and then spits on the floor at her feet. She is from Mauritius, she tells him, a teardrop-shaped island in the Indian Ocean.

One afternoon she hands Joseph a thick cream envelope over the counter. His name is written in looping turquoise ink, which means it is from Harry. He thumbs it open and reads it on his walk home, treading the solitary donkey track back to the house.

So you are the old man's muse! the letter begins. Joseph can hear Harry's red-faced wheeze, the rumble of his laugh and the slap of palm against pin-striped thigh. He closes his eyes and is thankful for the privacy of the empty road before reading on:

> *Joseph Adelaide, you sly dog. Young Man with Orange indeed! I never thought you'd get Tartuffe to talk, but now look at you. This*

makes an excellent piece. Much better than an interview, I think. Give me an insider's account on the workings of the master for next month's issue. Write down everything. I want to know what the old fart eats for breakfast and how he brushes his teeth. Does he have masterpieces stashed in every corner of the house? What's he up to next? And what does he think of the Dadaists' latest stunt? Pester him with questions and leave no stone unturned!

We'll call the piece "Musings from the Muse." Or: "The Subject Speaks"!

Plough on and deliver me some words by the end of the month. I'm keeping a 12" column for you so mind you fill it.

In eagerness,
Harry

PS—Watch the old rascal keeps his hands off you. Ha!

Crickets whir and heat beats down on Joseph's head. It is a relief to sink into English for a while. It has been alienating living so much of his life in French and this return to his native tongue is like plunging into a cold pool. A small reprieve from the language of his dead mother.

He can picture Harry ensconced in his club: plush chairs, chandeliers, taxidermied pheasants. The low murmur of other white-moustached gentlemen with rounded bellies. Gleaming watch chains and waistcoats straining at their buttons. Harry will be squashed in his favourite armchair, his recumbent figure as much a part of the furniture as the Persian rugs and crystal decanters. A sheaf of correspondence will be in his lap and his turquoise ink pen will fly back and forth as he signs off articles, reviews, letters, and cheques.

A cricket flits into Joseph's open shirt, and he feels a thousand miles away.

Joseph's response to Harry is brief: thank you for the praise, the words will come. But, he stresses, the piece will be about Tartuffe. It will be a study of the master, not his subject—certainly not, Joseph bristles, his "muse." Better to call the piece "Dispatches from the Studio." Something neutral.

The genius lies not in him, but in Tata.

As Joseph pulls the smock over his head at the end of one morning's session, he wanders around the edge of Tata's canvas. The outline of the painting is taking shape. He can see the curve of his mouth coming to life, the furrow of his brow. There is a blank space in his hand where the orange will sit.

"Do you always start from the inside?" he asks.

Tata does not respond.

"Do you start painting in the middle of the canvas and then work outwards?"

Tata is busy foraging in his paint chest like a fox inspecting a bin. He tosses a screwed-up tube of white onto the table.

"Do you prefer to begin with the light or the shadow?" Joseph tries again.

Nothing.

"Do you always outline in the same colour? I can see you've used blue here—"

"Why are you asking me these questions?" Tata snaps.

"I . . . I think it would be useful for my article," Joseph says. "I need to write about—"

"To hell with your article!" Tata barks. "Do not talk to me about your so-called "article" when you are in my studio! This is my space, do you understand? There can only be one artist in here and it is me!" He is panting, flushed with the effort of this outburst. He points to the canvas, gesturing at the accumulation of lines that make up Joseph's face. "You are the Young Man with Orange and that is all! Do you understand?"

Joseph is numb, an electric tingle shooting through his limbs. "Yes, Tata." He nods. "Yes, I understand."

Back in the safety of his attic bedroom, Joseph flips through his notebook and finds an empty page to scribble everything he remembers from the morning:

Tata sees not only in terms of colour, but temperature.

He favours a long-handled brush. Stiff bristles and a well-worn grip.

First come the lines. Then blocks of colour.

The smell of turpentine is overpowering.

Tata stops painting when the sun has passed overhead and no longer pours through the open window. The cycle of the day is his god master guide. He is attuned to, and always aware of, the light. Sun as light/colour/heat???

He has marked the positions of the easel and stool on the floor with chalk. They must not be moved.

He said he would flay me alive if I sneezed.

What can he do with these piecemeal observations? What can he divine from these scrappy encounters? He has been here for a week already but his subject refuses to talk. He needs to find a way in. No one has ever been allowed this close to Tata before but somehow he has been granted entry into the great man's world. He has one shot to crack this volatile, elusive genius.

But how can he write about someone who rebuffs him at every turn?

It feels as if he is circling; coming around before landing. He has not yet caught sight of what it is he needs to pin down, and so for now he circles.

ETTIE

"I hear there is a young man in the house."

Ettie ignores this. Lafayette the framer is leaning on the back of a chair, his eyes tracking her every movement as she walks around his workshop. It reeks of sawdust and sharp, sickly varnish. She runs a finger along a smooth frame and feels his gaze crawling up her back.

"I hear he is a foreigner," Lafayette continues.

Maybe the walnut, thinks Ettie as she wanders. *Or perhaps the silver?* She traces a series of carved wooden leaves with her fingertip.

"Which wood is this?" she asks. It is always she who makes decisions about frames. It is she who pedals her mother's old bicycle to the far side of the village, and she who subjects herself to Lafayette's idle gossip. It is she who commissions the frame and returns a week later to carry it home, slung over her shoulder as if she herself is a painting.

"Swiss pine," Lafayette replies quickly, his eyes still on her. Then, unable to help himself, "We didn't see the young man for several days after he arrived. We were worried your papa might have bitten his head off—"

"He's not my papa."

"Sorry." Lafayette bows his head a little. "Your uncle." He watches as she bends down and unwinds a measuring tape. "We were wondering how long this young man would be staying?"

Ettie takes the frame's dimensions. Calculates. When Lafayette says "we" she knows he means the village as a whole. The whispering cluster on the hill. "We" refers to a community which does not include herself and Tata.

Perhaps a plain wooden frame will work this time. It is only a small study of some cherries, after all. Yes, a simple Swiss pine. No decoration, no moulding. No gold or silver leaf.

Tata will not allow her to bring the paintings into Lafayette's workshop and so she must go by measurements alone. She gives Lafayette each picture's dimensions and he will either make her a frame or find one that meets her needs. Sometimes she brings back the frame and Tata says it is not right, too thin or too elaborate, too heavy, too bright, and so she cycles back to the workshop, returns the frame, and starts all over again. She once did this six times for a small study of a tulip.

"What's he doing in there then?" Lafayette presses. "What's the young man doing all shut up in the house? We didn't know what to think that first day when he didn't come back by nightfall . . . We were going to send out a search party."

"There was no need for that," Ettie says sharply. There is a pause. Lafayette is scrutinising her, still awaiting an answer. "He is here to write about Tata," she says eventually. "He thinks he can crack him."

"Ah," says Lafayette with a knowing nod of his head. "And do you think he will succeed?"

Ettie looks at him plainly. "There is nothing to crack."

JOSEPH

My dear Flora,

Of course I have not forgotten you! How could I forget you, my sweet, sweet Flora? I am sorry for not writing. Life is strange and time moves unexpectedly here. Whole hours are filled with sitting still and then time races forward and I find myself disorientated and confused. Often I am doing something wrong, though I do not mean to.

This is a bewildering place.

Tata (as Tartuffe insists I call him) has installed me as his sitter. I am to be the model for his latest painting: a portrait which involves me wearing a sort of biblical smock and holding an orange. I am honoured, of course, yet never have I felt so aware of my own skin. I see my face being built up day by day in layers of paint and I cannot decide if it is myself or a stranger looking back at me. It is intimate, being stared at for so long each day. Intimate and unnerving. I feel as if Tata must know all my secrets by now.

I do not know when I will come home. I am allowed to stay here for as long as Tata works on the painting and then I must leave, but it is not clear how long that will be. If I ask I get no answer.

Tata is as temperamental as everyone warned, rather like a firework about to go off, but I am learning to navigate the explosions. There is to be no noise when he is working or sleeping. No sudden movements when he is staring into space (this counts as working). No asking questions before midday. He must have his breakfast laid out in the studio each morning: one egg (boiled), a cup of coffee (black), and an orange (peeled). He likes to have his letters read aloud to him and does not deign to respond to them himself. He eats honey with his fingers. Do not point out if he has dropped food in his beard.

I have gradually learned that the following subjects should not be mentioned: "jazz" music; Titian's later period; the work, life, and opinions of Paul Cézanne; motion pictures; newspapers; novels; the selection committee for the Salon d'Automne; Americans; Joseph Duveen; the inhabitants of the nearby village; communism; sport; vegetarianism.

I am sure the list will expand.

My article is coming along in much the same manner as a fly trapped in a room. I keep bumping into things, and then running headlong into something else, and every time I think I have seen where I need to go I crash into a barrier I didn't even realise was there. I must have written thousands of words by now and thrown them all away. My wastepaper basket is an embarrassment, always overflowing with at least five crumpled-up drafts (I say wastepaper basket, it is in fact a watering can, purloined from one of the cupboards. I think it was used in Tata's Garden in Midwinter, *do you remember that painting? It is in the Walker Gallery, should you ever be inclined to see my wastepaper basket).*

How is it I am able to write so easily to you but as soon as I need to describe paint on a canvas my hands cramp up as if I am a rheumatic? Perhaps I am blinded by the light. I should not fear Tata as much as I do but there is something terrible about him, like looking into the eye of the sun. Or God.

Tata has a niece who lives with him. She is a strange creature. She has her hair cut short like a flapper and stares at me in the most intense way. She does not seem to blink as often as most people. She has the disarming habit of appearing without warning, almost as if she is creeping up on me except I do not think this is her

*aim. She is just very silent. Even when I know she is in the room I
have to look closely to make sure she is not a trick of the light. I am
hoping she will warm to me so I can ask her questions about Tata
as the old man himself has been less than forthcoming (yesterday
he told me to "go boil my head" when I asked if he'd like milk with
his coffee).*

*Do not think I have forgotten you, dear F. Tell me about home.
Have the lupins you planted in the spring come out yet? Do draw
me a picture. Show me the garden. Draw me in it and imagine I am
there with you.*

I miss you too. You know this.

Your brother,

Joseph

At the end of a tense morning—in which Tata has snapped two
pencils, squashed a tube of cobalt blue underfoot, and painted a
magnificent thumb—Joseph joins Ettie in the kitchen. She is sitting
at the long wooden table cleaning paintbrushes while Tata snoozes
in his frayed wicker armchair outside, a pot of honey gleaming in
the sun. Joseph takes a seat next to her. For a while they scrub in
silence, each head bowed low over the brushes, damp rags of turpentine turning their hands raw.

Joseph glances at Ettie's fingers. They are nimble as little birds.
The nails are bitten to the quick. A rime of paint lines their edges.
"Did your uncle ever teach you to paint?" he asks after a while.

Ettie keeps her eyes down. "No."

Joseph is surprised by this. He would have thought it would be
impossible to grow up in this house and not learn how to paint.
There are canvases stacked in every corner. You cannot retrieve a

fork without coming upon a stick of charcoal or a rusting palette knife. "Not even drawing?" he asks.

She shakes her head.

An idea comes to him. Perhaps this is how he can get Ettie to open up. Perhaps this is how he can extract some answers. "Here," he says, casting around. "I'll teach you." He plucks a lemon from the fruit bowl. He finds paper and a mangled tube of cadmium yellow which he squeezes onto a plate. "Start with a lemon," he says, placing it in front of her. "Anyone can paint a lemon because a lemon doesn't look like anything else. It is impossible to paint a bad lemon." He beams. He remembers this task from the Slade. *A lemon can be as plain or as detailed as you like*, his tutor had said. *But it will always be a lemon. It is the very best place to start.* He holds out a brush to Ettie. He is smiling at her, encouraging her. Trying to prise her out of her oyster shell.

But Ettie eyes him with a cool look that could be hatred. She stands up and leaves the room.

ETTIE

He is not looking properly.

JOSEPH

The following morning Tata is out of the house, stomping across the fields and swishing his way through the long grass, an easel over one shoulder. He is painting *en plein air* today, catching the soft yellow light as it caresses the hills. He wants to capture the sunflowers, he says, before they blacken and wither in the deep summer.

Joseph wanders onto the terrace, adrift without the subject of his study. Ettie is sitting at the long wooden table shelling peas.

"Can I help you?" he asks, putting down his notebook. Ettie does not look up but shakes her head. "Do you mind if I ask you some questions then? About Tata?" he says, easing himself into a chair. He might as well get straight to the point.

Ettie shrugs, still not looking at him.

"Well . . ." Joseph clears his throat. "I'll just start then, if that's all right?"

Silence.

"How long does it take Tata to finish a painting?"

There is a protracted pause as Ettie extracts a pea from its silvery lining. She places it in a bowl, then takes another and says slowly, "It depends."

"A month?" Joseph prompts. "Six? A year?"

She shrugs again. "Sometimes it's several months. Sometimes fewer."

He writes this down in his notebook. "How many paintings does Tata work on at once?"

Ettie looks thoughtfully at her hands as she picks up another pod, splits it open. "A few."

Joseph keeps his eyes on her, willing her to say more.

"Maybe . . . three?"

He scribbles this down. "All right . . . how does Tata know when he is finished? Is he always satisfied, or can he keep adding and amending forever? Are his paintings ever really finished?"

Ettie looks at him strangely. "They are finished when he stops painting them," she says. "That's all."

Joseph writes. Crosses out. Moves on. He is getting nowhere. "Does Tata choose his themes carefully or do they spring organically from this work?" he asks. "Mortality and decay, for example, is that a conscious theme he works into his paintings, or does it appear spontaneously? Does he think about his body of work as a whole or does he focus on one painting at a time?"

Ettie throws down a pea pod. "What does it matter?" she asks in exasperation. "What does any of this matter?"

"I . . . I need to get my article right."

"Joseph . . . art is not about being right," she says. Her voice is hoarse, as if she is not used to using it with this much force. "Maybe Tata is inspired by death, maybe he isn't. Maybe he paints one painting at a time, maybe he paints seven. What does it matter?"

He must look crestfallen because Ettie softens and says, "Tata is never going to read your article, Joseph. You can write what you like. Make up whatever facts you wish. What would happen if you wrote something that wasn't true? What if you misquoted him, or said he wakes at seven in the morning when really he wakes at six? What would happen, hmm?" She leans toward him and whispers, "Nothing."

Joseph is stunned. "But . . . what about truth?" he says. "I want to tell the truth. Isn't that the very point of art? To articulate a truth there is no other way of expressing? To clarify something, to give it a shape?"

"Tata is creating art," says Ettie. "That's all that matters. Just the fact that he is doing it."

Joseph sits back, deflated. He reads through the questions he had prepared.

Would you say Tata's recent work is inspired by Cubism, or could it be seen as a reaction against the movement?

Has Tata ever been tempted by abstraction?

Does Tata's work evoke a sense of nostalgia because he is resistant to change, or because he is deliberately concerned with articulating the past?

He strikes a line through everything.

"Fine." He looks up at her. "Tell me how long you've lived here."

"I thought you were writing about Tata."

"I am. But I'm interested in you."

Ettie looks at him warily, then reaches across and closes his notebook. She slides the pen from his hand and lays it on the table. "There. Now ask."

He leans back. "How long have you lived here?"

"All my life," she says, returning to her peas.

"How long is that?"

"Twenty-seven years."

Joseph takes a moment to digest this. It is longer than he thought. Something about Ettie's mute, childlike manner had disarmed him, but it turns out she is older than he is. He does some quick calculations. "So Tata left Paris and moved here around the time you were born. Do you know why?"

Ettie shrugs. "My mother lived here too for a while."

Joseph waits, willing her to say more. He is close to something here, he can feel it. After several moments in which it becomes clear he will not break the silence, Ettie goes on. "I never knew my father," she says slowly. "It was always just the three of us: my mama and Tata and me. And then it was just the two of us."

Joseph wishes he could write this down but his notebook lies closed on the table. He has never come across Tata's sister in any of the books or articles he pored over. Somehow she has slipped through the gaps in the record.

"What happened to your mother?" he asks.

"She left," Ettie says curtly.

He can feel her clamming up, her body curling away from him. *Why did she leave?* he wants to ask, but he holds himself back. He needs to ask his questions tactically. One misstep and Ettie will snap shut like a locket. He tucks the question of her mother into an imaginary envelope. Saves it for later. Instead he asks, "What about you? Do you ever leave the village?" He wants to know more about this strange, silent woman who moves like a shadow through Tata's house.

Ettie frowns, then says, "I went to Avignon once."

"Did you like it?"

She wrinkles her nose. "It was big. And far."

Joseph knows the town is only twelve miles away, having traveled the distance in a milk cart, but he does not say this. Instead he asks, "Don't you want to leave Saint-Auguste? Explore a bit? See some other—" But Ettie is already shaking her head.

"No," she says. "No, no, no." Then more emphatically, "*No.*"

"Why not?"

"I know what happens to people who leave." She says it very quietly, and Joseph wonders if he has heard her correctly.

"What do you—"

"My mother ran away to New York when I was seven." She looks up at him. "They brought her back in a coffin." The peas are done. She throws away the pods.

ETTIE

He is asking all the wrong questions.

Ettie was seven when she first understood that Tata could not look after himself. It wasn't that he was incapable of learning—any grown man with responsibility for a small child is capable—it was that he did not want to.

Tata was standing in the doorway of the stone kitchen, pointing to a pile of potatoes on the table. Ettie, barely tall enough to reach the kitchen sink unassisted, looked from the mound to him with wide, unblinking eyes. Her mother had been gone for some days—a week? Maybe more? Time moves differently when you are a child—and the house was silent and empty. The flowers on the windowsill had wilted. Ettie's hair and teeth were unbrushed. She and Tata had been surviving on leftovers, which had now finally run out.

Marie, the once-a-week lady, had brought potatoes and cabbages along with the usual basket of laundry she washed and pressed for them, but Tata would not have her in the house. He shooed her away as soon as she had deposited the vegetables on the kitchen table. The words "Where is—" had barely escaped her lips before Tata slammed the front door in her face, and silence descended upon the house. Ettie and her uncle were alone.

He gestured to the potatoes and told her to make something with them.

"What should I make?" she asked.

"Anything." Then he nudged her into the kitchen and shut the door between them. His footsteps receded, stomping away to his studio across the field. Ettie picked up a potato. She had seen her mother cook them before but had never done it herself. She bit into it, trying to see if she could get away with serving it raw. She could not. She looked around and found the heavy pot that was usually filled with water. She was not strong enough to lift it to the tap, so instead she scooped water into a single cup and decanted it over and over until the pot was full, shuffling back and forth across the kitchen.

How to summon fire? The large iron range was usually kept hot by her mother, but for days now it had been cold as stone. She peered into the fuel hopper, a metal drawer that still contained a few lumps of coal. She took one of the matches that were always in her mother's apron and tried to light it, but her fingers were small and soft, and the movement or the alchemy or the trick of it was beyond her. She rubbed the matches against the box. She snapped them. She struck match after match along the kitchen floor but it was no use. It was like trying to walk in a straight line after spinning around and around in the garden.

Eventually, brow sweating, tears streaming down her cheeks, she managed it. The flame caught and she watched the little orange bud tick down the stalk of the match. Blue, orange and white. Creeping, crawling like a caterpillar, all the way down . . . The pain was hot and sharp. Ettie clutched her burning fingers to her mouth, salty tears stinging her eyes. Two fat blisters appeared on her fingertips. She blinked through the pain, dried her eyes and tried again. And again, and again, and again.

That night Tata ate his single boiled potato and Ettie was proud.

Over the next few weeks she learned to cook more things. Her mother had taught her to read a little, and she was just about able to decipher the words in the cookbook on the windowsill. She made the recipes with pictures at first, mimicking the images which showed step-by-step how to coddle an egg, how to debone a fish, how to turn tomatoes into soup. She found a little stool and dragged it around with her, day in, day out. Ettie's cooking was always accompanied by the sound of the stool in those days, its three wooden legs scraping over the flagstone floor.

It was a long winter that year, and her mother did not return.

The days grew shorter and then longer again, snow fell and thawed on the distant hills, and blossoms were dropping from the crab apple trees by the time they had word of her. It was Tata who received the news, from a boy with flailing arms running along the donkey track. Tata met him at the gatepost and Ettie watched from the shadow of the doorway as Tata bent his ear to the boy, stopped frozen as if struck by a spell, and then shoved him roughly away. The boy turned tail and ran back up to the village and Tata stormed across the field, away from Ettie, away from the house. He walked for a long time, and when he came back his cheeks were wet and he said in a crackling voice, "Get inside. She's not coming back."

Two months later a pale coffin was delivered to the village church, and a fresh plot was dug in the corner of the cemetery.

Marie the once-a-week lady had a little girl, Marguerite, who used to run along the donkey track to play with Ettie. Marguerite was small and sweet-smelling with two plaits down her back. Rosy cheeks that shone like cherries when she blushed. She and Ettie used to play down by the well at the bottom of the garden, making fairy dens and mud pies. They splashed in the stream in thin, cotton dresses. They caught newts and frogs and built them palaces of sticks and stones.

Marguerite was afraid of Tata. She kept her games with Ettie to the bushes and the long grass, to the deep shadows of the stream. But one day Ettie clasped her friend by the hand and brought her into the kitchen. She showed her the little stool. Her special bowl for mixing. Her heavy knife. Marguerite peered around the kitchen, eyes wide. She examined her reflection in the mirror of a copper pan. She picked up a lump of coal from the scuttle.

But then she froze. Beyond the kitchen door there came a low rumble. A rough tread. The sound of an adult body moving through the house. Marguerite dived under the kitchen table just as the door opened and Tata's bare feet appeared on the flagstones. His body seemed to change the very air in the room. His earthy scent was salty and sharp.

He stood there for a moment, and then Marguerite let out a whimper, and with an ominous creaking Tata lowered his knees to the floor, bent his great shaggy head, and looked under the table. He reached out a hand and dragged Marguerite by her two perfect plaits. He yanked her all the way to the terrace, her chin scratched and bleeding, her knees raw. He told her to run.

Marguerite never came back, and neither did Marie. Word spread in the village. People stayed away. The priest from Saint-Auguste's crumbling church came down one afternoon, his black robes billowing like smoke, but Tata would not speak to him. He sat in silence for the hour the priest lectured him on the terrace, drinking the lemonade Ettie had fetched for them. When the priest had said his piece Tata stood up, unbuttoned his trousers, and urinated onto the flower bed.

The priest did not return.

No one came down the donkey track after that. The knocker on the front door rusted over from lack of use. The postman refused to deliver letters to the strange house down the abandoned track. And with Marie gone the housework fell to Ettie. The cooking, the cleaning, the shopping, the pressing of sheet corners into tight little squares.

When Ettie was nine she found a bird on the terrace. It had flown into the window and lay in a fluttering heap on the ground. Dazed. Barely alive.

To her surprise, Tata allowed her to keep it. He even brought her a paintbrush in a glass of water, and together they lay on their tummies in the winter sun, feeding droplets of water to the bird from the end of the brush.

"Goldfinch," said Tata.

"Goldfinch," repeated Ettie.

The bird's eye twitched open.

Tata brought down a birdcage from the dusty room at the top of the house, an old prop from one of his paintings. They nestled the bird inside, tucking it among scraps of cloth and a bundle of lavender stalks.

Over the following weeks the bird grew stronger. It began to hop around its cage. Its breast inflated with song. Ettie fixed the cage in the kitchen, high up near the window, so she could talk to the bird while she worked. She pressed sunflower seeds through the bars and watched its quick, enamel beak snap them up.

Ettie loved that bird. She loved its streak of saffron feathers, its dark, glossy eyes. She chattered away to it as she sliced onions, as she strained honey. Finally, she had someone to talk to. The scrape of her stool was replaced by the gentle babble of her voice, and the little bird sang back to her. It hopped along its perch, back and forth, back and forth, crying out through the bars.

Until one day Tata slammed into the room. He broke open the cage and grabbed the bird in his fist—the little thing was no bigger than a chicken's egg—and squeezed until it stopped singing. He threw the mass of feathers and skin to the kitchen floor and pressed it beneath his bare toes.

That was how Ettie learned to be silent.

JOSEPH

Each night without fail there is an event: a moment where Tata stands up, his belly juddering the table, and cries "Stop!" He holds out a hand for either Joseph's or Ettie's plate and, like silent disciples, they offer them. Sometimes Joseph has finished eating, with nothing but chicken bones left on his plate, but other times Ettie has taken barely a bite when Tata claims her dinner as his own. He disappears into the dusk, stomping down to the studio to set up his latest composition.

Each time this happens Joseph smiles at Ettie, as if to say, *This again!* But she does not smile back. She stares across the inky field, at the sliver of river beyond, her eyes dark.

She twists a napkin around and around in her hands.

Tartuffe is a luminary . . . No, not luminary. Too similar to "luminous," which he has used in the previous sentence. "Master"? *Tartuffe is a master who challenges our perception of art* . . . Not "challenges," that sounds too combative. "Questions"? *A master who questions our perception of art* . . . Is "perception" the right word, though? Perhaps "understanding" would be better. *A master who questions our understanding of art.* That seems a rather bold claim. *Our understanding of what art can be?* A little tempered, a little better. But has he tempered the sentence so much now that it just seems weak? Would "luminary" be better anyway? Perhaps "luminary" is not the problem and he should change "luminous" in the previous sentence. But that brings the issue of finding another word for "luminous" when he has already used "radiant," "lustrous," and "shining." Joseph scraps the sentence entirely.

Joseph wonders about Tata's odd, white eye. It has long been a source of speculation, but how did it happen? What does it mean for his art? If the great man cannot see, if he is gradually turning blind, then surely his painting days are numbered. What a scoop that would be for Joseph's article. *Young Man with Orange* may be one of the last paintings Tata ever completes. Perhaps—Joseph's heart races at the thought of it—this compromised eye accounts for Tata's unusual perspective? His paintings are always a bit jumbled up. Objects aren't quite where they should be. What is the story behind that eye?

He broaches the topic with Ettie one night when they are alone in the kitchen, washing up after dinner. "Are you worried?" he asks. "About Tata's eye?"

Ettie looks up from the plate she has been drying with a ragged cloth. "What?"

"His eyesight. The . . ." Joseph does not know what to call it. "The *white* eye."

"The dead eye?" she says. "It's been like that since he was a child. One of the boys on the docks threw a stone at it."

There it is. One hundred rumours quashed with a simple explanation. He will have to write to Harry and tell him it was not a duel with Cézanne or a fight with Van Gogh that blinded the great Tartuffe in one eye. It was a small boy with a stone.

A late lunch. Bread and fresh sardines. Tata is sitting back in his favourite wicker chair, his face tilted towards the sun. A plate of fish spines rests artfully at his elbow.

Joseph eats slowly while Ettie sifts through a pile of letters that have come for Tata. She reads them aloud and without opening his eyes, Tata gives his verdict.

"There is an invitation to the *Salon Dada*."

"Ignore."

"A request for a family portrait from the mayor of Marseille."

"Ignore."

"A message from Monsieur Diaghilev to ask if you would design the costumes for his latest ballet."

Again and again comes the command: "Ignore. Ignore. Absolutely not. Ignore."

Joseph comes upon Tata crouched outside the studio. He is on his hands and knees, watching a caterpillar inch its way along the path. A wide smile fills Tata's face and his whole body shakes. He is laughing. With a thick finger he helps the caterpillar across the path, out of the danger of trampling feet. When the creature is safely ensconced in the grass Tata squints up at Joseph, and the wonder on his face is that of a child, reveling in the sweetness of the world.

Most days it is so hot Joseph can barely think. He starts to work at night, or wakes early in the morning while the air is still cool. One night, in the strange hours between midnight and sunrise, he gazes through the circular window in his room and spies a movement in the grounds below. Something quick: a shadow flitting through the olive trees. He blinks and it is gone. He falls to his knees and presses his eye to the grimy glass. Is someone out there? He angles his head but cannot see anything more. Perhaps he imagined it. But as he eases himself back into his chair the night ripples again, and he thinks he sees a figure dart out from between the trees.

The studio begins to reek. A trail of ants crawls single file along the floor, winds itself up a table leg, onto a plate of melon slices. The ants swarm hungrily, then scatter across the table, up the walls, into the cracks in the bricks. The studio appears alive. Even when he lies in bed and tries to sleep, Joseph thinks he can hear the soft *tick* of hundreds of legs.

Joseph helps Ettie lay the table for dinner. Tata must have his special cutlery. The knife with the pearly handle. The fork with three tines instead of four. He arranges these hallowed objects on the table while Ettie brings out bread. Wineglasses. And then a plate of oysters that smell like death.

"Are you . . . are you supposed to eat oysters in June?" he asks. The evening sun is turning their milky shells to amber.

Ettie frowns. "We eat them whenever Tata wants to paint them."

"But aren't they rather off in the summer months?"

The frown deepens. "Tata wants to paint them," she says.

"But are they safe?"

"Of course."

They eat the oysters, and Joseph spends the rest of the night throwing up in a tin bucket in the dingy bathroom off the hall. His stomach roils, hair stuck to his clammy forehead, his body convulsing in shivering, tremulous waves. Salty acid hurtles up his throat. It is like drowning in reverse.

His misery echoes around the stained tiles of the little room but the rest of the house is silent. He is the only one afflicted. It is yet another reminder that he does not belong here, that even his body is not made for this place.

In the morning he feels like a shell of a man.

"This is not the right kind of paper!" Tata bellows. "It is too smooth! Why is it so smooth?" He flaps a piece in the air, his face contorting.

"It is the same paper as always," says Ettie, stooping to pick up the sheets he has thrown to the ground.

"It's not! This is not grainy enough! Why is it different? Where is my paper?" Tata casts around the studio table, knocking over a tin of paintbrushes. "Where is my paper? I cannot work without the right paper!"

He has been trying to make a pen-and-ink study of a fish spine all afternoon but has given up, blaming first the light, then the dust, then the sound of Joseph's breathing. Now finally he has decided it is the paper: too smooth. Inferior quality.

Ettie shuffles the sheaf of pages and returns them to the table. "The paper is the same, Tata," but her uncle has wound himself into a rage. He throws down the ink pen and one hundred black exclamation marks spatter across the floor. Tata wrestles the apron over his head and tosses it into the corner of the room. "I cannot work like this!" he bellows, dashing the inkpot to the ground, and storms out of the studio. Crickets whir loudly at his departure.

Joseph stoops to pick up the pen but Ettie is already there. She pulls a rag from her apron and begins to dab at the ink. Her hands are quick and well-practised.

Joseph reaches for the paintbrushes that have rolled across the floor.

"Leave them," she says coldly.

He straightens up, feeling useless. The morning has been marked by shouting, by upturned inkpots, by Joseph always somehow being in the way. And now Ettie is *psh psh*–ing him aside. She scoops the paintbrushes into their tin, returns them to the tabletop. Picks up the rumpled apron from the floor. Joseph watches the hunched figure of Tata thrash his way up the field, his steps becoming more laboured as the incline increases.

He is only trying to help. All he can do is be persistently kind.

This is the price we must pay for art, Joseph thinks later that night, when he is lying awake in his room at the top of the house.

Life with Tata is unpredictable. One moment he is jovial, buoyed with good humour and a bright, childlike glee. But the next moment he can sour, spitting poison at anyone who comes near.

Would the greatest painter alive have achieved what he had if he were not so particular? So firm in knowing exactly what he wants and how he wants it? The shouting, the storming, the throwing of anything within arm's reach . . . it is all part of Tata's process. And who is Joseph to say he should not work like this? Could he have produced *Bathers at Arles* without breaking some paintbrushes? Could *Caged Songbird* have been painted without bursting some blood vessels?

Joseph shifts and turns on the uncomfortable bed. *This is what we must endure*, he thinks. *This is the cost of genius.*

ETTIE

Ettie cannot remember her mother's face. It is one of the things that pains her most, makes her clutch her stomach at odd moments. No matter how hard she tries, casting her mind back to the furthest recesses of her childhood, she cannot picture her. There is no face to accompany the gentle woman who carried her to bed when she fell asleep on the terrace. No face for the fragrant blur who fed her madeleines for breakfast and put lipstick on Ettie's cheeks when she was small. Her mother only exists in a faint waft of cigarette haze.

Did she have dark hair? Ettie wonders. *What colour were her eyes? Did she have freckles just like me?* There are no photographs to help her.

Once, when she was about eleven, she asked Tata if he had ever painted a picture of her mother. He had stiffened but, "Yes," he said. "Yes. There is a painting." Ettie's heart had leapt. But he had sold it, he said. Years ago. It had disappeared into a private collection and he could not remember the name of the person who bought it. There was no hope of seeing it again.

Ettie tore through the house like a blizzard. She was looking for something—anything—that could lead her on a breadcrumb trail to the painting. There must be a draft somewhere. A preparatory sketch. There had to be something that could point her in the right direction; a clue in the treasure hunt that ended with her mother's face.

But there was nothing. The house revealed no answers.

She knew the painting existed, though. That was a comfort. On wild days Ettie used to think, *I will search every building in France until I find her. She is out there, somewhere, waiting for me.* Her mother's image would be hanging in someone's hallway, or perhaps a lady's dressing room. Her beautiful eyes would survey these wealthy, anonymous people, watching over their daily lives as she had not been able to watch over Ettie's. She would bear witness to their screaming rows and their small, tender moments. She would watch with a smile—Ettie is sure she smiled—and a knowing look in her painted eyes. Her mother was preserved forever in that painting, in a way she could not be preserved in life.

It was some years later, when Tata was drunk, that he admitted he had not sold the portrait of Ettie's mother at all. He had painted over it.

He was in need of a canvas, he explained, and painted over the old one to reuse it. He wouldn't tell her which one. He claimed he couldn't remember.

Ettie wanted to claw open every one of his paintings. To strip the image from the surface and reveal the lost woman underneath; to free her mother who was buried beneath someone else. Hidden, smothered, trapped. Which painting was it? The study of cobras in Morocco? *The Apple Peeler?* The great seascape *Boy with Kite?* If only Ettie could find the right painting she could rescue her!

But of course she could not. Ettie could no more peel paint from a canvas than skin from her body. She was no more able to unearth her mother from a painting than bring her back from the dead.

Ettie wanted to burn the house to the ground.

JOSEPH

Tata finished with Joseph hours ago and all he has done since is hole up in his room and succeed at writing nothing. The days are slipping through his fingers, June inching inexorably towards July. His deadline looms.

He is sitting on his bed, notebook against his knees, trying to find a way to describe the buildup of paint on Tata's canvas. *Impasto* is the technical word for it, but he must find a way of describing it to readers who have not spent a year at art school. The layers of paint? The strata? He chews the end of his pencil. He wants to say the paint is like furrows of tilled earth. Like the frothy gills of a mushroom cap. Like the tightly furled petals of a rosebud, thumbed-over pages, artichoke leaves, feathers, mulch . . .

It is hot and airless up in his attic room. The clothes he brought with him are too thick, ill-suited to this sunbaked climate, but he has no others. He undoes a few of the buttons on his shirt. Then pulls it off entirely, up and over his head. He shimmies his trousers off too, kicking them to the end of the bed. The air is a sweet relief on his skin. He lies back, reposing like a slain hero in a painting, and closes his eyes.

It is hard not to feel lonely here. He has been at the farmhouse for over two weeks but Tata mainly communicates with him through grunts and sharp tugs at his body: *Move your arm here*, his hands seem to say. *Breathe in. Chin down. Keep your eyeballs still.* He is content one moment, thunderous the next. There are bursts of good humour followed by long silences and sudden explosions. It is like living with an ever-changing storm.

Joseph's body thrums with the sharp vibrato of constantly being on edge. Sometimes he feels that even his breathing is too loud. Ettie must have learned to walk on her toes. To slip silently through the house. He wishes she would talk to him but she always seems to be just out of sight, out of reach. So for now he is lonely. And hot. And wretched. Trapped in a suffocating house speaking the language of his dead mother, every word a silver ghost in his mouth.

Joseph peels his eyes open. Tilts his notebook towards himself, and then tosses it across the room. He reaches instead for the one book he brought with him: *The Odyssey* by Homer. It is his brother's copy. A ridiculous book to take to the front lines of a war, but Rupert was determined. This copy is battered and browned, its corners soft. Joseph flicks through it, pausing at the passages his brother has underlined in faint pencil.

The Odyssey is not a story about going on an adventure, their mother always told them. It is a story about coming home. This was the book their mother—eccentric daughter of an eccentric Classics scholar—used to read to her three children. It is the story they performed in the garden on long summer evenings: pillowcases for tunics, washing basket for a ship, one-eyed cat for a Cyclops. This was their story. Rupert and Joseph and Flora's. He would give anything to go back to those days of handmade costumes, of bare feet running through grass, of shrieks and laughter and a sun that never seemed to set. But those days are long, long gone.

"Are you ready?"

Joseph gives a start. Ettie is standing in his doorway, a wicker basket over one arm.

"I didn't hear you coming," Joseph says, suddenly aware of his nakedness, of his sprawling limbs, his dishevelled bedroom. He hastily pulls the bedsheet up to his chest.

Ettie has tucked her hair into a silk scarf today. She is surveying him, taking in the crumpled shirt on the floor, the trousers kicked to the end of the bed. Then a smile appears like a hook under her cheek. "I need you to carry things from the market," she says. And that is that.

The donkey track shimmers in the heat. Joseph's head swims and he wishes he had grabbed some water from the house.

"Doesn't Tata have a motorcar?" he asks as they make their way along the dusty road. With all that money Tata could certainly afford one. Joseph has seen his auction records.

"He doesn't need one," Ettie says simply. "He never goes any-where, and anyone who visits him brings their own." It is one of the longest sentences she has ever said to him. "I am the only per-son who needs to leave the house," she continues, as if unable to stop now she has started. "So I walk. Or I take my mother's bicycle. Perhaps Tata thinks that if he gets a car I'll use it to escape." She says it like a joke, though Joseph can tell that neither of them finds it funny.

He glances at her from the corner of his eye. There is a free-dom to her movements out here. Her face is open, her chin tilted towards the sun, as if she has finally come out from under the shadow of the house.

"Has Tata always been . . . like he is?"

"Like what?"

Joseph is embarrassed at having to elaborate. He wants to say "like a tyrant," ruling over the farmhouse like a despotic emperor.

Tata can be so full of poison Joseph doesn't even understand some of the words he flings at Ettie. But then he has gentler moments too, when he smiles or cracks a joke, and light seems to radiate from him. In the universe of the farmhouse Tata is the sun around which everything else revolves. Joseph tries to find a diplomatic way of saying all this. "So . . . particular."

Ettie shrugs. "He's just lived alone for a long time."

"But he has you," Joseph presses. "He's had you for twenty-seven years. And before that he had—"

"I mean he lives in his own head," says Ettie. "He doesn't engage with the world. He's . . . turned away from it."

Joseph has an image of an old man rolling over in bed, turning to face the wall. "But why?"

"Some things don't have a reason," she says. "They just happen."

Joseph ponders this, kicking up dust as he walks. It is a relief to be talking to Ettie at last. He has been so adrift, so out of place, but here it feels as if he is finally getting somewhere. He turns over a question in his mind, one that has been blazing through his thoughts since he first arrived. "What happened between Tata and Cézanne?"

Ettie keeps her eyes fixed on the road ahead. "They were friends. And then they were not."

"But what happened?"

"I don't know. I wasn't there."

"But you must know—"

"It all happened before I was born." She closes her mouth, and the set of her jaw tells Joseph she will not say any more on the subject.

He shoves his hands in his pockets. Fine. Perhaps there is no mystery. No scandal. Perhaps Tata is just a man who has tired of the world and chosen solitude. Perhaps there is no puzzle for Joseph to crack.

They reach the village and step into the cool shade of its cobbled streets. An old man pauses a moment from sweeping his doorway. He straightens up, leaning on his broom, but does not raise his hand in greeting. He merely tracks them with his eyes, a taut silence stretching between them. Farther along the street two women sit on a bench mending lace. Their heads are bowed in conversation but as Joseph and Ettie approach they look up, fall silent. Joseph feels their eyes following them all the way up the street.

"Why do they stare at us?" he asks.

Ettie shrugs. "They always stare."

Joseph glances up at the shuttered windows of the houses they pass, imagining the eyes and ears lurking behind them. The whispers that will swirl as soon as he and Ettie are out of sight.

The market is busy. Wooden tables have been placed end to end throughout the square and spread with papery onions, plump tomatoes, bushels of parsley. Wizened old women, their hair tucked under white cotton scarves, roll nectarines from hand to hand before selecting the best. Children chase each other in zigzags and Joseph's nose is tickled by the scent of donkeys, garlic, straw. Cheese oozing in the sun. Fruit hammered into pulp underfoot.

It is so different from the cold morning markets he is used to: the damp pavements and stall sellers hawking their wares with fogged breath. Here, the square is a riot of colour. Joseph's head is turned by apricots, plums, and strawberries. There is a table in the shade of a plane tree spread with glossy pastries: towers of cream, raspberries, and pistachio. Sugar gleaming like dew.

Ettie pulls a piece of paper from her pocket and Joseph peers over her shoulder. In neat, thin handwriting she has written:

Peaches
Lemons
Cherries
Lobster

"What's this for?" he asks. The combination will make an odd meal.

"We are not buying food," Ettie says. "We are buying props." She starts to walk the length of a trestle table, inspecting the fruit. There are swollen watermelons, shining apples, and a crate of peaches so soft they look like sleeping animals.

"Here, this one looks nice," says Joseph, picking out a peach. Sunset pink turning to butter.

Ettie gives it the briefest of glances and shakes her head. "It's too perfect," she says, selecting another. This one is squat and yellow, as if it has been pressed flat by the heel of someone's hand. "Much better," she says, putting it in her basket. "This one is worth painting. We are not buying these things for the taste," she explains. "We are buying them for their colour, for their shape."

Joseph savours every detail Ettie feeds him, storing it away to write about later.

"Is this food for *Young Man with Orange*, then?" he asks.

"No . . . no, it's for something else. Another painting."

Joseph knows Tata works on several paintings at once but he is still bruised to think that the great man's mind might be on anything other than *Young Man with Orange.* He does not want to think of what will happen when he is no longer needed here. "What else is Tata working on?"

Ettie shrugs. "He's planning something . . . something big. Something about food."

"A still life, then?"

"No . . ." She holds up another peach to the light. "More like a portrait. But without any people."

Joseph is about to ask what on earth this means when Ettie reaches out a sharp arm and selects quite possibly the ugliest peach he has ever seen.

"This one!" She beams. It has a puckered bruise on one side and is already shrinking under a soft white mould. Ettie adds it to their collection and hands the seller a silver coin.

They repeat this exercise until they have nine knobbly lemons and a bag of bloodred cherries in their basket, and then follow their noses to the putrid sluices of the fishmonger. The ground beneath the stall is slick with water. The fish are silver-grey, their eyes gelatinous. Ettie selects the most colourful lobster from a basket on the ground ("Speckled, Joseph, speckled! The shell must have an interesting pattern!"), and the gently twitching creature is placed in a wooden crate and loaded into Joseph's arms. Its claws are tied with string, a damp newspaper laid over its back to keep it cool. Joseph feels the salty brine seep into his shirt.

Finally they turn from the market, stopping briefly at the tobacconist to collect letters, and then point their feet towards home.

Ettie busies herself with the letters as they walk. She reads each one silently and then slips it back into its envelope in a deft, practised movement: unfold, read, refold, return. Then she comes to a letter written in bright turquoise ink.

"Your editor wants to know when he can see a draft of your article," she informs him.

Joseph is skewered by a needle of anxiety. His latest draft is scrunched up in the corner of his room. He has nothing to show Harry, nothing at all. He takes the letter awkwardly over the lobster crate and glances through it. He will have to gloss over the facts. Tell Harry it's all coming along nicely.

But his sharp feeling of guilt is mixed with indignation that Ettie has taken the liberty of reading his private correspondence. Has she done this before? Perhaps she is so used to doing it for Tata she does not know it is rude. He is about to hand the letter back to her when he realises something.

"Wait . . . you can read this?"

Ettie has her head in the next letter but she gives a curt nod.

"You can read English?" he demands. "You can . . . speak it?"

She looks up. "I can read . . ." she enunciates in very slow, careful English. "Speak . . . not so much."

"Why didn't you tell me?"

"You never asked." She has already reverted to French.

"Where did you learn English?" he presses. He has been feeling so lonely, yet here is someone who speaks his native language after all.

Ettie pauses for a long moment, sucking in her cheeks. "I worked in a hospital during the war. Three villages over. I looked after a lot of soldiers. French, English, Algerian . . . I used to read to them. I learned it that way."

Joseph is oddly touched by this image of Ettie in a starched white cap and apron. "What did you read to them?"

"Poems, mainly. We only had what the soldiers brought with them so there wasn't much choice. I had the strangest vocabulary for a while," she says with a laugh. It is an odd sound, her laugh, like someone trying it out for the first time. "I can tell you all about daffodils and clouds. How the birds sing in the morning and which flowers bloom in the spring. And what it looks like where the Thames meets the sea and how the wind blows on the hills in Wales. I can tell you about stars and mountains and snow, and larks and swallows and . . . well, nothing very useful, really," she says, suddenly shy, tucking a lock of hair back under her scarf. "What about you?" she deflects. "What did you do during the war?"

Joseph's heart sinks. They have arrived: the war. The Great War. The war to end all wars. An itchy feeling comes over him, like dry grass on the backs of his legs. He squints at the hazy horizon. "I was too young to sign up," he says, hoping this will be the end of it.

But now Ettie has started talking there is no stopping her. "That didn't prevent some people," she says. "I had soldiers in the hospital who lied about their age. Sixteen, seventeen . . . one of them I swear was only fourteen."

He could brush this off. He could lie. He could say that his eyesight is too bad, that he is flat-footed or deaf in one ear. That he has a heart condition, or an abscess of the lung (he has memorised all the criteria for medical exemption).

Or he could tell Ettie the truth.

Joseph stops walking and looks at her, his arms straining under the lobster crate. He could just come out and say it. There is no one but Ettie to hear.

"I am an objector," he says shortly. "A pacifist."

He had never been able to say the word in front of his father without stammering. He had never been able to hold his gaze or stop his hands from shaking, but here he says it quite plainly in front of Ettie: "I objected to the war. I refused to sign up."

The air is still. Ettie looks at him thoughtfully and then, slowly, she nods.

Joseph had been too young to serve when war first broke out, but his father wanted him to sign up anyway.

"Why don't you enlist?" he boomed. "What's wrong with you, boy, don't you want to fight?"

It felt as if his father wanted him to die. Each year Joseph hoped that the war would end before his next birthday, that he would never be old enough to sign up, but each year it did not. As the war raged on for another one, two, three more years, Joseph knew what was waiting for him: death. The knowledge that he must kill or be killed. Perhaps both. It would be the end of his life as he knew it.

He attended lectures by political philosophers. He marched alongside protesters and joined his voice to the thousands shouting outside Whitehall. He signed petitions, distributed pamphlets, let white feathers be pinned to his chest. But always he removed them before he came home. With shaking hands he pulled the pins from his lapels, stuffed the pamphlets into his pockets, and sprinted up the stairs before his father could see him.

He thought briefly about the loophole of training for the clergy, but he knew that his heart was not in it. He must be true to what he believed in: pacifism. Disarmament. He refused to join a war that saw young men walk patriotically to their deaths while politicians sat in shiny offices and drew lines on a map.

Then, for his eighteenth birthday, Joseph's father gave him an enlistment form as a present, and Joseph could hide the truth no longer. Over a breakfast table spread with cards and well-wishes, he announced, "I will never join up. I am an—an objector."

Joseph's father had nearly choked on his kipper. The argument that followed had been colossal. It was hot and acidic. "A coward!" his father called him. "A disgrace to this family's name! A disgrace to your country, Joseph, and a disgrace to *me*." He reeled dizzily between outrage and disgust. "A milksop!" he called him. "A shirker!"

There were weeks when they did not speak to one another and then they collided like two irreconcilable comets burning themselves out in the sky. Joseph's refusal to fight became a stain on his character, a blemish on the Adelaide family name, and caused a rift between father and son which could never be bridged.

"Look at what Rupert's doing," his father used to seethe. "Your brother's out there serving his country and becoming a man. That's what it means to be a *man*, Joseph."

Rupert was the soldier. Rupert, four years older, exuberant and handsome. Blond hair that always appeared sunlit whatever the weather. He had their mother's strawberry-blond eyelashes, disappearing into a face so freckled he appeared permanently tanned, and a smile that reached all the way to his eyes, blue as meltwater.

"My brother . . ." he manages to say to Ettie as they start walking again, "he fought in the war. And it destroyed him."

Two boys. One dark, one golden. Rupert's childhood warnings were "not so fast," "climb down," "hold back." Joseph's were "hurry up," "sit straight," "pay attention."

Rupert wanted to be an aviator. A sailor, an inventor, an archaeologist, no actually a pirate, a polar explorer, a lion tamer. Joseph never knew what he wanted to be. Mostly he wanted to be Rupert.

Joseph trailed after his older brother wherever he went. He was the shadow of Rupert, the dark imitation that followed him everywhere. He grew up at the end of Rupert's outstretched hand, their younger sister Flora clinging on to the other.

But then there came a day when their hands slipped from one another.

Rupert had a place at Oxford to study "greats": Cicero and Plato and all the ancient thinkers of the classical world. "One last hurrah to stretch the brain before joining the family firm," he had joked. This was the agreement. There would be no polar exploring or lion taming for the Adelaide boys. A degree would be tolerated, and then a desk job in their father's timber firm was lined up for when they finished.

But Rupert had barely reached Oxford when war split the continent apart. He was plucked from his first year of Latin lectures, Greek translations prised from his hands, and sent to the underground hell of the trenches. He had taken his copy of *The Odyssey* with him, that great story about coming home. "If Odysseus can make it home from Troy, then I can get back from bloody Belgium." He had beamed at Joseph, radiant even in the gloom of their father's study. He was eighteen and knew nothing of the world.

Rupert had looked so handsome in his uniform. Their mother had arranged for a photographer to take his portrait just before he left, and sent the photographs to everyone she knew. And when Joseph screamed himself hoarse at pacifist rallies, he was really screaming for his brother to come back. All he wanted was for the war to end so Rupert could come home.

He kept Rupert's photograph in his wallet. He keeps it there still.

Ettie has slowed her walk as if to delay their return to the house. She is putting one foot very carefully in front of the other.

"Do you judge me?" Joseph asks her. He cannot help it.

"No," she says eventually. Then: "I don't judge anyone who chooses life over death."

Why can't time run backwards? Why can't Joseph undo everything that happened? He would give anything to roll up the spool of the last three years and start again. He would lock his brother in the house, confine their mother too, prevent either of them from going out into the world which was plotting so many ways to hurt them.

Life had so many tricks up its sleeve.

ETTIE

Deep night. Moonrise. Ettie is down by the river, washing the night's smell off her. It has seeped into her hair, under her nails, into the damp patches beneath her arms. She lies back, her body pearly in the moonlight. Her clothes float eerily nearby, the cool of the current cleansing them.

The moon is a sharp scythe tonight. Ettie dips her head under the water and lets the cold pierce her brain. She closes her eyes, runs her hands softly through her hair, letting the river flow through it. She lets it carry everything away.

There is something delicious about being awake when everyone else is asleep. It is a treat she gives herself: these satin-black hours when no one knows what she does or where she goes. She can slip from the house when there are no ears to hear the scrape of the door. No eyes to spy her silent tread through the garden. She can be herself at last.

She floats on her back, looking up at the slowly winking stars. A pair of bats streak across the sky. She runs her hands up and down her body, seeking out the dirt and the sweat and the grime, and her mind turns towards Joseph.

Joseph, sprawled on the bed. His body elongated, pale neck tipped back, hair wild against the wall. The long fingers of his hand rolling a pencil between them. Joseph is usually so alert, so poised and upright, it had been strange to see him unguarded. She had glimpsed him through a crack in the door and then been unable to look away. His limbs spread carelessly. His skin smoothed over undulations of muscles.

He looked so vivid. So alive.

Did Tata notice that they disappeared to the market together today? Was he aware that they were gone for longer than usual? That Ettie's movements were lighter when she returned?

She closes her eyes. Lets the water ripple around her.

Everything Ettie has learned about people she learned from Tata. She knows to treat them with suspicion, to keep them at arm's length. But something about Joseph is different. He is kind. Curious. Gentle. Easy to talk to; his presence calming. Sometimes she watches through the studio door while the men are inside. Tata bustling about, huffing and knocking things over. But Joseph is so still the only movement is the subtle rise and fall of his chest, swelling like a wave and then subsiding.

She wants to inch closer to him. To spin some thread of connection between her life and his.

But she does not know how.

The lonely church bell strikes three in the morning. Time is rolling onwards. Like an eye slowly closing, the night shortens by degrees.

She steps out of the water and lets the warm air dry her before wrapping herself in a fraying towel. Her clothes she wrings out on a nearby rock, then bundles them into her arms and begins the swift walk up the field. She brings her nose to her arm. The smell is gone. Her body is clean.

She glances toward the house. There is a light in one of the windows, up in the room beneath the eaves.

She is not the only one awake tonight.

JOSEPH

A visitor is coming. Joseph is surprised, for in the weeks he has spent at the farmhouse no one has troubled their doorstep. No one has even crossed the threshold.

He is oddly annoyed. He has become used to the three of them: he and Tata and Ettie, the gentle rhythm of their days and the pattern of their movements. They have fallen into a comfortable existence, Joseph inching forward with his article and Tata with *Young Man with Orange*. Ettie flitting like a sparrow between them. But today they must pause their careful choreography. Today a man is coming to the house.

"Who is "The Man from Paris"?" Joseph asks when he finally finds Ettie scattering corn for the chickens around the side of the house. "Tata said he isn't painting me today because 'The Man from Paris' is coming."

Ettie sighs, straightening up. "His real name is Raimondi."

Joseph stoops down and scoops a handful of corn. This name is familiar. It is one of the few that appears alongside Tata's in articles and sales records.

Raimondi is Tata's dealer.

Joseph had written to Raimondi—in his very best French—when he first had the idea of interviewing Tata. He had received a curt note in reply: *Monsieur Tartuffe does not give interviews. If you wish to make a purchase of his work, you will be obliged to go through me.*

"He comes down about once a month to collect Tata's paintings in person," says Ettie, "and then takes them back to his gallery in

Paris to sell. He sends Tata the profits. Sometimes brings those in person too." Ettie wrinkles her nose as if this displeases her. "Usually he brings money but occasionally he pays Tata in wine." She bends down to inspect one of the chicken's wings where the feathers are askew. "Raimondi's the only person Tata usually allows through the door. I think he enjoys being Tata's only friend . . ." She squints up at Joseph. "I'm not sure what he'll make of you."

The Man from Paris arrives in a sleek black motorcar. It crawls up the drive like a great shining beetle, a trail of dust spooling behind it. Ettie is there to open the car door to a man who springs forth like a jack-in-the-box. He is clad in a sharp black suit and wears a scarlet cravat around his neck like a slit throat. He has a thin moustache and dark, beady eyes. "My dear Tata!" he exclaims as he strides across the drive, holding his arms aloft as if to say: *Behold!*

Raimondi clasps Tata theatrically about the shoulders and kisses him on both cheeks. "A moment away from you is a moment too long. And . . . who is this?" He takes an exaggerated step backwards, looking Joseph up and down.

"This is Monsieur Adelaide," Tata says brusquely. "My model for *Young Man with Orange*."

Raimondi raises an eyebrow. "For *Young Man with* . . . I see. Well then, I am delighted, Monsieur Adelaide," and he squeezes a tanned hand around Joseph's.

To Ettie, he says nothing at all.

They make their way down to the studio where Raimondi prowls around the canvases. He lifts the corners of sketches to see what lies beneath. He fingers tubes of crinkled paint. He moves with an ease that shows he is at home in the studio, familiar with the mess and the paintings and the artist at their centre.

"Still not finished?" he asks, pulling a half-painted canvas away from the wall.

"Leave that!" roars Tata and Raimondi chuckles, returning the painting. "You have been busy." He nods approvingly, running his gaze around the stacks of paintings. He is here to pick up two of Tata's studies of food: a plate of silver anchovies, slimy and slick, and a handful of cherries on a white tablecloth. He says he thinks he can get a good price for them. "The major collectors are in Europe for the summer," he explains. "Americans, mostly. The ones who come along with a measuring tape and buy paintings according to how big their walls are. But what I am really excited about . . . is this."

He places himself in front of the easel where *Young Man with Orange* reposes. Joseph suddenly feels protective over it. *Do not look!* he wants to say. *It is not ready!* But Raimondi is already nose-to-nose with his half-painted face. His quick eyes are appraising Joseph's, taking in the dabs of paint like fingermarks. The rushes of colour. The canvas shimmering as if seen through a storm.

"When do you think it will be ready?" he asks, not tearing his gaze from the painting.

"It'll be ready when you stop badgering me," Tata grumbles, and Raimondi grins.

"Very well then, just two for today." He takes a last sweeping look around the studio as if to see if there are any more treasures he might have missed.

"Take them away, take them away," says Tata airily, "and come and have a drink."

They make their way back up to the house. It is not yet eleven but Tata sidles onto the terrace with a bottle of wine in one hand

and three glasses dangling from the other. "You will join us, Joseph," he calls over his shoulder. It is not a question.

Joseph looks back at Ettie but before he can invite her to join them she has given him a cool look, and slipped silently into the kitchen.

The three men sit beneath the arbour dripping with grapes.

"So, *Young Man with Orange*," says Raimondi as Joseph pours the wine. "Quite a radical departure, no?"

Tata leans back in his chair, his white and blue eyes gazing out at the field. "I have wanted to paint it for quite a while . . ." he says slowly.

Raimondi leans forward, and Joseph too is poised, his ears alert.

"It has been a long time . . ." says Tata. "A long time since any-one . . . Since I have . . ." But then he snaps out of it. He twists to Joseph and Raimondi, meets their eager expressions, their hungry eyes. "Does a man need an excuse to paint what he paints?"

"No, of course not," Raimondi says hastily.

"An artist must paint what he needs to paint!" Tata booms. "And if he requires a model to sit still and do nothing then that is what he shall have!"

"Of course, of course." Raimondi takes a sip of wine, and then turns his scrutinising gaze to Joseph. "Are you good at doing noth-ing, then, Monsieur Adelaide? Sitting still and keeping quiet?"

"Yes, I mean—good enough." Joseph cannot tell if Raimondi is making fun of him. "I am a journalist, actually," he says, sitting up a little straighter. "I'm writing an article about Tartuffe—about Tata."

"Oh?" Raimondi raises an eyebrow. He turns to Tata, eyes wide as if to say, *And you allow this?*

Tata shrugs and puffs on his cigar. "An eye for an eye. I paint him, he writes about me."

"I see," says Raimondi, turning back to look at Joseph with newfound interest. "And where will this article be published, if you don't mind my asking?"

"*The Inkling*," says Joseph stiffly. He feels defensive, aware of Raimondi's sharp eyes all over him. "It's a magazine in London. Just founded last year, the editor is Harold Makepeace—"

"A magazine in London, you say?" Raimondi twists his black moustache between two tobacco-stained fingers. He appears to be sizing Joseph up, perhaps remembering the letter he dismissed all those months ago. Reappraising him now that Joseph has wormed his way in. "Well . . . I am sure you can imagine, Monsieur Adelaide, how difficult my job is with Tata's refusal to publicise his work . . . this is certainly a change. Do you think your article will be published before *Young Man with Orange* is completed?"

"I . . . I don't know," Joseph falters. Harry needs the article by the end of the month, which is only a few days away. Suddenly his time at the farmhouse feels unbearably short. "I don't know how long it will take," he says carefully. "I just observe things. I study how Tata works. What he creates . . ."

Raimondi leans in close. "Are you studying us now, Monsieur Adelaide?" He blows a thin trail of smoke into the space between them. "Watching our every move . . . stealing our secrets?"

Joseph does not know how to respond. He shifts uncomfortably in his chair but Raimondi laughs and claps him on the back. "I think we need a nickname for you!" he cackles, and then he says a word that takes Joseph a moment to understand. At first he thinks Raimondi has called him *auteur*: author, and a warm glow spreads through his chest. He is a real writer at last. The author who will uncover the great Tartuffe.

But then he sees that Tata is laughing, and he realises what Raimondi has actually said: *vautour.*

Vulture.

It conjures up a sickly feeling in his stomach. He is a scavenger, scraping at whatever he can find: sketches, dried paint on a palette, the furrow of Tata's brow as he steps back from the easel. How his eye turns from milky white to fiery amber as the sun pours through the studio window. Joseph notes it all. He consumes it. He feeds on it.

Raimondi has seen him for what he is.

ETTIE

Raimondi departs mid-afternoon, the pair of canvases clutched under one arm. Ettie has wrapped them carefully in brown paper, giving them a final look-over while the men were drinking on the terrace. She has run her finger along the edges to make sure they are dry. Slotted them into the frames she commissioned from Lafayette. She has checked that Tata's signature is on the corner of each one.

At the door Raimondi kisses Tata on both cheeks. "Keep an eye on our friend the vulture," he murmurs, lingering on Tata's bushy jowl. Then he is away, walking briskly to his car. He places the paper-wrapped paintings on the seat beside him and, with a wave of his hat, reverses up the drive, disappearing in a spiral of dust. Ettie watches until she's sure he has gone completely, then closes the door and bolts it.

As she knew it would, a cloud descends upon the farmhouse. It is the same every time.

"I don't know why you let me give those paintings away," Tata grumbles as he stomps onto the terrace. "Awful little man. Trying to screw me over. He's out to get my money, the little weasel. My paintings and my money—that's all he wants." Ettie picks up the broomstick Tata has knocked over in his agitation. "He's a damned drunkard." Tata paces back and forth. "He'll crash that ridiculous car of his and my paintings will be covered in his little . . . weasel . . . blood!"

Tata is always unmoored after he releases his work to Raimondi. He does not like to let anything out from under his grip.

Ettie has found that nothing placates him when he is in one of these moods except time. She leaves him to his fuming.

For the next few days Tata shouts at Joseph, who looks as confused and wounded as a dog that does not know what it has done wrong. He tries to make amends, fetching Tata his cigar, praising his charcoal sketches, asking him about the other paintings he is working on, but Ettie knows he is only making things worse. One morning Tata grabs Joseph by the arm, pulls him close. They are in the studio, about to begin work for the morning but something is wrong. Tata holds Joseph's arm up to the light and drags his fingernail along the skin. "You are getting too dark," he murmurs.

"Too dark?" asks Joseph.

"Young Man with Orange is pale, not dark," says Tata, still trapping Joseph's arm in his grip. "Your skin must be pale."

Joseph's skin has changed in the weeks he has been here, rosy alabaster mellowing to nutty brown. The hair on his forearms has lightened. His collar reveals a line on his neck from the sun. Ettie has noticed all of this. Life here has warmed Joseph, filling his body with colour.

But this is not what Tata wants.

"Stay out of the sun," he growls, dropping Joseph's arm as if it has stung him.

From then on Joseph sticks to the shadows. He stays indoors while the sun is at its highest. He rolls his sleeves down to cover his arms. He only emerges onto the terrace in the evening when the sun has slipped beneath the hills, and does not come out of his room except to resume his position in the studio where Tata shouts and seethes.

He has become another captive of the house.

Ettie wants to reach for Joseph, to tell him Tata's anger is not his fault. But she does not know how to do this. She has never known how to forge a connection with another person. So she watches Joseph from a distance, cold and lonely with longing.

After Ettie's mother left, she dreamed of putting a hex on Tata. She would run down to the stream at the bottom of the field, beyond the trees where he couldn't see her. She would stir the mud on the bank with a stick. Drop one or two petals from the purple irises that grew at the water's edge. Sprinkle in some leaves. Mix the potion and wish, wish, wish him away.

She had a superstitious belief that if Tata left her mother would return. She would give him up in an instant if it meant she could have her mother back. She would do anything.

If I close my eyes for ten seconds he will be gone when I open them. If I hold my breath for one minute he will disappear. If I dig my nails into my palms and make eight perfect half-moons he will leave.

She was a small, lonely child, and having no real power in the world led her to invent her own power. It was a power of mud potions and silent incantations and touching things with her hands. She arranged snails along Tata's windowsill. Scattered cloves in the corners of the house. Touched her elbow three times, bit the inside of her cheeks, crossed her fingers while he was talking to her.

If I stay awake all night he will be gone in the morning.
If I do not eat for an entire day he will fall down the well and die.
If I refuse to look into his eyes he cannot hurt me.

She wanted to put a spell on Tata that would make him get up from his wicker chair, pack his easel over one shoulder, and leave the farmhouse forever. She spat in his soup. She collected his beard trimmings and buried them down by the stream. She drew a picture of him and threw it into the fire of the kitchen range.

She developed a need to touch things. She held on to chairs, doors, window latches, as if by anchoring herself to the house she could make sure it didn't abandon her too. She trailed her hands along the plaster walls. She pushed her palms into the wet grass on cold mornings. She dipped her fingers into the liquid wax of burning candles.

She ran her hands through the dresses in her mother's wardrobe, pressing her face to the cotton and silk she had left behind. In those early days the clothes still smelled of her, but as the months grew longer the scent grew thinner, until the wardrobe held only the stale musk of absence. The smell of a life that had faded into nothing.

Still to this day, when Ettie is nervous she reaches for something to touch. A peach stone. A cigarette. A paintbrush.

JOSEPH

For once, Ettie knocks.

Joseph is shut up in his bedroom at the top of the house, peering out of the small circular window that will not open. The sun blazes onto the fields below. The grass is bleached and brittle. It is a relief to be out of Tata's orbit for a while, away from the snorting and the hot, bilious words that have spewed from his mouth since Raimondi's visit. He is just trying to turn the handle of the window again when there is a gentle tap on the door.

"Come in?"

Ettie appears. She has a pinched look on her face, and a pair of heavy kitchen scissors in her hand. They stare at each other for a moment and then she says, "Your hair is too long."

"I'm sorry?"

"Tata says your hair is growing too long. Young Man with Orange has shorter hair."

"Oh." Joseph runs a hand over the back of his neck. Of course. He is not Joseph, he is the Young Man with Orange. Ettie holds up the scissors and Joseph understands what she has been sent to do.

She indicates the corner of the bed opposite the mirror, and Joseph sits. Ettie arranges herself behind him, kneeling on the mattress so they can both see the reflection. She eases the scissors open. Ochre rust dots the blades.

Silently, Ettie runs her fingers through his hair. It is the first time she has ever touched him. A fizzing sensation spreads across his skin. He keeps his eyes down as she slides her fingers up and down his scalp, and then begins to snip.

He concentrates on his hands in his lap. On the soft *strrp strrp* of the scissors.

A tuft of hair drifts down his back. He is sharply aware of Ettie's breath on his neck. Her knees resting against the base of his spine. Her fingers working carefully, trying to transform him back into the stranger he was when he first arrived.

Neither of them speaks for several minutes, then her soft voice says from behind him, "Tell me why you dropped out of art school."

Joseph is startled that Ettie remembers this. He thought he had been careful to omit mention of his time at the Slade—and particularly his ignoble dismissal—but Ettie has remembered. He looks up, meets her eyes in the mirror. "I didn't drop out."

Her hands are still on his neck. He is unsure how much to tell her, but something in the open curiosity of her face prompts him onwards and he says, "I was asked to leave."

Her body shifts on the mattress behind him. "Why?"

It is a simple question but Joseph's tongue feels papery in his mouth. Tendrils of something hot and shameful gather in his chest, filling it like a gas.

"I was there for a year . . ." he begins. It could have been the happiest year of his life. It should have been. He was going to become an artist. He had escaped his father's demands that he join the family timber firm or sign up to the army, and he was going to pursue something he loved instead. His grandfather—that kindly old Classics professor entrenched in a library in Switzerland—had wired the money for tuition. Even the war was limping to a close, and soon Rupert would be back from the Front.

It was all thanks to his mother. "I don't have my own money, Joseph," she had said, "and I don't have the authority, legal or otherwise, to grant you permission to go to art school. But I can take the blow from your father when it comes. So go. Go with my blessing. And make the most of every moment."

Climbing the steps of the Slade that first day he had rested his hand on the wide stone colonnade and vowed to make his mother proud. He arrived on time. He sat up straight and asked questions. He absorbed everything with wonder and attention. And he found his people. Here were the other bespectacled men and women with ink stains on their fingers and permanently rumpled clothes. There were even other conchies: young men who had rejected the war just like Joseph. They had a notably unhaunted look about them, these men. The whites of their eyes were too pure. Their hands a little too steady. For once Joseph wasn't made to feel strange for his refusal to sign up. He had found a home. And each day he remembered his mother's words and savoured every moment.

She died three weeks later. He had twenty-one days of blissful study, of perching himself behind an easel with charcoal in hand, of arranging lemons on a cloth, of measuring distance with a pencil, before Death tapped him on the shoulder: *You really thought you could outrun me?*

Was this the price he had paid for his freedom? Had his mother traded his future and paid for it with her own life? Or was this somehow a twisted punishment for his attempt to escape the war? Charcoal, lemons, and pencils meant nothing anymore. A black cloud descended upon his life, and nothing he did could dispel it.

November rolled around and brought the end of the war with it, but Rupert did not come home as he should have. The days grew darker at the edges. The nights were laced with frost.

It was Christmas morning when everything came to a head. Joseph had slunk downstairs into the parlour, cold and lifeless without its usual fire. He had paused, barefoot and pyjama-clad, and suddenly in the black dawn a rush of emptiness swept over him. There was no Mother that year. No Rupert. He and Flora were alone with their father, and the house was silent as death.

But there on the hearthrug, he saw quite clearly a little boy. He had untamed black hair and wire-rimmed glasses. Joseph stared at this vision of his younger self, this little boy who had no idea what was coming. Who basked in the golden years as if they were endless. This boy who did not believe, who could not imagine, the loss and terror that awaited him. And Joseph saw the boy turn to him, reach out his arms, and he wanted more than all the world to embrace his younger self and never let him go. Never let him grow up, never let him know what the years had in store for him. And he actually moved to do it, he stumbled forward and tried to throw his arms around the little boy but the only thing he found was air. He embraced nothingness. He could not reach himself and he could not save the boy from all that was to come.

And something inside him broke, like a snapped violin string.

Later, Joseph read the psychologist's assessment which came addressed to his father. "Joseph cannot cope . . . displays a proclivity for vulnerability . . . a certain weakness of character . . . perhaps inevitable considering his political leanings." The diagnosis was "a total collapse of the nerves."

His father refused to look at him after that.

1918 shrugged into 1919, and Joseph slumped up the steps to the Slade each day and sloped home at night. What he did in between he had no idea.

The war was finally over but traces of it were still visible on London's streets. A melancholy hung in the air that could not be lifted despite the patriotic bunting that fluttered between pubs and shops. It was a damp, foggy winter. The sky darkened in midafternoon and the sun did not rise until late the next morning. Mists gathered thickly on the pavements.

Joseph tried to think about art. He made himself focus on nothing else, tried to drive the black clouds from his brain, and for a while it worked. But when he attempted to create something himself his hands faltered. He tried chalk, oils, watercolours. But the easel in front of him remained bare. There was nothing inside him left to paint.

He dragged himself through the rest of the year, but when June swung around his tutor sat him down and made it clear that his efforts had not been enough. Joseph would not be returning to the Slade in the autumn.

Walking down those steps for the final time, Joseph had buckled under the weight of everything he had lost. His brother. His mother. The education she had given him. More than anything, he felt that he had failed her. He sat down there and then and sank his head into his hands. What was he supposed to do with his life now?

In the end it was a stranger who saved him. Harold Makepeace came across Joseph slumped on the steps of the Slade and sat down beside him. He extended a plump hand. Enquired what Joseph was doing sprawled in such a public display of misery. And he listened as Joseph told him—in halting, gasping self-pity—all the while twirling a bowler hat in his hands. Then he stood up and invited Joseph to lunch.

He was launching an art magazine, he explained as they strolled along Piccadilly. He had just been discussing it with some old chums at the Slade. Could Joseph string a sentence together? Was he *au fait* with the ins and outs of the art world? Did he have an opinion on those rogues who called themselves the Dadaists?

Over lemon sole and buttered greens in Harold's club they agreed on the particulars: five guineas an article, one article per issue but more if Joseph had ideas. The work would be freelance at first, for a trial period of three months. Harry—as Harold insisted Joseph call him—would extend this if Joseph could promise to file his pieces on time, have a basic respect for spelling and grammar, and come up with something interesting once a month.

For some reason it was the fact that Harry called Joseph "my boy" that convinced him. "Come now, my boy, what say you?" He beamed over coffee. This kindly, velvet-clad figure was like the father Joseph had never had. He seemed proud of Joseph already.

They shook hands and Joseph walked onto the streets of Piccadilly a little lighter. The cloud had not lifted but Harry had given him an umbrella for when the rains inevitably came.

"It's embarrassing," Joseph says to Ettie when he has finished his story. "Breaking down like that . . . not being able to cope. I didn't even go to war and I was the one who fell apart." The memories he has tried to drown have suddenly come simmering to the surface. Hot and spitting.

Ettie's body shifts on the bed behind him. Very gently, she brushes the hair from his neck. In the mirror he sees her open her mouth and then close it again, as if she wants to say something but cannot find the words. Then she gathers up Joseph's severed hair, sweeps it into one of his handkerchiefs, and removes herself from the bed.

At the door she turns. "Your mother would be proud of you," is all she says.

And the blinding white light of the sun in the mirror makes Joseph's eyes sting with tears.

Each day is hotter than the last. The air is so thick Joseph wants to chew it. June is shimmering towards its end and Harry's letters are becoming more urgent.

Have you got a draft for me yet, old boy?

When can I see something?

Send me whatever you have as soon as possible.

Any day now, Tata will throw down his paintbrush and declare that *Young Man with Orange* is finished. And then what? What if Joseph has to leave before his article is finished? Could he write it in London, back in his childhood bedroom with his father pacing outside the door? Could he summon this heat and the light from that dismal grey city, where every brick and stone is steeped with memories he would rather forget?

He is terrified of going home empty-handed. Of returning to his father. Of being dragged back to the life he has, so briefly, escaped.

"Can you tell me why you mix your paint on the canvas and not on the palette?"

It is the first time either of them has spoken for several hours, and the first time Joseph has ever interrupted Tata while he is working. They usually sit in a long, stretched-out silence, but today Joseph is desperate.

Tata ignores the interruption.

"I . . . I need to know, Tata. I need to know how you do it."

A bushy face appears from behind the canvas. "Quiet. Boy," he says slowly. The face retreats.

"But Tata—" The face reappears.

"I need this," Joseph pleads. "For my article. I need . . . I need to know how you do it." He is emboldened by the shocked silence of the studio. "You have to give me something. I am giving you my body. My face. I just need—"

"Give? *Give* you something?" The words are louder than Joseph could have imagined. A burnt colour floods Tata's cheeks. "I do not have to *give* you anything."

"But—"

"I am letting you stay under my roof!" Tata bursts. "I am letting you watch me work! Do you know what people would do to be admitted in here? Do you know how much I am giving you already?"

"I'm only asking for a few answers—"

"You ask too much!" Tata has stepped into view by now, abandoning *Young Man with Orange*. He kicks at the easel. "You drink my wine. You eat my food. You breathe my air and you watch me paint. I give and I give and yet you say you want more. I owe you nothing!"

Cold, acidic panic courses through Joseph's body. He wants to stop, to take everything back, to repeal this moment. Go back to the stillness and the calm of a few minutes before. But Tata is already huffing like a tethered animal. Breathing through his nose. "I do not owe anything to anyone," he snarls. The paintbrush trembles in his hand. "Perhaps I would not need to explain my work if you learned how to look properly."

Joseph opens his mouth to retort—in protestation or appeasement he does not know—but Tata snaps, "I cannot look at you anymore! Cannot look at this." He gestures to the painting, and for a wild moment Joseph thinks he might smear it with the paintbrush. Then he is fumbling with the ties of his apron, forcing it over his head and throwing it to the ground. A box of charcoal tumbles to the floor. "Look what you have done!" *Snap!* A pencil becomes two twigs. *Crack!* A tin of paintbrushes scuttles under the table. "Do not claim I give you nothing!" he shouts. "Put that in your article." *Smash!* "And that!" A wet rag is hurled against the wall. He swings his fists wildly and Joseph flinches, thinking Tata is going to hit him, for he has worked himself up into a whirlwind. "The day is ruined! I cannot paint anymore. No, no—" Joseph has got to his feet but Tata pushes him back. "Do not speak. Do not move. I do not want to waste one more thought on you." A jar of honey shatters into shards. The door slams. Tata is gone.

Joseph slumps in his smock. The studio is a battleground strewn with debris: brushes, paint tubes, splintered charcoal sticks. He reaches for his glasses under the stool. "He's wanted to paint this for a very long time." Joseph whirls around.

Ettie is standing with a bundle of sheets in her arms, a cigarette tucked behind one ear.

Joseph runs a shaking hand through his hair. "I didn't hear you come in," he says, embarrassed to think how much she has witnessed. He never hears her come in. His shoulders sag and he feels bruised with the weight of the day.

Ettie puts down the dirty sheets and stands in front of the painting. "Freshness," she says.

"What?"

"Freshness. That's why Tata mixes his paint straight on the canvas. If you mix it on a palette then the colour is already secondhand by the time it gets to the painting. It has to be fresh. It has to be born in the painting."

Joseph nods. "Thank you."

Ettie contemplates *Young Man with Orange*. "It's beautiful."

Joseph slides off the stool and stands beside her. The paint is almost crawling off the canvas. Raw as a wound, the impasto shiny, Tata has made it feel as if Joseph is trying to break free from the image. Writhing and seething and alive. "I just wish I knew what it means," he says.

Ettie positions herself behind him. Very gently, she holds her hands on either side of his face, blinkering his vision until all he can see is the painting between her palms.

"Look," she says.

"But—"

"Don't speak. Look."

And so he looks—really looks—and tries to see what Tata has been able to see all along.

"You think too much," Ettie murmurs in his ear, her breath on the back of his neck. "Use your eyes, not your brain. Look at the painting without thinking."

Joseph tries to ignore Ettie's hovering hands. He focuses on the square of his vision and lets his eyes throb with the image.

The Joseph on the canvas is sitting forward, his face staring directly at the viewer. A shadow hangs under his unruly hair—rendered here by quick swishes of brown—but his eyes are bright. In one hand he holds an orange and the other lies open and empty like a shell in his lap. He sits in front of a window showing a parched landscape. Deep shadows. Blue sky. Scraggly trees are dotted about but there are no oranges on their green boughs. The only fruit is the one in Joseph's hand. The orange is no more than four broad strokes with a brush.

Ettie's hands slip away. She comes to stand next to him and they contemplate the painting side by side.

"Why can't I write about it?" he croaks.

"You're getting in your own way. Take yourself out of it. Imagine it's not you."

Joseph swallows and tries to imagine that he has stumbled across this painting in a gallery. That it is not his face looking back at him. He notes that Tata has echoed the shape of the orange in the young man's billowing shirt. In the curve of his empty hand and the crescents of leaves on the trees. Joseph takes in the flat background and the frenzy of paint in the foreground, brushstrokes peppering down like rain. Tata has made scratches in the paint with the handle of his brush, or sometimes with the grimy curve of his fingernail. The painting has a clawed-at quality, as if the brushstrokes are marks left by desperate fingers.

"Tata is not telling you that the sun is shining," explains Ettie. "He is making you feel the warmth on your skin." She reaches out a hand and touches it lightly to Joseph's cheek. "He is putting the feeling here."

Joseph's skin tingles.

"See the brushstrokes, not Tata's hand behind them," she says. "Remove Tata. Remove yourself."

He knows what she is saying. That he worships Tata too much. That he is blinded by the light. "Take Tata away," she whispers.

"Take yourself out of the painting . . . what's left?" Texture. Colour. Light.

"A sensation . . . an impression," Joseph says haltingly. "A young man with an orange."

The painting is the feeling of youth. Of fleeting moments, of afternoon sun warming your bones, of luck caught in the palm of your hand. It is a painting of innocence. Of a future filled with promises. Of someone trying to grasp them.

"But how do I express that in words?"

"Perhaps you can't," says Ettie. "There's a reason Tata painted it in the first place. Perhaps it's a feeling beyond words."

"But I *need* to put it into words," he says, desperation rising in his chest. This has been his fear all along: How to transform a painting into writing? It is the paradox that has tormented his days and nights.

"If you try to put a painting into words you'll have to lose something of it," says Ettie simply. "You have to accept what you'll lose."

Joseph nods. There is a lesson there: in accepting what you must lose. He can never know what Tata saw when he looked at him, sweating in an oversized smock, perched on a three-legged stool. But what he can see is how Tata interpreted that moment. What he chose to distil: the heat, the light, the ambrosial vitality of youth.

And then Ettie says something which unlocks a door for him.

"You are not holding fruit," she says. "You are holding colour."

It is as if she has translated the painting. He sees it now: the young man holding a bright ball of colour.

The *Young Man with Orange.*

His heart beats quicker. The painting is the feeling of the colour orange: fresh, bright, alive. The trees in the background are stripped of fruit but the man holds one perfect orange in his palm.

"Ettie," he says. It is a full sentence. He takes her by the hand and just . . . squeezes it. He would kiss her if he could. Then he is off, running across the field towards the house.

With Ettie's words still ringing in his ears Joseph jams himself in front of his typewriter. He wants to remember everything she said, every golden, illuminating word. She has cracked the world open for him.

It is not the article he thought he would write. It is better. Ettie has shown him how to see the art beyond the man: sweep aside the artist, the gossip, the possible scandal. None of that matters.

Ettie has handed him the key to the door.

Remove yourself. Remove Tata.

The relief is physical. He can write.

Young Man with Orange is a painting of a colour. Everything points towards and culminates in that one burst of orange: the lines of the man's arm sweeping down towards it, the branches of the trees reaching for it, the brushstrokes radiating from it. Tata has summoned all the light in the world and put it in the young man's palm. It is as if he is holding the sun. It is a painting about clutching the future in your hand and weighing it up.

Joseph writes with a sharp, searing clarity. The words pour out of him. *Young Man with Orange* was never about the young man, it was about what he was holding. What he is showing you.

His fingers beat down upon the keys, fueled by the feeling that yes, yes, yes, finally, it is working. He has grasped it. He is holding it in his hand. He has something to show the world.

ETTIE

Tata has been secretive these last few days. He hasn't needed Joseph and has banished him from the studio. The old stable door has been bolted. He has demanded silence. Only Ettie is allowed in, bringing madeleines, coffee, turpentine.

Young Man with Orange is finished but Tata cannot let it go. He sits in his studio, brooding. He does not wish to relinquish control of the painting. To finish a painting is to give it up, to hand it over to other people who will offer their thoughts, their opinions, their feelings. If Tata never lets this painting go then it will be his and his alone.

Ettie had known that the painting was nearing completion ever since Tata's argument with Joseph. It is the same every time: the scalding words, the broken brushes. She knows how to read the signs.

Tata drags his old wicker chair down through the field and positions it in the studio in front of *Young Man with Orange*. He sits there for three days as if guarding the body at a wake. He smokes cigar after cigar and occasionally starts, springing up from his chair and grabbing a paintbrush, only to lower it slowly, retreat.

There is nothing left for him to do.

On the third day Tata finally stands up, wipes his hands on his trousers, and moves towards the canvas. He picks up a brush, the usual one. He chooses a colour, different this time. Earth-brown, to match Joseph's hair. With a creak of his knees he bends and makes one final mark upon the canvas: a practised up, down, and along. His signature. *E. Tartuffe.*

He turns away, unable to look at the painting any longer.

Dusk falling. The evening air rotten with grapes. A celebration is in order. Ettie has laid out crystal glasses. A plate of snails, cooked until tender, their shells stuffed with garlic and parsley. She has put bottles of champagne in flowerpots full of ice.

A toast: "To the *Young Man with Orange!*"

Clink.

"To success!"

Clink.

"To a finished painting at last!"

The glasses come together, then part. Toothpicks are inserted into the coiled snail shells. The moon climbs steadily beyond the treetops, the evening soft as velvet.

More toasts, each louder than the last: "To painting!"

"To art!"

"To me!"

They finish one bottle of champagne. Then another. Ettie has one meagre glass. She sips it slowly, holding the celebrations at arm's length. She must keep a clear head tonight. Tata is sitting with his feet up on the table while Joseph talks animatedly about the painting. He praises the cascading brushwork that looks as if it has been blown across the canvas. Each mark so casual yet deliberate! Like a collage, he is saying, a collage of autumn leaves stamped into the ground. But the colour! Oh, the colour, says Joseph. The colours are as bright as stained glass.

They toast to that. *Clink.*

Now that Joseph no longer needs to be the Young Man with Orange he can unbutton his shirt. Free his skin. He bends his arm at the elbow to undo a cuff. Squeezes out the button like a lemon pip. He fumbles with the other and takes the material in his mouth, releases it. Pushes back the thick cotton to reveal his forearms, long and slender. Smoothly strung with muscle. He wipes the back of his neck with the cup of his hand. Ettie darts her eyes away.

Tata brings out the absinthe. They have eaten nothing but a few snails apiece: each delicate, salty mouthful drowned by gulps of champagne. Ettie had prepared bread to soak up the alcohol but then had second thoughts. She was halfway through cutting the baguette when her hands stilled. She gathered up the slices up and hid them in the back of the cupboard. Tonight she wants heads to be heavy, ears muffled.

Joseph offers her some of the eerie emerald liquid but she shakes her head. She knows better. Absinthe is poured for the two men and the toasts begin again:

"To genius!"

"To France!"

"To life!"

Ettie watches Joseph, this shy boy curled around his absinthe glass. A sweat has broken out across his brow and he is struggling to keep up with Tata's relentless pace. She wants to reach out and brush the hair from his eyes. To run her fingers down the skin of his cheek. Rest them in the damp hollow of his collar.

Just as Tata does not want to let the painting go, Ettie does not want to let Joseph go. She has grown used to having him around the house. She likes the way he looks at her, the way his hand reaches for hers when he wants to tell her something, the way his eyes light up when he watches Tata paint. She likes the way he asks if she wants coffee, clementines, croissants? The way he stands in the field each morning, arms aloft, feeling the tips of the grass when he thinks no one is watching.

She likes that he questions her life here. Why do you read Tata's letters for him? Don't you have any friends in the village? Have you really never been farther than Avignon?

She looks at this pale boy who has been undone by art. By the sun and the freedom of being far from home. She remembers his halting presence that first day, his tentative walk around the house when nobody answered his knock. She had watched as he stumbled on a fallen roof tile in his ill-fitting boots. He looked like a newborn deer that day, all shaky legs and fearful eyes. Eyes waiting to be opened.

Tata belches loudly and Joseph's head slips off his arm where it had been resting. The black flies of the daytime have long been replaced by mosquitoes, and the stars are appearing one by one. Joseph looks around himself and a streak of sadness crosses his face. It is there only for a moment, but Ettie catches it. There is longing in his eyes: the longing to draw out this moment. The longing to stay.

She has already glimpsed his knapsack lying open in his bedroom. It is ready but not yet packed. He has not been able to bring himself to tidy this life away, not yet. Raimondi will be coming in the morning. *Young Man with Orange* will leave and Joseph will follow a few days later. The train timetable has been cut out of the local newspaper and pinned to the kitchen cupboard, a time circled in red pencil. It counts down their final days.

As Joseph looks around the darkened terrace his eyes seem to be drinking in this moment. Savouring it. Then he blinks. Shakes his head. He takes the hand Tata is offering him and the older man pulls the younger one to his feet. Ettie watches as they stumble inside and soft sounds fill the air. The hollow clink of empty bottles. The uneasy sway of feet on the stairs. Doors fitting into frames. The household turning over.

The night beginning.

JOSEPH

The *heat*. He cannot sleep. It is as if there is a hairy creature sitting on his chest, its claws sunk into his skin. He needs to shake it off, to free himself. His head throbs from the champagne and the absinthe and the snails, and he wants to throw up. He kicks off his covers. A sheen of sweat coats his body. He jams his glasses onto his face and grasps around for his water jug, but it is empty.

He trips down to the kitchen, cool and blue in the moonlight. Gulps a glass of water. Feels his lungs expand. The pounding in his head subsides.

He catches his reflection in the dark window: hair askew, white nightshirt clinging to his chest. The night beyond the window looks fresh and inviting. He will take a walk to clear his head. He slips through the kitchen door and out onto the terrace. The open air is a relief. The wind blows his shirt open, cooling the sweat on his feverish skin.

The silence of the night is eerie. Even the cicadas are quiet at this hour. There is a dampness to the air: a greenness that isn't there in the day. His fingertips brush rosemary and lavender as he wanders through the garden, their scents deep and heady. He stumbles onto the donkey track as if in a daze. Dark the garden. Dark the sandy path. Dark the twisted olive trees. Dark the air and dark the sky.

But then—just there beyond the tangled fingers of the trees—something flickers. A light.

Joseph pulls himself to a halt, feet faltering in the dust. The distant light is uneven, as if from a candle. It wobbles, half-glimpsed through the trees, somewhere over by one of the abandoned outhouses.

Like a moth, Joseph is drawn towards it. The ground is warm underfoot. His bare feet find thorns and stones but he treads carefully, as if pulled by an invisible string. He can see the shape of the outhouse now. The light is coming from within and there, through the window . . . there is a figure. Someone is standing quite still, bobbed hair silhouetted in the quivering orange light.

Joseph draws nearer. His hands find the stone wall, his feet press softly into the dirt. He is careful not to make a sound, though his heart pummels like a piston in his chest.

He peers inside the outhouse.

Ettie is there, and so is *Young Man with Orange*. She is staring at the painting. She looks at it for a long time, gazing at Joseph's painted face. And then finally she takes the painting from the easel on which it rests and places it on the floor. She kicks away some of the straw surrounding it.

Then she strikes a match and sets the painting on fire.

The next morning, *Young Man with Orange* is back in the studio.

Joseph cannot make sense of what he saw. Did he dream it? Last night he had been able to do nothing more than stare. To stagger backwards through the darkness, away from the violent amber light pulsing like a heart beyond the window. Away from the dark figure, away from the crack of wood and canvas and the smell of burning paint.

But now *Young Man with Orange* is back on its easel. It has even been slotted into a wooden frame.

Raimondi arrives, his suit and car immaculate. He inspects the painting, nods, and Ettie wraps it in brown paper. She loads it into Raimondi's car and he drives away down the dusty path. He does not stay for a drink.

Joseph's head throbs. As soon as Raimondi has gone he goes back to the outhouse, back to the scene of that strange apparition from the night before. But the little stone building is cold and empty in the morning light. What is it he saw? He casts a hand over the flagstones, feeling around for . . . what exactly? He sifts through the straw and the dust. He sniffs the air.

There is nothing. No sign of a fire. No ash. No trace of whatever it was that went on here in the dead of night. Whatever he thought he saw, it does not exist in the morning. Is he hallucinating again? Are his senses playing tricks on him? Is he losing his mind?

And if he cannot trust his own eyes, then what can he trust at all?

PART II

THE WRITER

JOSEPH

Joseph does not want to leave. He rolls his socks into a ball and places them on the bed. He cannot bear the thought of going home. He slides his pencils into their case, slots his typewriter into its box. He does not want to think that he has had his last sleep, his last meal, his last morning waking to the bright call of larks and crickets. He folds a shirt that has been soaked alternately with sweat and turpentine, now pressed and white again, as if none of it ever happened.

He stoops under the bed to retrieve his ink pen. His comb and razor he shuts into a case. He has misplaced one of his handkerchiefs, lost to the chaos of the room. A final search does not reveal it. He flicks open his passport, weighs it in his hand for a moment and has a sudden urge to fling it into the field. But no. He closes it carefully and slips it into the outer pocket of his bag.

He splashes his face with water from the jug Ettie brought him that first day. He can still picture her, poised in the milky sunlight. He will miss her, in a strange, hot, surprising way. He will miss trying to catch glimpses of her as she flits in and out of the studio. Trying to talk to her, trying to understand her. He runs his hand over the place on the bed where she knelt while cutting his hair. But the impression of her body is long gone.

He packs with unnatural slowness, trying to drag out the process. He wants to cling to the bedstead and refuse to leave. To gulp great lungfuls of air, to swallow it down in the hope that some golden mote will stay inside him forever. How strange the way a place can change you. Just by being here, something has come loose within him. He has opened up like a fist unclenching. He catches sight of himself in the mirror. In the month since coming to the farmhouse he has begun to stand taller. His chin is lifted. Wine and heat and summer fruits have added a healthy flush to his skin. He wears two more buttons undone than he would ever dare at home.

He tries to remember the smell of this room, of the dusty olive trees, the warm scent of the kitchen. He will miss the sun on his skin. The long, heady days. All he wants is to eat peaches and melon slices and little French cheeses and anchovies and apricots on the terrace for the rest of his life. He can picture himself: the sun warming his back, the terrace table spread with notes, his shirt-sleeves rolled up to the elbows. Tata is there, holding forth at the head of the table while Joseph writes. And Ettie . . . Ettie is near. She moves in a silent arc, her fingers brushing his as she pours coffee, slices peaches, sifts letters. There is a breeze and the circling of swallows and the endless, endless days.

Joseph pulls the drawstring of his knapsack, folds over the top.

There is one last thing to pack. It rests on top of an old bird-cage. He picks up *The Odyssey*, his brother's copy, taken to the front lines of the war with him. Rupert had underlined parts of the book in grey pencil when he was yearning to come home. All Rupert wanted was to come home. Joseph sinks onto the bed and turns the soft pages, searching for a sign of his brother.

And then, Ettie is calling his name. He comes to the head of the stairs and looks down. She is standing in the hall next to a large wooden crate, her freckled face looking up at him.

She has a letter in her hands.

ETTIE

Ettie stands in the wide entrance hall, the open threshold between in and out. It hums with warmth, the air suffused with lemony sunlight. Joseph is making his way slowly down the stairs, each tread sending a creak through the house. Coming up the field, she knows, is Tata, heading in after a morning's work. She has aligned herself perfectly between the two men.

In her hand is a letter from Raimondi. He has written from Paris, bringing the news that *Young Man with Orange* has sold—sold for more than he had hoped—to a buyer from London. Someone had read about the painting in Joseph's article and, from his description, known he had wanted it. The buyer had known the painting belonged in his collection and put in an offer the very day the article was published. He wanted *Young Man with Orange*, whatever the price.

Folded inside the letter is a cheque. The number is larger than Ettie has ever seen.

As Joseph's foot reaches the final stair Tata pushes open the front door, right on cue. Stage left, stage right. Both men enter.

Ettie turns to her uncle first. She stands just behind the wooden crate, the better to foreground it. A shaft of sunlight from the open front door shoots towards it, illuminating it like a spotlight.

"From Raimondi," she says, indicating the crate. She has angled the side bearing the champagne-maker's crest towards Tata. "A token of what is to come."

Tata wipes his hands on his smock. She can tell he has had a good morning by the bounce of his gait. Without looking at her he lifts the lid of the crate—nails already slid out by Ettie—and counts the bottles. He slots one out to inspect the label.

Joseph, Ettie knows, is hovering. But it is not him she needs to keep an eye on. His movements are predictable. He will wait.

Ettie says, casually, that Raimondi has written to say that *Young Man with Orange* has sold. It has sold well, and it is thanks to Joseph's article. She makes it clear that this is Raimondi's professional opinion.

The crate of champagne came with a note. In thin, slanting writing Raimondi has written:

Keep the vulture around. He is good for business.

It is this note which Ettie weighs in her hand now. Tata is busy with the champagne, twisting off the cork and pouring it into a glass he finds conveniently waiting on the sideboard. Of course Raimondi sees the financial gain in keeping Joseph around. Joseph's words are all the publicity he needs. With Joseph's writing alerting the world to every new Tartuffe painting, all Raimondi has to do is sit back and wait for the buyers to come.

Of course it makes sense.

Ettie holds the note steady. She can do one of two things in the next moment: she can crumple the note in her hand and lose it in the pocket of her apron. She can help Joseph pack his belongings and wave him goodbye. She can watch him walk down the donkey track, knapsack over one shoulder, until he is out of sight and forget about him entirely.

She could do that.

Or she could read the note aloud and unleash into the air the suggestion that Joseph stay a little longer. She could suggest that Joseph might be of some use, that his writing will serve Tata well. It is Raimondi's idea, after all.

Her heart pounds. She has two props at her disposal, and she hands the first to Tata, giving him the cheque and pointing to the amount with her finger. It only takes a glance at the number of zeroes for the sum to register in his mind. Then she clears her throat. "We have orders from Raimondi," she says, holding the note aloft. "Keep the vulture around," she recites. "He is good for business."

Joseph blinks. He turns to Tata, who is slugging champagne down his throat. There is a pause. A long, drawn-out balance between silence and speech. Then the old man wipes his mouth on his wrist. His eyes, the blue and the milky one both, meet Joseph's. He shrugs. "Stay, then." It is as simple as that.

Joseph's face cracks like a sunbeam. "Really?" he says. He is like a child, so radiant and clear in his emotions. "I can stay? I can write another article, about your new painting?"

Tata waves his hand, "Write whatever you want." Ettie knows Tata's mind works fast like hers, but his face gives nothing away. He refills his glass of champagne and hands another to Joseph. "Just keep out from under my feet." He is as gruff as ever but there is a gleam to his pearly eye. Ettie is familiar with the currents and twists of his thoughts. There is a telltale lightness to his movements. He knows that this is a good deal. He knows he will be the one to profit from this arrangement. He downs his champagne in one.

Joseph, hardly able to contain his excitement, does the same.

And Ettie too has a smile about her lips, though she has already slipped from the scene, and retreated into the wings.

JOSEPH

It is several days later that Joseph's article arrives. Harry sends a copy and Joseph unwraps it in a fervour. Page seven, there it is. "Dispatches from the Studio." And there, underneath, is his name: Joseph Adelaide, reporting from Saint-Auguste-de-Provence. He casts his eyes over the text and yes, yes, those are his words, the words he scribbled in his notebook up in his bedroom beneath the eaves. The words he pressed into the keys of his typewriter, imprinting them onto paper which he folded and sent to Harry (paying far too much for stamps, but he wanted to make sure it got there), the sealed envelope winging its way across fields and ocean waves before being slit open, its contents spilled, edited, typeset, and finally printed. Yes, yes, those are his words.

Joseph proffers the article to Tata but he bats it away, assuring Joseph he has no interest in reading a word, so he brings *The Inkling* instead to the kitchen. Ettie is hunched over a colander of potatoes, her head down. He places the article beside her.

"It's here," he announces, unable to keep the ceremony from his voice. Ettie leans over the magazine and spots his name, then brings her face very close to the print and begins to read. He watches her anxiously, her eyebrows pinching together as she drags her finger under the rows of type, digesting the words slowly, taking everything in.

He reads the article again over her shoulder, just for the thrill of it.

In the land of the blind, the one-eyed man is king. [Joseph had been proud of that opening.] So may it be said for Edouard Tartuffe, whose land is the golden countryside of southern Provence. Though he has only one eye to give him sight, this luminary painter is able to capture more in one painting than his fellow men may hope to in a lifetime.

Are we blind, compared to this master of the brush? It is a question I have asked myself readily over the past few weeks, privileged as I am to share the same views as Tartuffe each day. We look upon the same landscape, we see the same hills each morning and the same ochre sunsets at evening time, yet his eye perceives more than mine. He does not see the world as we do.

Tartuffe's latest work is his first to feature a person since *The Lace Makers* in 1893 (winner of the Prix de Barbizon that year), painted when the artist was still living at the centre of a thriving artistic community in Paris. This new work, entitled *Young Man with Orange,* is a return to life for Tartuffe and a move away from the morbid paintings of his recent years, which have been charged with an uncharacteristic current of darkness. But no longer. Life and light have returned to Tartuffe's canvas. Sitting as his figure for the titular Young Man, I have had the rare opportunity to study the artist at work.

To watch Tartuffe is to observe an alchemist: a man who takes basic elements and transforms them into pure gold. It is his treatment of light which distinguishes him from his contemporaries, as if he has bottled sunlight itself and poured it onto his canvas. When he paints, Tartuffe does not tell us that the sun is shining; he makes us feel the warmth on our skin.

I do not believe I am premature in declaring that Edouard Tartuffe is a Master of Light, and *Young Man with Orange* a masterpiece. The painting's background, a scrub of fields and trees glimpsed through an open window, ripples as if seen through frosted glass. The figure in the foreground is fragmented. No matter how closely we press our eye, no matter how hard we squint, the image does not become clearer. We must step back, and let the parts arrange themselves into a whole. For it is then that we see that the young man is not just holding fruit, but a burst of colour. In his palm Tartuffe has placed a ball of purest orange, as if he is clutching sunlight itself. It is a masterstroke. Youth, colour and vitality coalesce in this young man's palm, which he offers to the viewer.

These have been dark years of late, but here Tartuffe is showing us something hopeful. The pall of war is being swept away and something bright remains. Among the rubble, something gleams.

In this painting Tartuffe is offering us life, once again.

After several minutes Ettie sits back. A flicker of hair has fallen across her face and he is seized with a desire to tuck it behind her ear. He clamps his hands behind his back.

"You make him sound like a god," is all she says.

Joseph is taken aback. "Well, he is a god, isn't he? A god of painting? A god of light?"

Ettie does not reply. Instead she turns the page of *The Inkling* and busies herself in the next article.

Joseph shrugs off her bluntness and flicks through the rest of the post. Nothing can dampen his spirits today. There are some envelopes for Tata which he piles next to Ettie and then, at the very bottom, a letter addressed to him. He knows this handwriting. Leaving Ettie with the magazine he slips from the kitchen and takes the stairs two at a time, retreating to the solitude of his bedroom. He locks the door. Then he sinks into the chair at his desk and thumbs open the letter from home.

Dearest, damnedest, most infuriating Joseph,

Are you alive? Have you been kidnapped by a band of absinthe-drinking painters? Should I rally around and put together a rescue party? (Please say no, as this would be such a nightmare to organise.) Weeks go by without a word from you and then The Inkling slips through the letterbox and I find out your article has already been published. Does this mean you are coming home? Or will we have no notice of that either?

Do try to write a bit more, you insufferable creature. Life is so dull here and I long for news of you. How is the great Tartuffe? Any less of a tyrant? Did you get an answer about why he had that fight with Cézanne? You mentioned he has a niece—tell me more about her.

You must picture me, dear brother, sitting alone in the drawing room with my face pressed against the window. From the study above I can hear Father boring on about import taxes and "the damn coolies" (his latest irritation), and it is all I can do not to smash through the window and make a run for it.

Father grows more cantankerous by the day. He doesn't speak of you but he takes The Inkling every month. He pretends not to but I see it pressed between The Times and his account books. I found him up in your room the other day, standing at the desk in the corner. He was running his finger around the inkpot, long dried-out since you left, just staring out of the window. I crept away before he could sense I was there.

Rupert asks after you. He asks after Mother, and Nanny Astrid, and Queen Victoria, and I haven't the heart to tell him they're all gone. Well, you're still alive of course, but you're gone too.

Come back soon. We miss you.

Flora

The letter trembles in Joseph's hand.

Rupert asks after you.

He slumps back in his chair.

Come back soon.

Rupert is in the hospital where their mother died, though he does not know it. He has been there for two long years. Their father does not see him. It is lovely Flora who visits and brings news.

"He gave me a daisy today!"

"He asked for you by name!"

"He has cut his wrists all the way to the elbows. They found him just in time."

When Joseph first saw Rupert after the war he had stared at the strange figure in the hospital bed. He knew it must be Rupert but still, somehow, he hoped it was not him. It couldn't be him. This was a hollow shell of a person. He had hoped that his brother would burst through the door with his usual high spirits and clap him on the back. That it was all a joke and Rupert would shout "Azah! Had you for a moment!" and they would all laugh and the doctors would wheel away this husk. This old man.

But the figure in the bed just turned his head and rested his cheek on the pillow as if it were the heaviest thing in the world. He had not looked at Joseph, but through him. His blue eyes stared at something nobody else could see.

Joseph sat in a chair by the bed, aware of the years of distance between them. He tried to reach across the gulf, across the oceans and deserts between him and this strange, unknowable man. He noticed the new furrows across his brother's forehead. The cheeks that were now sunken and gaunt, the eye sockets hollowed out as if with a spoon. But the thing that had chilled Joseph most was the stare. Rupert's stare was the haunted gaze of a man who had left this world behind. Someone who was caught between places. Searching for a way back.

"How goes it, Rupes?" their father had boomed, clapping his eldest son on the shoulder. "Nothing like a bit of R and R after a big adventure, eh?" His tone was ridiculously, unbearably cheerful. The idea that all Rupert needed was rest and relaxation had sickened Joseph. He looked at his broken brother, at this empty carapace of a person, and wanted to weep. He pressed his face to the bedclothes, twisting the sheets in his fist, and Rupert had done nothing. He had not even been able to lift a hand to reach for his brother. He was somewhere else entirely.

And then: "He's not coming home with us," their father had announced. His voice was suddenly brusque. "He's staying here. Just for a while."

Joseph had not understood. "Why—why can't he come home?" he asked, throat tightening. *Don't cry*, he told himself. *Don't cry, don't cry, don't cry.* "Why isn't he coming?"

Their father had not answered, the outline of his fist clenching and unclenching in his trouser pocket. Then a nurse came in and started fussing about Rupert's sheets, announcing that visiting hours were over and they had best be on their way.

Rupert stared at them as they left. He did not return Joseph's wave. He just shook his head, and went on shaking it and shaking it until Joseph was out of sight.

Rupert was to stay in the hospital until he got better, they were told. Just until he was able to look after himself again. But Rupert did not get better. It had been two years and despite the electric shocks, despite the cocaine prescribed each week by Dr. Yealland, despite the curtained room kept free of light and sound, Rupert's mind tore itself apart. His words became tangled. He stopped blinking.

There was a new term for it, for what had happened to these men who returned unmendable from the war: shell shock. Joseph's father refuses to say it. "Just a case of jangled nerves," he insists. "He'll be over it soon enough."

The last time Joseph had seen his brother was in late spring. Rupert had been confined to a wheelchair, his spine twisted from the electric shocks, his feet turned inwards. Joseph and Flora had wheeled him into the clear sunshine of the park next to the hospital. A nurse had been stationed behind a nearby rhododendron bush just in case, but the three siblings were allowed this afternoon together. With an effort—an immense, tragic effort—Joseph had lifted his older brother onto the grass and propped him against a tree. Rupert's face was a wrecked ship. His mouth a storm-torn sail. His hands two empty bowls in his lap. His once golden hair was now lank and dull.

They brought a picnic. Flora laid out bottles of lemonade, triangles of sandwiches, even a trio of jam tarts she had made herself. Rupert turned away when Joseph offered him a sandwich, the egg and cress limp in his hand. He and Flora tried to talk, nudging the conversation along, talking about home and about Father and the plans Flora had for the garden. They glanced over at Rupert, leaving pauses in their conversation so he could join in if he wanted. They asked him how his back was feeling? Did he like his new nurse? Was he getting enough to eat? But Rupert did not speak. He stared into the distance, his eyes juddering from side to side. As Joseph and Flora talked Rupert ran his hands through the grass, twisting it in his fingers and ripping it up by the roots. Twisting and ripping. Twisting and ripping. His hands did not stop trembling.

Then suddenly—a sharp cry. Something sailing through the air. An object soaring in a high arc and landing with a thud on the grass nearby. A child's ball, thrown wide. Joseph reached for it and was about to throw it back when he was stilled by a shriek. It was a noise such as he had never heard before: a noise like the end of the world. Rupert was cowering, his arms over his head, pressing himself into the ground. He coiled himself into a ball, curling away from them, screaming into the ripped-up grass. He pressed himself into the earth like an animal. Rolling over his twisted back, clamping himself tighter, clawing at his ears, screaming through a mouth pressed so tightly closed the scream sounded as if it were coming from beneath the earth itself. From someone who had been buried alive. Footsteps, across the grass. Nurses running. Something yellow spooling out of Rupert's nose. Flora's cries and Joseph, the ball still in his hands, standing helpless. His last glimpse had been of Rupert, shaking from head to toe as if he were being shocked with an electric charge. Three nurses pinning him down. Something silver, a needle, and then his brother shuddering, falling still. His body twitched irregularly, like a snake decapitated. And then from deep in his chest there came the most terrible sound of all: a broken, childlike cry.

ETTIE

Paints. Brushes. Flashes of sun. The tang of turpentine in the morning. Ettie has swept the studio, sending crumbs scuttling, and lined tubes of paint along the table just the way Tata likes them. A sense of expectation hangs in the air.

The large canvas Ettie ordered is propped against one wall. It sits like a beached whale in the studio, blank and unassuming. It had to be specially requested from Paris, stretched by two men and delivered by a third. She can just about carry it with her arms stretched wide. She has primed it herself, using the flat brush Tata stipulates, and tested the tautness of its surface with her own fingers. Tata prefers a thick weave for his canvases, so the paint can cling to the texture.

It is early morning and she sits cross-legged on the studio floor looking up at the empty white square. No one is awake yet. A rosy dawn seeps through the open window.

She hears a drumming of footsteps and turns around, but no one is there. She is alone, and the sound is only the echo of all the years she has spent in the studio, doing exactly this. Priming, prepping, cleaning. She sees herself as a little girl, running her fingers along the downy tips of Tata's paintbrushes. Whenever she picked up a pencil Tata would lift her beneath the armpits, swing her high above his work, and put her down outside the studio. "Not for you," he used to say with a chuckle. He said it again and again over the years whenever Ettie reached for a paintbrush. "No, no, that's not for you." It became a mantra. It became a warning.

While Tata makes preparations for his new painting, Ettie buries herself in *The Inkling*. Tata does not allow reading material in the house. She can only read newspapers if she picks one off the ground in the village and discards it before she gets home, but she has sequestered Joseph's copy of *The Inkling* and pores over it whenever she can. It is like a signal flare from the outside world, a portal into the bright, radiant lights beyond Saint-Auguste. She finds a review of an exhibition on postwar women artists. An article about someone called Nina Hamnett (the name is strange on her tongue), whose paintings are "architectural" and "penetrating" (penetrating!).

These pages are filled with words that seem to say: *There is life elsewhere.*

She keeps returning to Joseph's article too. She had been put out at first, on reading his piece. She had hoped to glimpse something of herself in there, to spy herself between the lines. But he has not even mentioned her. He has written "Dispatches from the Studio" without mentioning the person who makes the studio turn on its axis. The person who prepares the paints and cleans the brushes, who sets up canvas and easel, who sweeps and scrubs and arranges and cleans so Tata can work.

She feels stung, in a childish way.

But this resentment perplexes her. For so long, she has been happy to live in the shadows. She has craved neither attention nor recognition. But now there is something inside her reaching towards the light.

After her mother left, Ettie tried to find a way of capturing her uncle's attention. He rarely looked at her. He never played with her. In fact, he seemed to forget about her entirely until food was placed in front of him each night, and then he would give her hair a quick ruffle. His attention was always on his pencils and his paints. Observing this, Ettie drew pictures on spare scraps of paper and left them for Tata to find. She was too shy to ask what he thought of them, but hoped that if he found her drawings he would be impressed enough to comment on them.

At first she sketched what she knew: a lemon, a cracked egg-shell, a dead lizard. She made still-life arrangements with her few possessions: hairbrush, button, spoon.

But Tata never said anything. She left drawings in his studio and on the terrace table. She even pinned them to the kitchen cupboards but in the morning they had always disappeared. Tata whisked them away during the night, and she never found out what he did with them.

She set herself bigger challenges. Perhaps she had not been ambitious enough. She attempted vases with patterns. Glasses which distorted her reflection. She experimented with perspective, placing grapes in front of apples to make them look bigger than they were. Tata ignored these too. Ettie could not understand why he wasn't interested in her creations. She wanted to make art with him. It could bond them together, tying a knot between their lonely, isolated lives in the farmhouse. But Tata was blind to all her efforts.

Was she simply not good enough? Once, on a fresh spring day when she knew he was in a good mood, she asked Tata if she could be sent to art school. Perhaps the same one he went to?

A look of alarm had flashed across Tata's face, and then one of sadness. "Oh, Ettie," he said. "Little Ettie, how innocent your dreams are!" He tousled her hair, the way one ruffles the ears of a dog. "The Académie is not for the likes of you."

"No, no," she hastened to add. "Not now. I mean when I am older. When I am grown up."

"It has nothing to do with age, little thing." Tata sighed. "You see, it is only men who are allowed to study at the Académie. They do not let women in."

Ettie had an image of women hammering on the great door of a castle. The Académie became an impenetrable fortress in her mind. Barricaded from the inside. A citadel of men who gathered along the ramparts and pulled up the drawbridge. Readied their bows and arrows over the walls.

Neither Tata nor the Académie would teach her, but that did not mean she could not learn. She would just have to teach herself, as she had always done.

But then one day when she was twelve, everything changed.

Still desperate to win Tata's approval, she had painted a bunch of wiry daisies that grew in the field behind the house. Their roots were tangled like ribbons and the way she had painted their petals made it look as if they had been blown across the page. The painting was less precise than her previous efforts. There was a looseness to her lines, and the final image had some of the freedom of Tata's technique. She had been studying him closely.

She watched from the safety of the kitchen as Tata unstuck the painting from beneath the honey jar on the terrace. He stared at it for a long time, as if trying to work out whether he had painted it himself and forgotten. Ettie saw him turn the paper over, inspecting the front and back. Perhaps this was the moment. The day when he would realise she was a fellow artist, a kindred spirit with whom he could share his life's work. Perhaps this was the painting that would grant her access to his secret world.

But then he raised his head and his white eye glowed with something she did not understand but knew to fear. His bottom lip trembled, and he appeared to grow in size on the terrace, swelling like a thundercloud gathering darkness.

She knew she had done something terribly wrong. Something irreversible. Tata locked eyes with her through the kitchen window, beckoned to her, his finger wrinkling like a worm. She tripped onto the terrace. The storm cloud was deepening, ready to burst. She looked up into Tata's face. Without a word, he held up the drawing. She did not speak, did not move. And then, very slowly, Tata tore her painting in half. He ripped it into smaller pieces. Smaller and smaller until the paper was nothing but petals in his hand and then he opened his fist and threw them into the wind.

Tata lowered his face to hers. A thick pulse throbbed in his neck. "Never . . . *never* do that again, do you understand?" And then he wrapped his hand around her wrist, jerking her closer so she could see the yellow of his teeth. "There is only one artist in this house," he whispered. "And it will never be you."

Ettie did not leave any more pictures for her uncle to find after that. She never let him catch her with a pencil in her hand. She made sure not to let him glimpse the longing in her eyes when she looked at his paintings.

She made him believe that he had won.

JOSEPH

Joseph writes to tell Harry he is staying, for the sake of another article at least, and Harry is happy. "Dispatches from the Studio" can continue as long as Joseph sends him another piece by next month's issue. Raimondi, too, is delighted. A crate of wine arrives addressed to *Our Esteemed Vulture*. And even Ettie, when Joseph catches her eye, has a smile about her lips.

Tata does not protest when Joseph watches him paint now. He is permitted a stool in the corner of the studio, which makes him feel like an oversized schoolboy. He perches, pencil in hand, notebook on his lap. He is there before Tata in the mornings and he lingers long after he has left. He draws a diagram of his palette and labels each colour. He counts the brushes. The paints. This time he can watch the master at work without the barrier of a canvas between them. And now that he is no longer required to be the Young Man with Orange, he rolls up the sleeves of his shirt. Lets the sun sink into his skin. Hides himself away no more.

Everything is going well. Joseph is happy. He is writing. For the first time since arriving at the farmhouse he feels at home.

And yet . . . And yet.

Something snags at the edges of his thoughts. It nudges him, when he catches a whiff of smoke on the breeze or when Ettie strikes a match to light a cigarette. When he glimpses his reflection in the dark of the kitchen window.

In all the excitement of his article being published and of being allowed to stay, of the fuss and the champagne and the train time-table being ripped from the kitchen cupboard, the thought had dipped beneath the waters of his mind. But now it bobs to the sur-face. What was it he saw that night in the outhouse?

He tries to busy himself in writing and in making himself use-ful. He cleans paintbrushes and feeds the chickens and fetches let-ters from the village. But still the thought tugs at him.

He catches Ettie after lunch one day. Tata is marching down the field with the afternoon's spoils: a platter of grapes and a curl-ing rind of goat's cheese. Ettie begins to clear the table but Joseph reaches out a hand and says, "Wait."

Her expression is cautious. He runs his eyes over her face, his mouth twitching with indecision at the words he is about to say. Then he lowers his voice to a whisper—afraid that somehow Tata might hear him, or perhaps he is afraid of voicing his mad-ness aloud. "What happened the night Tata finished *Young Man with Orange?*"

Ettie puts down the plate she is holding. "What do you mean?" Her voice is equally low.

Joseph swallows. "The night Tata finished the painting. I saw . . . I think I saw something. Something I can't explain."

"What did you see?"

"I saw a light . . . a light in the outhouse." Joseph swallows again. "I followed it and looked through the window and I saw . . . I saw the painting. *Young Man with Orange* was there. And you were there too." He is describing the scene as if in a dream. The night exists in a somnambulant haze, the details ungraspable. But an image burns in his mind. "I saw the painting . . . and I saw you set it on fire."

Ettie's expression is unreadable.

He grips her arm, urging her to believe him. "How can a painting that was destroyed by a fire be whole again the next morning? How can a painting come back from the dead, as if no flame ever touched it?"

Ettie raises a cool hand to his forehead. "The heat," she says quietly. "It plays tricks on you." Her fingertips brush the hair from his brow. "It was a night fever." Her voice is calming, smooth as honey.

Joseph closes his eyes. "But it felt so real. The painting was there and I thought . . . I really thought I saw you. You set the painting on fire."

"Absinthe," Ettie says, her voice harsher now. "It makes men mad." Joseph feels a flare of shame. Perhaps it was the absinthe. Perhaps his mind was addled and his eyes were playing tricks on him.

Ettie steps closer and holds Joseph's face between her hands. "Do not trouble yourself," she says. "You saw nothing."

She turns from him, taking the stack of plates, the clinking cutlery, the breadbasket and the crumpled napkins, and vanishes inside the house.

Joseph throws himself down on his bed. It is stifling up in his attic room and he tries to find a way of prostrating himself so his limbs are not touching any other parts of his body. He lies starfished on the sheets.

Is he losing his mind? He has hallucinated once before in his life, that terrible Christmas morning. It cannot be happening again. He is half-tempted to write to Flora and tell her what he saw. He even jolts towards the desk a few times and picks up his pen. But then he is stilled. He does not want to worry his sister with two mad brothers. The pen is returned to the desk. His body flung back on the bed.

He reminds himself that there was nothing in the outhouse the next morning. He checked, his fingers turning over dry grass on the ground. There were no scorch marks, no traces of burnt wood or canvas. No signs that anyone had been there at all. And besides, he pounds his dull head, the painting was back on its easel the next morning. He saw Raimondi collect *Young Man with Orange* and load it into his car to be taken to Paris. Someone has bought the painting already—bought it for a considerable sum—and now it is hanging on their wall. *Young Man with Orange* has not been destroyed.

If only it was as easy as Ettie said: *Do not trouble yourself.* But is he troubling himself or is something troubling him? He feels wretched. His grasp on reality wobbling loose like a tooth.

Ettie, Ettie, Ettie. He cannot work her out. Perhaps it was a hallucination, as she said. If it was, then part of him longs for another night of fever. He wants to glimpse her again, to see her unguarded, to wear the cloak of night about his shoulders and walk through the darkness unseen. The loneliest part of him wants her to press his face between her cool hands again, and tell him he saw nothing.

ETTIE

A quick glance around Ettie's bedroom does not reveal much. A narrow bed. Wooden wardrobe. Well-swept floor. But behind, inside, and underneath what meets the eye, certain items have been hidden.

At the back of the wardrobe: Two small canvases. Sketches on brown parcel paper. The July 1920 edition of *The Inkling.*

Inside the lining of an old coat: Three paintbrushes, snapped in half by Tata, glued back together by Ettie. A stick of charcoal.

Beneath the pillow: Joseph's missing handkerchief.

Under a loose floor tile: A peach stone taken from the mouth of a man in the garden of a convent which was once, during the war, a hospital.

Tucked inside an old recipe book, the pages coming loose from their binding, the cover splattered with oil: A handwritten piece of paper. The paper is torn from a notebook, the handwriting is loose and exuberant—that of a child.

It is a list of names.

A short while after her mother was consigned to the smallest plot in the village cemetery, Ettie decided it was time she found out who her father was. She was eight and had never asked the question while her mother was alive. She had never given the absence much thought because it did not feel like an absence. But now her mother was dead and there was a hole. She had tried, once or twice, broaching the subject of her paternity with Tata, but he reacted as if she had stung him. He became brusque, and it was a brusqueness that turned to anger if her questions went too far.

She took matters into her own hands.

Wandering the cobbled streets of Saint-Auguste, she scrutinised every man she came across. She peered at the butcher. Perhaps her mother had fallen in love with him? She looked keenly into the milkman's face, trying to see if there was any resemblance to her own. She stared at the other children in the village. Did she share a parent with any of these clean, rosy-cheeked boys or girls?

She kept a list of suspects hidden between the pages of her mother's recipe book. At night she took it out and added or removed people according to her deductions.

Jean-Luc the pig farmer

Emile the farmhand

Monsieur Lafayette who makes Tata's picture frames

Girard the rat-catcher—no, too ugly. Her mother would never fall in love with a man who had hair sprouting from his ears *and* nose.

Monsieur Dubonnet the mayor—no, this did not make sense either, because if the mayor was her father then surely he would send a secret envelope of money each year, to keep her in good dresses and well supplied with madeleines. No such envelope had ever arrived.

Father Le Brun—crossed out when Ettie learned that priests were not allowed to marry or have children. Rewritten when she discovered that the priest had in fact fathered one of the children in the village. Crossed out again when she observed the child's fiery red hair, matching exactly that of the priest. Ettie's hair was a dark chestnut.

So went the list of nearly every man in the village, married and unmarried, of siring age and right up to old Père Abélard, the blind man who lived in a cave.

One time Ettie asked the cobbler, "Are you my father?" She had been watching him for a few days and found the evidence most compelling. See how his skin was freckled, just like hers. And the way he had lost a front tooth, just like she had! But he hissed at her and shooed her away with a wave of his hand.

Ettie crouched by her mother's grave to watch if anyone secretly left flowers on it.

No one ever did.

When the list did not look promising enough, Ettie wondered whether her father had been a traveler, perhaps in a circus or with a band of musicians. If ever she saw a particularly handsome stranger, she added him to the list.

The man with green eyes and a pony, walking through the village on Midsummer's day—yes, she reasoned, perhaps he had come back to look for her after all these years. She positioned herself prominently in the village square, waiting for him to notice her. She presented her face the way a sunflower tracks the sun, but either he did not recognise her or did not want to. He passed straight by. Did not glance back.

Ettie never found her father. The list of names remains unfinished. Folded and hidden, between the pages of a book.

JOSEPH

July blooms like a ripening fruit. Joseph has been at the farmhouse for over a month now. The leaves on the trees have curled in the heat. The river has reduced to a stream.

He tries to put the fire out of his mind. He refuses to dwell on the night he cannot explain. Occasionally his thoughts flash with the image of a burning painting but then he shakes himself. Focuses instead on what is in front of him.

Before starting on the large canvas, Tata dashes off smaller studies of food. Then he paints over them and starts again. A plate of ham becomes a dish of anchovies. A jar of honey turns into the cragged shell of an oyster. A hunk of bread into a coil of lemon peel.

But the great white canvas in the corner remains blank.

Why will Tata not begin? What is he waiting for?

As Joseph does not know what this new painting will be about, he decides to write his next article about the influence of landscape on Tata's work. He wants to know what it is about this hot, crackling place that first drew Tata in. Why did he come here? Why has he never left? And why has he pushed the world so far away?

Ettie has started to meet Joseph's eye. There was a time at lunch when Tata was enumerating the failings of the Académie des Beaux-Arts. Spit flew through the air, and beneath the volleys of half-chewed tomato pips Ettie's and Joseph's eyes connected, and for once she did not drop her gaze. Since then their eyes have found each other across the table, through the kitchen window, along the terrace, communicating words they cannot, or perhaps do not know how to, say aloud.

Joseph perches on his stool and watches Tata paint a red pepper. It is just a quick study. It will probably be painted over later. The pepper looks quite ordinary: bands of red and amber smeared with a palette knife. A stub of green for the stem. But then Tata takes a small brush. He adds a sheen of reflective white to the pepper's surface, and suddenly the painting comes alive.

Tata turns around to look at Joseph, as if knowing he will appreciate this trick. "You just follow the light, Joseph. That's all there is to it. The light will show you what to paint."

Tata has never explained his work before. A door has opened, just a crack.

Joseph notices that they only eat food that Tata can paint. Everything they consume must have a clearly defined shape because this is what looks good in a painting. Tata rejects anything that could melt into a brown blur. He will not paint beef stew or fish pie or anything with a homogenous, saucy look. There is no mince, no pâté, nothing jellied. Soups are only considered if they are served in a particularly distinctive bowl. There is a reason why very few casseroles appear in the history of art.

Instead they eat food chosen for its shape and colour. Oranges. Radishes. Nectarines. Seafood is particularly artistic. The black spines of a sea urchin (no matter that they taste disgusting), the serrated shell of a scallop, the curving claw of a lobster. Whole fish, eyes and tail intact. Grapes, excellent (Joseph has learned you can drape these like beads). Red currants, gleaming and bloody when scattered across a tablecloth.

Joseph tries to eat his meals in particularly interesting ways. He arranges certain textures on his plate, combines different colours, in the hope that Tata will fling out a hand and take his dinner down to the studio. He is always flattered when Tata chooses his plate over Ettie's. He has contributed, in some small way, to the master's work.

One morning, a week after the publication of his article, Joseph settles himself in the corner of the studio. Tata is setting up for the day, bustling about with paints and brushes, sunlight filling the room like air inflating a balloon. Joseph has pulled his stool up to the wooden table. He has taken one of his pencils and a blank page from his notebook, and is trying to sketch the plate of sardines Tata dashed off on a small canvas the day before. It is slow, painstaking work.

The pencil is slippery in his fingers and he cannot replicate the freedom of Tata's lines. The harder he tries the further he strays from Tata's painting. He needs to be both spontaneous and precise. Careful and carefree. The mimicry is harder than he expected. He cannot get the looseness of the shapes quite right, nor the freshness of the image.

Tata sees him with a pencil in his hand and frowns. "What are you doing?" he growls.

"I am sketching a copy of your sardines for my editor," Joseph explains, "to accompany my next article." Harry has suggested illustrating his pieces, and this is the best he can do.

Tata peers over his shoulder. "Jesus Christ, boy," he snorts. "I thought you said you could draw. Even Ettie could do better than that." He bustles around, shuffling through papers on the floor.

"Here. Send this instead."

"I can't take this!" Joseph says. Tata is holding out a preparatory sketch for the painting. An original, a draft straight from the hand of the master!

Tata slaps it onto the table. "You just did."

He strides back to his easel and Joseph holds the drawing carefully in his hands. It is beautiful: dashed off in an instant, the fluidity of the lines showing the impulse with which Tata works. The shapes are free and pleasing. He has used nothing but blue pencil yet he has captured perfectly the essence of the slippery fish. Slick and wild. Almost alive.

This is one of Tata's golden moments: a rare glimmer of the man who emerges like a ray of sun through clouds, placing beauty into his palm.

Joseph takes the drawing up to his bedroom. He slots it into an envelope, careful not to crease the paper, and seals it. Then, with a sharp tug of his heart, he addresses the envelope not to Harry, but to Rupert.

Ettie deposits a pile of fresh sheets on the tin drum in Joseph's room. He is embarrassed that she has come upon him—as silently as always—when he is meant to be working. Instead, he is sitting on his bed rereading *The Odyssey*. She is about to leave when she catches sight of the book in his hands. "Adventure stories?" she asks.

Joseph shakes his head. "*Nostos*," he says. "Homecoming, in Greek."

Ettie takes a step forward. She runs her finger along the book's well-worn pages. "One of the soldiers in the hospital told me there are only two stories in the world," she says. "A stranger comes to town. And a man goes on a journey."

Joseph turns this over in his mind. "Is that all?"

"Yes. Just two."

"What about women?"

Ettie's mouth becomes a thin line. "There is only one story for women: they stay at home."

They stare at the book in silence together, at its faded cloth cover and its unnerving brown stains. Joseph thinks of his brother, the boy who went on a journey but never really came home. He thinks of Ettie's mother, the woman who did not stay at home and was brought back in a coffin. In his own story he is the man who has gone on a journey, but for Ettie he is the stranger who came to town.

He is aware of the closeness of the two of them, the silence of the house and Ettie's soft, still presence in his bedroom.

"I hope he got home," he says eventually. "The soldier, in your hospital. I hope he had his *nostos*."

Sometimes Joseph jolts awake, his body thrumming with the knowledge that *something is on fire*.

But no. Nothing is burning. He lies back down uneasily, his body sinking into the sweat-sour bed. His mind twitches with the image of a painting. His own face going up in flames. *Young Man with Orange* obliterated, and then whole again. Destroyed. Reincarnated.

Each time he dreams of the burning painting he wakes with his throat dry as sawdust. His heart throbs and his blood churns as if he has been running from something. All he can do is close his eyes and try to sleep again, thinking of Ettie's lips forming the words: *You saw nothing.*

Joseph finds a peach outside his door. Not a mouldy one for Tata to paint. This one is plump and ripe. The sort he'd like to eat.

Joseph must kill a chicken for dinner. Ettie has been sent to the framer's for the afternoon and so it has to be him. He has never killed anything before and looks down at the tools Tata has given him for the task: a mallet and a pillowcase.

Out in the yard there are several hens scrabbling around in the dust. He chooses the nearest of them: a feeble creature with moulting grey feathers. She does not run as he steps towards her, but squats as if to make it easier for him to pick her up. She is pleasingly warm; alive and clucking and soft. He sighs and takes a step around the back of the house, where he forces the poor bird into the pillowcase, wings suddenly flapping and, turning his eyes away as if the moment will be less awful if he does not see it, he finds the bird's neck, and twists.

There is a hollow snap like a twig underfoot. He glances down. The pillowcase blooms with blood. But the bird is still moving, juddering and spasming. He has done something wrong. The blood spreads, seeping onto his hands. There should not be this much blood. A sharp bone pokes through the pillowcase.

He wishes the bird would die quicker. She is twitching in his hands, not alive but not yet dead either; her nerves fraying and fizzing. Black spots appear in front of his eyes. Why won't she die? He feels around for her head. Grabs the mallet. Turns his face away and swings. There is a violent crunch. A last, desperate flutter. And then nothing.

Joseph steps back into the kitchen, spattered with chicken blood. It has leached through the pillowcase, staining his hands, his shirt, his chest.

Tata takes one look at him and issues a short bark of a laugh, "Ha!," and continues on his way out onto the terrace, jar of honey under one arm.

Joseph deposits the chicken on the kitchen table. Bile rises in his throat and he retches, but nothing comes up.

Back in his room he tries to clean himself. He crouches on the floor and plunges his arms into the earthenware jug, rubbing them up and down, trying to rid his skin of the blood, the warmth, the death. He paws at his shirt but the red splatters only burst into explosions of pink. The fabric sticks to his chest. It is no use, it is no use. He is skeined with blood. He is hot and suddenly more tired than he has ever been in his life.

He rests his head against the rim of the jug.

"What are you doing?"

It is Ettie. She is standing in his doorway, frowning at him squatting on the floor. Damp and wild and bloodied.

She seems to sense something desperate in him, and says, "Come."

Joseph is weary; weary of being ordered this way and that, of the heat and the blood and the twitching chicken refusing to die. He wants to stay crouched on the floor here. Forever, perhaps. He wants to moan, "No." But Ettie says, "Come," and pads softly down the stairs.

He gets to his feet. Laboriously, achingly, he follows her footsteps until they come to a wooden door and emerge around the side of the house, blinking in the bright sunlight. Joseph's shirt fills with air. Dust sticks to his itchy skin and he wants nothing more than to peel it from his body.

He follows the silent Ettie as she leads him away from the house, down the crackling yellow field. She glances over her shoulder just once, in the direction of the terrace. Tata is snoozing, a straw hat pulled down over his eyes. A jar of honey glows in the afternoon sun like a lantern.

Ettie reaches back and grabs Joseph's hand. Her fingers are dry and chapped. She pulls him down the field, through the spiky burrs and brittle grass, heading for the dark patch of trees at the bottom of the slope where a towering willow looms high. They reach its shadows. Slip beneath the fronds.

The river makes barely a sound, slipping sleekly over wide pale rocks. The water is clear as glass. Joseph wants to plunge into it, to hurl himself bodily into the cold.

Ettie turns to him. She steps very close. Close enough for Joseph to see the dust caught on her eyelashes. Gently, without a word, she takes the edge of his shirt in her hands. She holds it for a moment as if weighing it, then slowly peels it upwards. Joseph's pulse is a drumbeat in his ears as she lifts the bloodied shirt over his head and pulls it from his body. She looks down at it. A crumpled mass of red and pink.

She steps down to the river, crouching on the bank and spreading the shirt in the water. It billows outwards like a cloud. She sits, resting her feet in the water and pulling the shirt to her, finding the parts with the stains and rubbing them slowly between her hands. The blood lifts and is taken away by the water. She rubs and rubs, seeking out the dust and the dirt and the death.

Joseph sits on a rock a little way along the bank. His feet slip coolly into the water, the ache and weariness leaving them. He looks down at his body. His arms are nutty brown from his time in the sun but his chest is pale. He brings the water up to his arms, to his shoulders, lets it run over himself. The dust swirls off him. The blood dissipates. He can breathe again.

Ettie shakes out his shirt. She wrings it like a rope, then flaps it out and places it on a rock to dry.

She looks at him. Her expression is unreadable, her chest rising heavily as she watches him running his hands up and down his body. Then she splashes through the river. Her skirt soaks up to the knees but she does not look down. She strides towards Joseph, stopping only when her feet are planted between his. She looks at him, then stoops, cupping a pool of water in her hands and lifting it to Joseph's neck.

She washes him, and he does not speak. His skin ripples with goosebumps. Ettie's hands run lightly over his body, her fingers tracing the veins in his arms, long after the blood and the dust are gone. He raises a cool hand to her face. Slowly, ever so slowly, he strokes his fingers across her cheek. She closes her eyes. He cups her face in his palm and she leans into it, her mouth resting against his thumb.

Suddenly her eyes fly open.

There, in the distance, he hears it too. A cry: "Sylvette!"

Tata tucks a napkin into his collar. Ettie has plucked and trussed the poor hen, basted it with lemon, orange, and salt, and cooked it until its skin is crinkled like leather. She places it on the table atop a bed of carrots and parsley.

Tata wastes no words or time in appreciating her efforts and leans forward to tear off a drumstick. He eats without cutlery, plunging his face straight into the flesh, juice and oil dripping into his beard.

Joseph wants to look at Ettie but she will not meet his eye. She is staring off into the darkness.

"Joseph. Eat," Tata says gruffly. "If I wanted to dine with a skeleton I would dig one up from the cemetery."

Joseph reaches forward and slides a knife into the chicken. He plates up slices for Ettie, and then for himself. The night is silent, save for Tata's muffled grunts.

Joseph manages to move food from his plate to his mouth but he is not aware of eating. He cannot focus on anything except the ends of Ettie's hair where it has curled around her ears. The echoes of her hands run up and down his body, a tingling shadow of sensation.

They do not talk about what happened at the stream. They do not speak at all over the next few days, but Joseph's mind is filled with images of Ettie's blazing, determined face. Of her strong hands wringing the blood from his shirt. Of her mouth resting against his thumb.

He wants to talk to her but whenever he enters a room it feels as if she has just left. She keeps her distance, as if she is trying to tread backwards, to undo what happened. As if she is telling him once again: *You saw nothing.*

When Ettie eats a peach she lets the juice run down her wrists and then licks it all the way back up.

ETTIE

Joseph is studying Tata's work almost as closely as Ettie is these days. She often finds his head bowed over the palette before she can get to it. His hands sift through the sketches before hers; his eyes linger over the paint-clogged brushes. She finds their movements more tangled than before as they tread an invisible dance across the studio floor. Their trajectories intertwine. When Joseph is not writing he helps her with the cooking, the cleaning, and the day-to-day running of the house. Their bodies orbit each other. Their arms, occasionally, brush.

One day Ettie comes upon him in the kitchen, reaching for the jug on the highest shelf. He stretches easily and as his shirt lifts she catches the briefest glimpse of skin. The smooth arc of his side. A pebble of his spine. Those soft striations of muscles she ran her fingers over when she washed the blood from his shirt in the stream. Then he grasps the jug and his body is hidden again, shrouded in a thick sweep of cotton. Joseph turns and catches her looking. Their eyes meet for one heartbeat.

She is so aware of his body. As July rolls on she finds herself drawn to the flicker of a pulse in his neck. The slice of his shoulder blades through his shirt. The pool of sweat at the base of his throat—a perfect hollow for her to place her tongue.

She shuts this thought down immediately.

Ettie has not been touched in so long. She exists in a world bereft of physical contact. Sometimes when paying for bread at the market she slips more coins than necessary into the baker's palm, so he has to return them to her, his hand brushing hers for a second time. Two touches for the price of one. Ettie has not been held, not been squeezed, kissed, or clasped in so long that sometimes she feels like an echo of a person. Insubstantial as air.

Ettie's was a childhood of having things taken away from her. If Tata saw that something made her happy—a book, a friend, a bird in a cage—he found a way of destroying it. This has been the pattern of her life. And so she must not let Tata know how much pleasure Joseph gives her. How her body untenses when he is near. How the air seems to clear.

Like all her most precious desires, she must keep these feelings secret from Tata. But that does not mean they don't exist.

When Tata forbade Ettie from painting he thought he had stamped out her hunger. But though he took the pencils from her hand, he could not quell the urge within her.

Ettie was a quiet child, but being quiet did not mean she was not curious, and in her teenage years this quietness gave way to secrecy rather than obedience. After she had gone to bed each night she would slide a chair under the handle of her door. She reached into the back of her wardrobe and extracted the near-empty tubes of paint that Tata had thrown away. Brushes he had snapped in half. For paper she used the backs of his sketches or cut scraps of canvas from the rolls he kept in the attic. She painted under the cover of darkness, ears alert to the tread of his footsteps in the house beyond. If Tata would not teach her, it did not mean she could not learn from him. She studied everything he did.

Her secret paintings had strange colour combinations, born of the necessity of scavenging whatever she could get. Sometimes she would squeeze a raindrop of colour onto a handkerchief and keep it alive with some stolen linseed oil. Her brushes were the odd ones Tata had discarded already. Her palette was a broken china plate.

In time, when she was put in charge of ordering Tata's paints and equipment, she started to order two of everything. Two canvases. Two fox-hair brushes. Two bottles of turpentine when Tata only needed one. She made sure he did not see her squirrelling these duplicates away. She found hiding places throughout the house.

She did not paint to win anyone's approval. She had learned by now that she would never get it from Tata. She painted only to satisfy a need within herself. She was trapped in a house with a man who tied her down with invisible ropes. She knew nothing of the outside world or how to get there. She had no money, no knowledge of people or places or customs beyond her limited life. But painting became a kind of freedom. She had found a way of escaping without taking a single step.

Did Tata forbid her to paint because he feared she might be equal to him? Or did he fear a life without Ettie in her place? Would he be able to paint if she was not there to cook and clean for him? To scrub his brushes and wash the stains from his apron?

Ettie knows that Tata fears a life without her. More than anything, Tata fears the life she dreams of.

JOSEPH

Joseph,

I saw the drawing you sent to Rupert. I don't know what it's of and can barely make out which way round it's meant to go but Rupert stared at it for hours. It transfixed him. He hadn't slept for eight days but after you sent him that picture he slept so deeply the nurses thought he was dead.

He wasn't. He was fine. He was just, finally, at peace. He hasn't let the picture out of his hands and it's gone all soft around the edges.

Thank you. You know he'd say it himself if he could.

Flora

From that moment on Joseph syphons more sketches from Tata's table. He does not steal them exactly, but once Tata has finished with a painting, once he has painted over it or consigned it to the stack of canvases in the corner, Joseph leafs through the preparatory sketches and sneaks one out for Rupert. An impression of a pomegranate. Cragged scallop shells. Rosy apricots. He imagines his brother pinning the sketches by his hospital bed and staring up at them in the lonely, moonlit hours.

Joseph wants Rupert to know he is thinking of him, because he is. Always. The latest sketch he has snaffled is of a cluster of grapes. Tata has drawn them loose and free: pleasing in their plump, endless spirals. Joseph hopes they will bring a moment of calm to Rupert's tormented mind.

There is a line in *The Odyssey*, when Odysseus has finally returned from war but tosses and turns in his bed, unable to sleep. The goddess Athena comes to him and says, "So, surrender to sleep at last. What a misery, keeping watch through the night, wide awake—you'll soon come up from under all your troubles."

Joseph writes this on the back of the envelope, and sends it with his love.

It is the feast of Saint Juliette, and the village is holding a dance. Joseph sees the poster pinned to a plane tree on his way back from the tobacconist. There will be musicians, and a punch fountain, and a whole roasted boar. There will be fireworks!

He turns the details over in his mind as he walks along the donkey track. The heat beats down on him and a dry wind sends up whorls of dust at his side. A spark of excitement crackles to life in his chest. Not for the first time, he finds himself walking towards the house, his heart hammering.

Why shouldn't he do it? Why shouldn't he follow his instincts for once, instead of the voice in his head that tells him this is a bad idea?

He is going to do it. He is going to ask Ettie to the dance.

He finds her in the kitchen, bent over a pile of brushes from which she is trying to extract the last glimmers of paint.

"It is Saint Juliette's Day," he announces from the door. The romance of the name has not escaped him.

Ettie keeps her head down. "Saint Juliette was burned at the stake."

"I'm sorry?"

"Saint Juliette. She was burned alive."

"Oh."

Ettie looks up, seeming to sense this was not the tack Joseph had intended.

"There's a dance," he says. "In the village. Tonight. And I thought it might be nice if we—well, if you . . . if you'd like to . . . come to the dance with me?" His face feels hotter than usual. "There's going to be music," he blunders on. "And fireworks. And a roasted boar." Perhaps the boar will swing it? Do women like roasted boars? A small frown pinches Ettie's brows.

"Only—only if you want to come, of course," he says.

It feels illicit, what he is asking. As if Tata could come upon them at any moment and wrench them apart. Joseph can so rarely get Ettie on her own and he wants to feel again the freedom of that day in the market. Or the afternoon when she cut his hair at the top of the house. Or the stolen hour down by the stream . . .

There is a long pause as Ettie twists a paintbrush in her hands. Then she says, very quietly and without looking at him, "I would like that very much."

"Brilliant!" Joseph beams. "Excellent. Thank you—I mean—well, brilliant. Shall we leave here at seven?"

Ettie glances out the window to where Tata is dozing on the terrace. "I have some work to finish up here," she says quietly. "I'll meet you there. Wait for me in the square."

Joseph nods, ecstatic and nervous all at once. This gives him time to wash his face and comb his hair. Maybe even do something about the ink all over his fingers. "The music starts at eight," he says.

Finally Ettie looks at him. "The music starts at eight." She smiles.

Lights are strung in the papery trees. The air is thick with crackling boar fat. Old women line the crumbling square at the top of the village and groups of boys and girls stand in clusters, eyeing each other in the lavender dusk. The old bougainvillea-clad church stands watch over everyone, its spire piercing a cloudless sky. Rogue notes from pipes and fiddles slip into the air as musicians tune their instruments, and all around is the chatter and laughter of high spirits.

Joseph does not know where to wait. He wants to make sure Ettie sees him when she arrives. He has found his cleanest shirt, and washed and dried a silk handkerchief before spending several minutes folding it perfectly into his breast pocket. He has shaved, and even shined Rupert's boots using an old rag and some shoe polish he found in one of the cupboards. He thinks he looks quite nice.

He buys flowers. They are expensive and deplete his already depleted funds but he does not regret it. He spends a long time choosing the shapes and colours he thinks Ettie will like most. He pays an extra coin for a crimson ribbon.

He tucks his hair nervously behind his ears. It is sticking up in the heat and no amount of Macassar oil has been able to tame it. The evening is humid and the flowers are sweaty in his palm, so he moves towards the punch fountain. Old Salomé from the tobacconist hands him a cup with a wink, and he presses it to his forehead, sweat mingling with the condensation of the glass. The coolness steadies him. He takes a walk around the square. There is the woman from the bakery where Joseph buys baguettes, and there is the man who sold him the lobster that day at the market. At the edge of the square is a small group of men in wheelchairs, pushed back from the crowd. War medals glint on their chests. Empty trouser legs flap in the breeze.

Joseph nods at them and continues his walk. A dark-haired woman catches his eye and smiles, but he glances away quickly.

The band strikes up. It is only just eight. He scans the heads of the crowd but Ettie is nowhere to be seen. She is not among the laughing girls or the jostling boys wearing paper hats. She is not among the men leaning on walking sticks or the women dispensing punch. He eases himself onto a bench and waits, his knee juddering up and down. The flowers have started to wilt and he rearranges them to make the freshest ones stand at the front.

The dancing begins. Men and women swirl into the centre of the square, boys hold out their palms to girls who smile and clutch their skirts. It all looks so simple. Couples intertwine their fingers and drape their arms around each other's necks. They move as they please. Children run between swivelling legs, chasing after dogs and cats and firecrackers. The music grows louder. Bodies squeeze closer.

Heat seeps into Joseph's clothes. The heady smell of roasted boar wafts towards him but he does not want to eat anything. He is clammy and restless so goes back for more punch. It is ice cold and tastes of something sweet but also bitter. Cherries? Or black currants, perhaps. He sips it while doing another round of the square. Perhaps he missed Ettie the first time?

But no, he could never miss her. She is simply not here.

He goes back for more punch—his third glass? His fourth? He does not know—and Salomé eyes him with a sly look. "You do not want to dance?" she asks.

"I do. I'm just . . . waiting for someone."

"Who are you waiting for?"

"Ettie."

She cocks her head to one side.

"Sylvette, from the house."

Salomé's eyes narrow. "Hmm." Her nostrils flare as she scoops punch for an old man behind Joseph. "You are wasting your time . . . That girl is no good. No good at all."

"She said she would come," Joseph says confidently.

Salomé shakes her head. Then she leans forward and hisses, over the crackle of boar fat and the bursts of music and laughter, "You are playing with fire."

Joseph does not want to hear any more. His brain is fizzy and he turns away, cradling his glass of punch. The music has grown louder. The lights hazy. And there is the dark-haired woman again. Her eyes are large and bright. Her hair is loose, tumbling in a wave down her back. She does not say anything but her presence seems to suggest something. Something that both repels and entices him. He pushes past her into the crowd, making for a bench on the opposite side of the square.

The church clock strikes nine, then nine thirty. Long shadows become longer still, and the summer sky is tinged with purple. Where is Ettie?

Joseph is sat among the war-wounded. These men do not speak, but watch the dancing with a look of desolate longing. Their severed limbs nudge in time to the music, and something about this makes Joseph want to cry. None of these men will ever dance again. He is drunk. He knows it by the blurring of his vision and the way the ground tips this way and that. By the sick, acidic taste at the back of his throat.

"She's not coming," says a voice close at hand. The dark-haired woman is back.

"I'm sorry?"

"Whoever you're waiting for. She's not coming." A smile plays about the woman's lips. "Dance with me instead." Joseph feels the limbless soldiers watching him. He feels their yearning gazes, the hearts that ache to dance again. Joseph looks at his wilted flowers. Is it really so obvious he has been let down? He feels hot and embarrassed. Did Ettie even say when she would come? He cannot remember. The loneliness that has been gnawing at his insides suddenly bites. He knocks back his punch and tosses the flowers to the ground.

The woman pulls him into the swirling mass of dancers. He feels her take his arms and wrap them around her waist, feels her press her hands to his shoulders. She is warm. The lights flit past as she whirls him around. The music is fast and his feet are slow, knocking about in Rupert's boots, but the closeness of another body makes his heart swell.

"What's your name?" he murmurs into her hair.

"Sabine." He can hear the smile in her voice. She ducks under his arm, forcing him to twirl her, and comes up facing him. Her eyes are dark. Then she is away again, twirling and spinning until they are pressed together once more by the crowd.

"You smell nice," he says absently. He does not know why he says this, other than that he is drunk and she is there and her hair is pressed against his nose and it smells of jasmine. She nestles her head close to his, and he feels her teeth on his earlobe. It is a horrible, jangling sensation. He tries to pull away but the crowd pushes them together and she guides him around the square, twirling and returning, pressing and looping his arms about her. She is throwing her head back, laughing, as if to say, *Isn't this fun?*

No, Joseph thinks. *This is not fun at all.* His head is pounding and he wants this to stop. Whatever this is, he needs to get away.

There is a pinched, keening feeling in his stomach. He wants to throw up. He needs to look for Ettie, to find the woman who should be in his arms. He cranes his neck but the square is a blur, the crowd flying past in a whirl of lights and bodies and noise. Sabine is in front of him. He is hit by the rushing, unstoppable force of her. Sabine, whose hair smells of jasmine and whose face is coming closer, closer, closer. Her lips are upon his. She presses her face to him, her hands on his cheeks. Her nails dig into his skin.

He recoils.

The band is still playing but he cannot hear it.

He shakes his head, stumbles away from her. The crowd rush on but over Sabine's shoulder he sees a woman. A woman in a white dress, a flower tucked behind one ear. A woman whose eyes have already found him.

Oh, Ettie.

ETTIE

Ettie turns and runs. Cold sickness swirls through her. She hugs her arms about herself, clasping her ribs, her lungs, her hollow heart. *No, no, no.* She strikes the ground with her feet, pushing it farther away from her. *No, no, no.* She was too late. Too late! It was not meant to be like this. She glances over her shoulder and sees Joseph tangled among the dancers. He is trying to follow, fighting his way towards her.

She runs faster. Cobbled alleys fly past. She turns from the village. Thorns clutch at her white dress, the dress she brought down from her mother's wardrobe and held against her body in front of the mirror. She claws at the daisy in her hair but it is tangled; the daisy she slid so carefully from the vase in Tata's studio while he was sleeping.

She can hear Joseph stumbling after her. *No, no, no.* She runs like a storm towards the house, pounding her feet into the harsh ground, dust sticking to the twin trails of tears on her cheeks. She wishes she could outstrip the wind, outrun the night. She runs and runs and runs.

Why had she been so late?

Tata had known. From the moment he saw the white dress he had known where she was going. The sight of his sister's old clothes had struck something wild across his face. Something furious. Something almost like fear.

"Ettie . . . just one thing," he had said. "Help me with this." The task he had concocted involved traipsing down to the studio. The light was fading and he had fumbled about with matches, rooting around for candles, asking Ettie to run back to the house to fetch more. "I need to rearrange these," he had said, sifting through the plates on the table. "Come here, hold this." Plate after plate had been piled into her arms, stinking food stacking up on top of each other. "Just one more," he had said, shifting more and more plates into her arms, weighing her down. If she let them go they would smash.

"Now give me this one—no, that one. Switch these, take this. One more."

It was only when she had set down the final plate with a slam that he had cracked a smile at her. A glint had come into his blue eye and he had laughed, ever so softly.

She is wearing silly, impractical shoes and she stops and rips them off her feet. Her name is being called across the wind and she runs faster, her bare soles battering the ground. She runs past the house, down the field, through the long grass, stopping only when she comes to the soft fold of the trees. Darkness embraces her. There is the stream. The moon a glistening oil slick on the water.

She doubles over. Clasps her knees and gasps, pressing air into the feeble paper packets of her lungs.

"Ettie!" a voice calls out.

She straightens up. Turns.

Joseph is standing beneath the fronds of the willow tree. His hair is plastered to his face and his eyes are dark and bruised. His shirt is open, sweat pooling at his collarbone, his chest heaving. He looks incandescent with despair. He shoves the hair from his face. "Don't run from me," he pleads. "Don't run."

Ettie does not move. She remains still as a deer in a field. Joseph takes a shaky step towards her. Not too close, but closing the gap between them until she can see the thump of his heart in his throat. His breath comes fast. His voice is broken. "Why didn't you come?"

"Why didn't you wait?"

There are no answers. Only words, and it seems that words are not answers. Not tonight. Nothing is an answer except the space between them, the silence pooling into an ocean at their feet.

Joseph takes another shaky step towards her. "I am so, so sorry," he says. Each word falls like a stone on the ground. "I am so very sorry." He takes another step, closing the distance by just one pace.

Still she says nothing.

She could reach out an arm and touch him if she wanted.

She does. Her fingertips find the damp cotton of his shirt. He closes his eyes and when he opens them again she has taken a step towards him. She lifts her hand and runs her fingertip along the hollow of his jaw. She wants to grip the front of his shirt, to clutch him to her, to press her salty lips against his.

And so she does.

JOSEPH

She tastes of peaches. She tastes of the stream, of its green fresh-ness and its cool, metallic grip. She tastes of lavender, and the warm sun on thousands of blades of grass.

She tastes of being alive.

ETTIE

All Ettie knows is Joseph. His arms around her. His mouth pressed against hers. The heat of his hands through the thin cotton of her dress.

She lifts herself onto her toes. She has his collar in her fists and she pulls him closer, squeezing tight the seam of their bodies until there is nothing between them. No air, no breath.

Kissing him is like finding land after a shipwreck.

Joseph's hands are trailing up her back, cupping her neck, threading into her hair. She does not want to burst this moment. She does not want to think about what it means. The night is endless with possibilities, thick with the hum of cicadas and the soft trickle of the stream. She wants this moment to go on and on.

They break apart. Somewhere in the distance, fireworks. Low, rhythmic booms shudder across the hills. She clasps Joseph to her and kisses him again. Again and again. She can feel his pulse through his skin. It is his pulse. It is hers.

Joseph pulls back a fraction, looks down at her. His face is silver in the moonlight. He takes her hand in his and raises it above her head, turning her in a small, careful circle. There is no music, only the faint crackle of fireworks, but they are dancing. Amber light showers through the sky like arrows.

Ettie's hand fits warmly into Joseph's; so soft, so strong. He does not take his eyes from her. She is aware that she has lost her shoes, and sinks her toes into the damp earth. Joseph is looking at her as if she is the most astonishing thing in the world. He slides the daisy from behind her ear. Presses it to his lips. Tucks it into the pocket of his shirt.

Ettie touches the warm hollow at the base of his throat. And suddenly the smell of the stone hospital fills her nose. The awful tang of carbolic soap. Blood. Paraffin wax. The scent of death close at hand. She scrunches shut her eyes, wills herself back to the present. Joseph's body steadies her. She can feel the heat of him, the slick sheen of his skin and she grips the front of his shirt again. He is so alive. Very gently, he brings a hand to cup her face. His thumb smooths her cheek. "Ettie . . ." he whispers.

She leans against him. Usually she is aware of every second ticking by, every grain of sand falling through the hourglass of her life, but tonight time is suspended. Seconds, minutes, hours mean nothing. The cascades of light have ceased to tumble through the sky, leaving only stars behind. The moon hovers like a scythe. The wind is warm on her skin.

She does not know how long they stay there, but the night lingers just for them. Ettie lifts her face to Joseph again, and her mind is sweet oblivion.

JOSEPH

There is a snake in the garden. It is dead; snipped in two by one of the chicken's beaks, but still it makes Joseph shudder when he steps outside the next morning. It lies like an omen across his path.

Images from the night before flash through his mind: Ettie's upturned face. Her parted mouth. Her eyes fluttering closed before she—

He rubs his pounding head. What is he doing? It feels as if he is being torn in two. One part of him wants to find Ettie, to pull her to him and kiss every freckle on her face. To run his hands through her hair, to press his mouth to the soft heartbeat beneath her skin. But the other half of him surges with an oily guilt. What if Tata finds out what they did? Joseph is only here thanks to Tata's goodwill and if he were to discover, if he were to suspect even for a moment, what happened down by the stream, Joseph would be cast out in an instant. Kicked along the donkey track. Never to return.

Sunlight creeps over the pale hills. He is meant to be writing about Tata. Landscape. Paintings. Horizons and cloud banks and orange trees and Ettie, Ettie, Ettie . . . In his mind he can still see her by the stream. He can still feel her body through the thin cotton of her dress. He can still taste her on his tongue . . .

Focus.

He is here to work.

In the sour pit of his stomach he knows he should never have asked Ettie to the dance at all. He should never have given in to the desperate longing of his heart, to the desire to reach out and forge a fragile connection with her.

He runs a hand through his hair. He will banish himself to the studio. Yes. He will focus all his energy on Tata. He will throw himself into work, lock himself in the attic to write. He will not stray, will not linger, will not even glance towards Ettie, though every thrumming particle of his body wishes he could.

ETTIE

Watch your step.

Ettie slips out the side door.

Careful there.

She steps over a chicken, skirts around a rusty wheelbarrow.

This way danger lies.

She strides along the donkey track, fists bunched in the pocket of her apron. It had been such sweet relief to let her guard down last night but now in the cold light of morning she feels a chill of trepidation. As if she has been peeled open. Exposed.

A mistake.

She does not know where she is going, she just needs to walk. She needs to move.

What a stupid thing to do.

She needs to shut out the voices in her head.

You cannot let him get too close.

But Joseph . . . Joseph. She feels hot and then cold when she thinks of him. A warm flare of desire fills her body before a flash of memory numbs her to the bone. She speeds up, tripping into a run along the donkey track.

You know what will happen.

She stops to catch her breath, her hand on the gatepost.

You know how this will end.

She sits down by the side of the road and rests her head on her knees. Ettie wants to be good, but she has dark thoughts. Terrible thoughts, the likes of which she knows Joseph could never imagine.

Would he still want to be near her if he knew the darkest recesses of her mind? If she cracked open her chest and showed him the ghosts that haunt the chambers of her heart?

She stuffs her apron into her mouth and bites it.

Ettie has violent dreams. In one she is walking among the pews of a church. She walks aimlessly, without design or thought to where she is going. She constructs her own labyrinth through the wooden benches until she comes across a child, crying. Always, a child crying. The wails echo up to the vaulted ceiling, resounding against the stained-glass windows. Ettie crouches down to the child—a little girl with a plait down her back, tears streaming down her flushed cheeks—and Ettie reaches out with her hands. She wraps them around the girl's throat. She strangles her.

In another dream Ettie is aware she has stepped on something. She lifts her foot and sees that she has trodden on a mouse. It is dead and fleshy under her heel. She tries to run but with every step there is another dead thing under her. Frogs, worms, a quivering bird, a snake. She leaves a trail of destruction wherever she goes.

And then there is the hospital. The familiar high ceilings, the stone floors. Ettie stands in a room of dying soldiers. Their organs spill out, their jaws hang off, their limbs are blackened and burned. Blood seeps into her shoes, and her ears are filled with the cries of men calling out in a multitude of languages for her, for God, for death. This is not a dream but a memory.

Whenever the hospital forces its way into Ettie's mind she wakes up in a cold sweat. Acid rolls through her stomach and she retches over the side of her bed, but nothing comes up. The darkness is entirely inside her. She drags herself to her bedroom window, trying to stop her teeth from chattering. She looks out towards the distant hills and her mind flashes with images of what lies beyond:

the white stone building. Nuns in bloodstained uniforms. A man with one ear.

Ettie grips her stomach and returns to her bed. She never wants to think about the hospital or what went on there but the images infect her mind like a disease. She wants to cough everything up, to pool her organs on the floor and scrape the past from her body.

She knows what happens when she lets someone get too close. Her memories are buried beneath those distant hills. The memory of a man, and a life she almost had.

JOSEPH

They seem to have reached a silent agreement not to mention the kiss. Not to allow their gazes to cross anymore. To stay out of each other's reach.

It is safer this way.

But Joseph is weighed down by all the things he must keep to himself. Each night when he lies awake at the top of the house his mind goes back to those stolen hours by the stream. Ettie's body moving like a wave. The glint of her eyes. The soft crush of her lips.

Sometimes he feels he is losing his grip on reality. His thoughts jumble with images of Ettie's skin, her fingers, her mouth. That sweltering afternoon when she washed blood from his shirt.

The delirious night by the outhouse. The painting. The fire. The strange circular riddle of it all.

The kiss is yet another nighttime apparition he must chase from his mind. He pictures Ettie holding his face and whispering again: *You saw nothing.*

He will be good. He will pretend nothing happened. He will focus on his work. He will play by the rules of the house.

Perhaps he is being optimistic, but as July slips into August, Joseph senses a mellowing in Tata. He has accepted Joseph about the house like a loose floorboard one learns to step around. He does not even seem to mind Joseph's persistent presence in the studio, notebook under one arm. He does not object when Joseph scribbles down something he says, noting the exact wording so he can feed it into his writing. Tata just snorts and shakes his head. Calls him a filthy vulture.

Joseph is treading uncharted ground. Somehow he has come closer to Tata than anyone else: the outsider allowed into the inner sanctum. But still he is missing something.

One evening, a dust storm sends them inside. They eat dinner in the formal dining room, somewhere Joseph has never been before, except once to fetch a silver platter for one of Tata's paintings. The room is austere and imposing with its heavy stone fireplace and dark walls. An old Corot landscape hangs above the fireplace, blackened with soot in a way that makes Joseph want to weep. Thinning Persian rugs cover the floor and stuffed animals perch on the cabinets. A hawk glares down at them, and a weasel twists in perpetual pain. The fire is lit, though the evening is hot. Joseph's collar itches.

Joseph avoids Ettie's eyes all through dinner and after they have finished eating she takes their plates and hurries into the kitchen. Joseph is about to rise as well but then he sees that Tata has pushed back his chair, refilled his wineglass. He seizes his chance and does the same.

Tata looks almost fatherly tonight, his recumbent figure rosy in the dim light. His eyes are lowered and for a moment Joseph wonders if he is sleeping, but then he notices that Tata's grip on the wineglass is tight. He is surveying Joseph through half-closed lids, his mouth slightly parted. Then he says, "The next painting is always the best painting."

Joseph sits up a little straighter.

"There is something about the next one . . . the painting you have yet to paint. It is always the best one."

Is Tata finally about to talk? Perhaps he will be in one of his golden moods tonight, softened by food and wine and the closeness of the room. Joseph hardly dares breathe in case he breaks the spell.

"You must always look forward, Joseph," Tata says. "Don't look back. There's nothing for you there. You must always look to the next thing."

Joseph fidgets uncomfortably. He is always looking backwards. Glancing over his shoulder, going over his past mistakes.

"Do you know what you need to be a true artist, Joseph?"

Tata's chair is positioned slightly higher than Joseph's so he has to look up to answer. He takes his time before saying, "Talent?"

Tata bats this away with a swipe of his paw.

"Dedication? A good teacher? Luck?"

Tata shakes his head. "*Silence*," he says, swirling the wine around his glass. "An artist needs silence. He must not be distracted, not be disturbed . . . Art is created out of silence."

Joseph slides out his notebook, uncaps his pen. He is inching closer, he can feel it.

"Beware of women, Joseph."

The pen slips from his hand. "I'm sorry?"

"Women . . . they get in the way." Tata's eyes gleam in the firelight.

Panic coils through Joseph's stomach.

"You're young, Joseph, you don't know women like I do . . . But take this as a warning: they disturb the silence."

Unease trickles down Joseph's spine. It feels as if Tata is peering inside his heart one chamber at a time, inspecting what's hiding inside.

"Women talk too much," Tata continues, his eyes still on the fire. "They *demand* too much. I have never had a woman because if I did I would never paint a thing. You must learn which you want, Joseph: your art, or a woman. Women get in the way," he says again. "They get in the way in here." He taps a finger against Joseph's temple. "And they get in the way here." He lowers his hand until it rests over Joseph's heart. He leaves it there for a warm moment, then retreats into his chair. "The head and the heart both need silence."

The conversation and the crackling fire are making Joseph's skin crawl. "What about Ettie?" he says before he can stop himself. He has never met anyone as silent as Ettie. She moves like a shadow. Tata's paintings depict a world in which someone has arranged food on a plate but the person is no longer there. And in his life that person is Ettie. She is the invisible presence hovering just out of sight.

"Yes, Ettie is a good girl," Tata says dismissively. "She does what she's told and she stays out of trouble. But . . ." He stares into the fire. "She is her mother's daughter."

The walls of the room seem to draw closer.

"There's an untamable streak there . . ." says Tata. "Do you know the mistral? It is the name of the wind that blows through this region."

Joseph did not know the wind had a name but he has heard it. He has felt it. It tears unstoppably through the fields. Whistles through the house.

"That is what my sister was like."

Perhaps this is the moment to ask. All Joseph knows about Ettie's mother is that she went to America and came back in a coffin. He leans forward and, very quietly, says, "What happened to your sister, Tata?"

"She was a whore!" Tata booms.

The word shocks Joseph. It is as if Tata has plunged his fist down Joseph's throat and he wants nothing more than to cough it up. He manages to sputter, "Tata! How can you say that?"

"My sister was a damn, filthy whore . . ." Tata downs the last of his wine, slamming the glass back on the table. "She was a fool, that girl. A whore who spread her legs for any man who would have her. Look what happened . . . first Ettie, and then if that wasn't bad enough she ran off with the next man who came knocking." Saliva bubbles on his lips. Blood vessels have ruddied his cheeks. "She said she would come back. *Promised* me she would . . . But that's what happens to people who leave. They don't come back. I was left to raise Ettie by myself because my sister ran off and died before she could return."

Joseph gulps down his shock. So Ettie's mother had followed a man. To New York, Ettie had said. A man had whisked her away to a different life . . . but it was not life that was waiting for her. It was death. "How . . . how did she die?" Joseph asks.

"Painfully." Tata shifts in his chair. "The scoundrel left her, of course. She made her way to a hospital but by then it was too late. Two souls died that day. Do you understand what I'm saying?" Tata's eyes narrow. "There were two souls. She'd got herself into trouble again. Stupid girl."

Joseph cannot help but think of that poor woman, thousands of miles from home, alone and scared in a foreign hospital, surrounded by doctors who spoke a language she couldn't understand. In his mind she has Ettie's face.

"Women, Joseph . . . they're unpredictable. You have to keep them under your thumb." Tata mimes twisting his thumb into the arm of the chair. "Keep them under your control."

Joseph meets Tata's uneven gaze. The white eye is amber in the firelight. Trying to keep track of Ettie would be like trying to catch hold of the wind. Like trying to bottle sunlight. Joseph stands up. He can bear it no longer, the heat and the resentment filling the room. He unsticks his shirt from the back of his neck with a hook of his finger, and nods once at Tata. "It is late. Thank you for the conversation." He closes his notebook, folding over the empty page.

Tata does not reply but stares deeply into the fire, his bottom lip trembling.

Joseph hurries from the room. He has never seen Tata so vulnerable, so broken. So poisonously cruel. Finally, he had got Tata to talk but it has left nothing but a sour taste in his mouth. Is Ettie's existence here some sort of punishment for her mother's betrayal?

Tata's words have shaken Joseph. He feels rattled and hollow. He pauses outside Ettie's door on the way up to his bedroom. Despite Tata's warning—or perhaps because of it?—Joseph wants to press his face to her neck and inhale every particle of her.

On an impulse, he raises his hand to knock on her door. She could be lying there, just on the other side of this wall, her heart beating against the darkness. He is about to knock, but then he is struck by another pang of guilt. What if Tata suspects the fire that burns in Joseph's heart? What if he is onto him? He lets his hand fall. Runs his palm softly over the wood. Turns away.

ETTIE

Why won't he come in?

Ettie is lying prostrate on her bed, fully clothed under the covers, her skin sweating. She listens to the pad of Joseph's footsteps on the stairs. She had been so sure he was about to knock.

She has been listening to Joseph and Tata's conversation. After so many years of silence even muffled voices in the house sound loud, and she could hear every word. She had been waiting for them to go to bed, waiting for the house to fall silent, for the night to be hers again. And then there were footsteps, hurried at first and then slow, and she felt Joseph's presence on the other side of her door. She listened to his steady breathing, willing him to knock. But then he turned away. Each of Joseph's treads on the stairs takes him farther from her.

Ettie rolls over and presses her face into her pillow.

She has been lying in bed thinking about Raimondi. He will be back in another week to pick up Tata's study of a lobster. She is counting down the days, a metallic anxiety curdling in her stomach. She dreads Raimondi's visits. She can already feel his eyes on her. His hairy, bronzed hand creeping towards her under the table. His wet lips curling into a smirk.

She remembers showing Raimondi into her bedroom. She must have been fifteen. Tall and filled-out enough to be a woman, jaded enough to know what that meant.

Tata was asleep on the terrace, snoozing after a bottle of wine at lunch. Ettie and Raimondi had put down their cutlery at the same time and looked at each other, and as the first snore rose from Tata's chest they both stood up, as if knowing what the other was thinking.

They moved silently through the house. Slick as a fish he slid into her bedroom: her haven, the only place she could ever be alone. The door closed behind them. Raimondi already had a smile on his face, had already sat himself on the edge of her bed. Her hands trembled at the thought of what she was about to do, and she clasped them behind her back. She had never done this before. "I have a favour to ask," she said.

"Oh yes?" Raimondi leaned back, his eyes darting up and down her body. "What is it you want from me?"

Ettie took a breath, and then opened her wardrobe. She scraped aside the hangers of cotton dresses, pushed away a mouldering shoebox, and from the depths of the wardrobe she brought out a small painted canvas. It was flimsy in her hands but the colours were intense: lake green, the colour of algae in the night. Black shadows. An underbelly of blue.

Raimondi looked at the painting, his fingers halfway to undoing his cravat. "What is this?" he asked.

"A painting."

"By Tata?"

"No." Ettie took a deep breath. "By me."

Raimondi's fingers retreated, curling into a fist at his side. He brought his face to the canvas. Ettie could hear his every breath in the hot, still air. Eventually he flicked his eyes up at her. "What?" was all he said.

"I painted it. It is . . . it is a painting of a feeling," Ettie said carefully. "It is the feeling of holding your breath underwater and not knowing how long you have been under. It is screaming with your mouth closed. It is trying to wake from a dream but not being able to move. It is the feeling of being trapped."

Over years of painting in the dead of night, Ettie had developed her art beyond the simple daisies and lemons of her youth. She had invented her own technique. It was nebulous. More wild even than Tata's. She painted moods rather than images. She channeled her dreams and desires, her thoughts and longings, her pain and desperation, through her brush and onto the canvas. Her paintings were as free as she could only dream of being.

Raimondi stood up and took a step back from the painting. She held it in her outstretched arms like a saint proffering her heart. He looked at her as if he had never seen her before.

"What is this?" He indicated a dark streak at the bottom of the canvas.

"It is ... this." Ettie touched a hand to her breast. "I have painted what is in me. What I feel." And then she asked the question that had been burning inside her since she first touched brush to canvas. "Do you think it's good?"

Raimondi looked as if she had asked him to eat his own hand. He was shaking his head, not necessarily in rejection, but disbelief. All pretence of charm and glitz was gone from his eyes as he whispered, very deliberately, "No. No, I do not."

"Wait," Ettie said, tears choking her voice. Maybe this had been the wrong painting to show him. "I have another." She turned back to the wardrobe and pulled out a different canvas, this one even smaller than the first, the dusty blue of a winter plum. Cloudy like a bruise. A ripening storm. "This is a painting of a nightmare," she said. "And this one"—another canvas, sickly yellow this time—"this is longing."

Raimondi took the blue canvas from her.

"You have a nerve," he said in a low voice, "to call this *art*." With a flash he tossed the canvas onto the bed. "What are you trying to do?" he hissed. "Do you think that just because you are Tata's niece the world owes you something?"

"No!" Ettie protested. "No, that's not what—"

"That you can ride on your uncle's coattails?"

"No!"

"And me?" Raimondi continued, advancing towards her. "You think you can use my good name, my connections, my reputation, for these . . . *attempts*." The word dripped out of his mouth. "A *monkey* could do better than this," he spat. Tears came to Ettie's eyes as the barrage continued. "Where is the skill? Where is your understanding of composition? Of line? Of tone? This is laughable," he said, though he was not laughing. His eyes betrayed only a chilling contempt.

Then suddenly he softened. He seemed to deflate, and he ran his hands through his hair, leaving deep furrows in the oiled strands. "Is it recognition you want?" he asked. "Do you want me to put in a good word for you in the salons of Paris? Maybe hang these paintings in my gallery?"

Ettie nodded. Yes, yes, that was all she wanted.

"Ah, but my dear . . ." Raimondi said sadly. "Young men are already begging for an hour of my time just to show me their latest landscape, their idea for a still life . . . I have no inches of wall to spare. Everyone wants a piece of Raimondi, but does no one think of what poor Raimondi wants?"

His hand, so softly she could barely feel it, began to lift the skirt on her thigh. His breath was at her cheek, and a lithe fingertip found a curl at the nape of her neck. "Perhaps if you were to . . . persuade me."

She shoved hard against his chest. There was a ripping sound as her skirt tore in his hand. "You monster!" she cried. Hot rage flashed through her. "You . . . are . . . disgusting!"

Raimondi stumbled backwards, and the moment she hated him most, more than any up to that point and any after, was the moment he began to laugh. "You silly girl . . ." he said. "You really think you can win? You think you can get anywhere? You are nothing," he spat. "*This* is nothing." He aimed a kick at Ettie's painting of a nightmare which had fallen to the floor.

Ettie was breathing heavily. "Tell me they're good," she said through gritted teeth. "Tell me they're worth something."

"No." Raimondi laughed. "They are worth less than dog shit under my shoe." He plucked up the doll on her bed. Mathilde, with her button eyes and the chequered dress her mother had sewn for her. "You are a child," he said. "A silly little girl. You need to learn not to dabble in things you don't understand." He threw the doll back on the bed. "There is only one Tartuffe, my dear. And it will never be you."

I'll show you, she thought. *I'll show you, I'll show you, I'll show you.* She was alight with anger. "I can be just as good as Tata," she seethed.

This seemed to outrage Raimondi more than anything else she had said so far. "Silence!" he hissed, advancing towards her.

"I can!"

But then Raimondi pressed his hand over her mouth. "I said *silence.*" His sharp eyes bore into hers. "Do you not think you have caused enough trouble by now?" They were nose to nose, only Raimondi's hand between them. "Do you not *realise*," he said poisonously, "that Tata is only here in this godawful place because of you?"

Ettie shook her head. She tried to speak but Raimondi clamped down harder. "Do you not understand that it is because of you— you and your bitch mother—that Tata is here at all?"

A cold numbness stole over Ettie. "Don't talk about my mother," she spat into Raimondi's palm.

"Good girls don't chase after married men," he whispered. "But your mother had to open her legs, didn't she?" He was so close Ettie could smell the onion and garlic he had eaten for lunch. "If it wasn't for that slut, Tata would still be in Paris," Raimondi went on. "But she had to get in the way, didn't she? And then *you* came along. Tata took your mother in when no one else would have her. He found a place for her when she had nowhere else to go. He gave up Paris, he gave up his studio, he gave up everything to protect her . . . and now here you are." He stepped closer, nudging her against the wall. "You think you can claw your way into the light? It is precisely because of you that Tata's light was dimmed in the first place."

He lowered his hand and ran his fingers along Ettie's lips. "You and your whore of a mother."

Ettie bit down, and tasted blood.

After Ettie's tears had dried, once she had washed the blood from her mouth and shoved her canvases back into the wardrobe, she slowly pieced together what had happened to her mother. Over the years she has cobbled together a story from whispers in the village. From Tata's rages when he was drunk. From Raimondi's cruel asides. Even old Salomé in the tobacconist could be persuaded to trade information for a good bottle of wine.

"Poor girl," Marie, the once-a-week lady, said.

"A shame." Salomé shrugged.

"Slut," said Raimondi. "She was a plague on Tata's career from the moment she showed up at his door."

From what Ettie has deduced, her mother's story is this: Gabrielle Tartuffe had been her brother's painting assistant in the days when Tata had a studio on the Left Bank. When he was working closely with Raimondi, when he was producing fifteen paintings a year. When the world lay at his feet.

Gabrielle had fled the industrial port town of their youth and joined her brother in Paris. He was older than her. He had his own studio. He had sold a painting for more than their childhood house was worth. He had friends who were poets and painters and dancers and absinthe drinkers. With Gabrielle working in her brother's studio, the two scrappy tearaways from out west had the run of the great city. There was money. There was novelty. There was life to be hungrily consumed.

But there is always a sting in the beautiful curve of the scorpion's tail.

"Your mother was a whore," Raimondi had hissed that day in Ettie's bedroom. Everything came tumbling down because of her.

All Ettie knows is that the man was rich. He was important. He was married. And he wanted nothing to do with Gabrielle or their unborn child.

Ettie's mind is assaulted with images of her mother, the faceless woman, no wedding band on her finger but a stomach swelling with every month. She imagines her desperate eyes, her work-worn hands. She imagines her mother begging Tata: "Please. Help me."

And so Tata, at the shining peak of his career, shut the doors of his studio. There was a place they could go. Somewhere he had been painting once before. A place where nobody knew them. He would take her and the moon-curve of her body away to avoid the scandal. Raimondi found a house for them—yes, they had Raimondi to thank for that. He turfed out the farmer who lived in the remotest house in the smallest village in that parched landscape, paid him in cash. Tata would be able to paint, and their self-imposed exile could begin.

But Gabrielle would pay for her transgression. She had been Tata's studio assistant and now she became his housekeeper, his cook, his cleaner, his secretary. As her belly bloomed she became his errand girl, gardener, messenger, and accountant. There was more work to do now they no longer lived in Paris. Water had to be pumped from a well, food needed to be procured from the land or the curious villagers, and each journey began with a sweltering trek up the donkey track. It was not the life she dreamed of, but what choice did Gabrielle have?

Ettie is sure people wondered why Edouard Tartuffe, golden boy of the Paris art scene, shut up his studio and retreated to the south of France. They would have speculated about the artistic reasons for the move: Had his inspiration dried up? Was there a creative rift with another artist? But for all the artistic reasons people wondered about, it was a matter of the heart that drove Tata away. He moved to protect his sister. He gave Gabrielle shelter when she was the worst thing a woman could be: an unmarried mother, a temptress, a whore.

And then, a few months later, came Ettie: a braying, bawling creature. Her mother was only just out of her teens when Ettie was born. Ettie thinks her mother loved her, but still she imagines that she would have felt robbed. Of a life, of a future, of a body. She could not have known how much attention this new creature would guzzle, how much time she would sap. Gabrielle used to be vivacious, Paris-living, adored. Now she was isolated, chain-linked to a child she had never intended to conceive, in a place where she knew no one.

What did she see when she looked down at her newborn daughter? Did she see the face of the man who had brought this upon her?

Gabrielle had no blueprint for raising a child but Ettie is sure she tried her best. She fed Ettie all the delicious things she could think of. Sang her songs from the nightclubs in Paris. Ettie has snatches of memories that slip and slither.

When Ettie was old enough to be left alone, her mother strayed farther and farther from the house. Saint-Auguste. Sainte-Victoire. Avignon. When she came back to Ettie she smelt of secrets. Lavender water (her own). Expensive cigarettes (other people's). Ettie felt the longing in her mother's brisk embraces, in her quickly dissipating footsteps. Her mother wanted nothing more than to leave the farmhouse forever. But the more she tried to flee the tighter Tata held on. Every time she mentioned Paris, or Nice, or Brittany, he shut down. *No, no, we must stay here.* He had grown accustomed to the solitude. To having everything done for him. To being the master of his own domain. As the years rolled on Tata spent more and more time shut away from the world. His every need was catered to. He was free to think of nothing but his art.

But the more he tied Gabrielle down the more she strained to escape.

And then one day a stranger came knocking. Ettie is not sure whether the man who came to the door was a traveling salesman or a carpenter or a farm labourer. Perhaps he was an art student looking for Tata. What is certain is it was not Tata who opened the door. It was her mother who came face to face with this unknown man. Perhaps she rested her body against the doorframe. Perhaps they arranged to meet in the village for a drink after nightfall. What is certain is it was this stranger who gave Gabrielle a glimpse of her old life, of the vibrant youth she had left behind.

Her ticket out was a man (it is always a man). He knew a place they could go. It was called Brooklyn and they would take a ship. But there was one catch (there is always a catch). He would take Gabrielle but not some other man's child. He would not be responsible for Ettie. Gabrielle pleaded, he refused. She begged, he compromised: "Maybe," he said (for this is a man's compromise). "Maybe, after a while, once we're settled, the child could join us. You can get a job, save up some money, and send for her. There's only enough money for the two of us right now."

If she didn't join him he would leave without her.

Ettie was seven years old. Her hair was tied in a plait with a bow, her eyes round as buttons. Her mother—the faceless woman—gave her a doll. "Her name is Mathilde," she said. "You"ll look after her, won't you? Just until I get back?"

Ettie nodded obediently. She had never been given a doll before. She took great pride in showing Mathilde around her bedroom: here was her hairbrush, here were the stones she had plucked from the river, here was the peach she was going to eat for lunch. She would share it with Mathilde. She felt a kiss on her head but did not look up. She was busy showing Mathilde the orange trees outside the window, and by the time she looked around her mother was gone.

Was that the last time she ever saw her? Does it even count, if she didn't see her go? There is a world in which her mother is still in that room. She has not yet turned from Ettie, not yet dropped her eyes from her daughter for the final time. Her fingertips still linger on Ettie's head.

Although the figure of her mother has no face—Ettie's mind has blocked it out, erased it in a cruel trick—she is there in a cloud of particles. Ettie will never know why her mother abandoned her. She will never know whether it was fear, or desire, or cowardice, or cruelty, or love.

Sometimes her mother is a monster. Sometimes she is a woman just as lonely and wretched as Ettie.

JOSEPH

One crackling afternoon while walking along the donkey track, Joseph opens a turquoise-inked letter from Harry. It brings the welcome news of an increase to his rate, and hearty encouragement for his next article. Joseph is alone, surrounded by nothing but empty fields, but he beams. Harry's letters are the scribal equivalent of a clap on the back. A jovial assurance that he is one step closer to making something of himself. To doing what he is meant to be doing. Then Joseph turns over the letter and notices a scribbled *PS* on the back.

One more thing, old boy. The Americans are in town. Scott and Ambrose etc., the Greenwich Village lot. Thought I'd send them your way. Eager to meet Tartuffe. They've been in Paris for two weeks and are bored out of their minds so I suggested they head south. They should be with you the day after tomorrow. Feed them something slap-up and for God's sake don't mention Hemingway.

"Oh no," Joseph murmurs. "Oh no, oh no, oh no."

"Ettie . . ." he gasps as he hurls himself around the kitchen door, panting from his run up the drive. "A disaster is coming."

She is sitting in the warm light of the kitchen. Curls of hair turning amber in the afternoon sun. Freckles spattered like paint over her skin. Her hands are busy in a bushel of mint leaves but she looks up as he enters, and for the first time in days their eyes meet.

Do not think about kissing her. Do not think about kissing her. Do not think about kissing her.

He hands her the piece of paper. They have not been alone together since that night by the stream. But this is no moment for averted gazes. They have an emergency on their hands.

Ettie's eyes dart quickly across the page. "You have invited people for dinner?" she says.

"*I* haven't invited anyone!"

"But people are coming?"

"Yes."

"And they are American?"

"Yes."

Ettie lets out a long, slow whistle. "What are you going to do?"

"What *can* I do?"

"You could construct a barricade around the house so they cannot physically come in."

"Ettie . . ."

Joseph crumples into a chair. This plan is so typical of Harry. Nothing could be more fun in Harry's mind than squashing people together like guests on a sofa at an overcrowded party. Shoving drinks into their hands and saying, "Talk! Get to know one another!" But nothing in the world could be less welcome for Tata. Joseph has worked so hard to worm his way into this house and now these interlopers are turning up at their door. Uninvited! In need of entertainment!

"Who are these people anyway?" Ettie asks.

"Some artist friends of Harry's from what I can tell. Painters from New York. That's where Greenwich Village is, isn't it?" Ettie shrugs.

"Do you think it's better or worse that they're artists too?"

"Worse," she says. "Tata hates competition."

"Then what am I going to do?" Panic shakes his voice like a rattle. "What if we all go on a trip, so we're not here when they come knocking?"

Ettie folds her arms. "Tata never goes anywhere."

"Do you think I have time to write to Harry? Head them off?"

She picks up the letter again. "It sounds as if they're already on their way . . . you have to tell Tata."

Joseph moans. "I think he's going to kill me."

Ettie looks over the words—Joseph's death sentence, as he thinks of them—once more. "What's a Hemingway?" she asks.

"Stumped if I know. I expect it's some chap they've fallen out with already. Oh *God*," he moans.

Against all odds, presuppositions, and expectations, Tata does not kill Joseph. When he returns to the kitchen half an hour later Ettie looks surprised to see his head still on his shoulders.

"Tata said . . . yes," Joseph announces from the door. He can barely believe it.

When Joseph had broken the news to Tata that people were coming for dinner the old man had cracked one eye open and squinted at Joseph from his recumbent position in the hammock beneath an orange tree. He had not spoken as Joseph babbled but then he held up a hand.

"How many?" he asked.

"How many people?" Joseph scanned the letter again. "It doesn't say . . . although, well . . . at least two, from what I can tell."

Tata gave a grunt.

"I don't imagine it would be more than two—" But Tata's hand was up again.

"Very well," he said, both eyes open now. He scrutinised Joseph from within the fraying cocoon of the hammock, and said, "Make it a feast."

"A . . . what?"

"A feast, damnit! Plates! Food! The whole table laid out! I want to see how people eat. What gets eaten first, what gets left. Where the greasy fingerprints land and how lips press against the glasses. I want to see how bread is torn and where teeth leave little marks in slices of cheese. I want a feast."

"Tata . . ." Joseph gulped. "Did you hear what I said? People are coming to the house. And"—he felt it best to give the old man some warning—"they are *Americans*."

"I heard you, I heard you!" roared Tata. "They can stay for dinner but no longer. Just make sure there is *food*. And wine of course, but mainly food. With colour. And texture. If you serve a soup I"ll boil your testicles and serve those instead."

"A feast?" repeats Ettie from her stunned position at the kitchen table.

"He wants to paint it," says Joseph. "That's what everything's been leading up to, isn't it? All the paintings of food. The half-eaten meals . . . he's painting a feast. Do you think . . ." *Do you think we'll be in it?* he wants to ask in a flash of vanity, but he stops himself. "Do you think we have time? We need to make a feast!"

"We?"

"We—oh—Ettie. Please . . . help me."

She slides a pencil and paper across the table. "We'll go to the market tomorrow," she says. "Write a list."

"A list, yes. Good idea. Right . . . what do artists eat for dinner?"

"Mainly, they drink. Put down two cases of red wine."

"Two?"

"And one of champagne. If you get them drunk enough it doesn't matter what the rest of the evening is like.

"Okay, but we had better feed them something." Ettie sighs. "*We* need to provide options."

"Of what to eat?"

"Of what to paint. This isn't about what would be good to eat. It's about what would look good on a canvas. So think colours, think shapes."

Joseph casts his mind back to that day at the market. "Lemons?"

Ettie rolls her eyes. "Some sort of fish, one that looks nice on a plate. Oysters, even though they're not in season. Bread, of course. A lobster if we can get one. Artichokes for their shape. Fennel. Radishes. Tomatoes in different colours. All the herbs you can think of."

Joseph turns the paper over and starts writing on the back.

"A wheel of cheese," she continues. "Roquefort, for the colour. How about some peaches?"

"Peaches, yes, good." Joseph scribbles hastily.

"A melon. One of the orange ones, Tata hates the green. A pomegranate, but let's cut it open and spill the seeds across the table." She is sitting up a little straighter now, her eyes alight. "Apricots cut in half so you can see the stones. Oranges with their skin unpeeled in a spiral. Some of the ham they slice ever so thinly at the butcher's so we can drape it like ribbons. Grapes and cherries and little silver sardines, and then I think those are most of the important elements ticked off."

She smiles, flushed with the thrill of designing Tata's great feast.

"Ettie, you're a dream," Joseph says. He could kiss her.

"Oh, and hazelnuts," she adds.

"Hazelnuts?"

"For a *tarte aux noisettes*."

Joseph hesitates before writing this on the list. "Will Tata allow you to make a brown tart?"

Ettie's face falls. "Well, if you don't think it's a good idea I won't make it."

"No, no." Joseph did not mean to offend her. He is so grateful she is helping him, so thankful they are talking again, and so he changes tack at top speed. "I think it will be wonderful."

At the market the next day, Joseph tries to look at food with an artist's eye. They do not buy the ripest tomatoes, but the ones with the most interesting colours. Radishes are chosen if their leaves are dark and frothy. Peaches only if their skin is bursting open in the heat.

"We want the feast to feel *alive*," says Ettie as they pluck textures and shapes from the shaded stalls. They buy fist-sized artichokes, purple and spiky like creatures pulled up from the sea. Bumpy lemons and waxy globes of fennel. Dusty baguettes from the baker and translucent flickers of ham from the butcher. The fishmonger loads their baskets with pewter sardines, a barrel of oysters, and a lobster whose claws have been bound with twine.

It is exuberant. Like being a child again; a return to the world of physical, tactile pleasures. They stagger home with their baskets heaving, arms straining beneath string bags filled with pink and yellow, green and purple. The sun blazes like a medal overhead. Long grass bows as they approach. The air is clear and sweet as nectar.

Finally, in the soft warmth of the evening sun they pluck oranges from the garden trees, and Joseph feels the familiar weight of the ball of light in his hand.

The following day is spent sealed in the kitchen. Joseph does not know when the uninvited guests will arrive and so they set to work early. Scrubbing. Plucking. Chopping. Scraping. They pull spines from the fish. Drop the lobster into boiling water. They steam artichokes and pick dirt from radishes and fennel. Cut peaches and apricots into moon-shaped segments.

As they work alongside each other Joseph sees that though this is Tata's painting, Ettie is the one who chooses what colours will end up on his palette. It is she who arranges rosy tomatoes between flourishes of parsley and crags of bread. She creates the painting before it becomes a painting.

Over the course of the day the kitchen fills with intertwining aromas: scorched flesh and citrus zest. The salty grime of ocean creatures. The bitter tang of herbs. And all the while Joseph is palpably aware of Ettie's closeness. He watches her hands sink into a bowl of water. Her lips smudge against the skin of an apricot as she takes a bite. Her tongue run up the back of a spoon. Occasionally she catches him watching, and in these moments her eyes linger too. Neither of them speaks, but their bodies draw closer. As the hours roll on the distance between them contracts, like the incremental pull of the tide.

But this heady proximity is tinged with dread. Every passing second is one second closer to the arrival of the unwanted guests. Who are they? How many of them will come? And what on earth will Tata do when faced with strangers in his house?

By early evening, the food is prepared. The house swept. The wine uncorked. Joseph has put the stinking Roquefort in the pantry, the oysters on ice. Now Ettie is holding court in the kitchen, making her *tarte aux noisettes*, and he has been given instructions not to come in until she has finished.

It is too hot to eat outside tonight, the warm wind whipping up a dry and itchy dust, so he sets up in the dining room instead. There are the taxidermied animals, and there is the sooty Corot landscape that makes him want to weep. But he has no time for weeping. He manages to find cutlery which vaguely matches and arranges it on the mahogany table. Wineglasses he wipes on the corner of his shirt. A water jug must be emptied of dying flowers before being placed on the table. At its head, where Tata will sit, Joseph places a selection of pencils and paper. A few paintbrushes. A pot of ink. Oh God—chalk! What if Tata wants chalk? Joseph dashes down to the studio, grabs some coloured chalks and a stick of charcoal, just in case. He lays everything within Tata's grasp: wineglass, cigar, fork, knife, napkin, pencil, sketch pad, brushes, ink, chalk, charcoal, rubber. The objects fan around the plate like a shrine.

When at last Ettie props open the kitchen door and lets him enter, she has a pink puff of pride about her cheeks. There, gleaming on the table, is the hazelnut tart.

"Ettie, you're a genius!"

"It's my mother's recipe." She beams, pulling a handwritten piece of paper from her pocket. It is stained with grease and torn around the edges. "One of the few things I have from her."

Joseph has not tasted the tart but he can smell the smoky roasted nuts, the caramel, the browned butter. It is dark and rich, shiny as a mirror, and oozes warm delight. He wants nothing more than to sit on the kitchen floor right now and eat it with Ettie, just the two of them. He would barricade the door with the kitchen table for a stolen hour with her.

But Ettie has already turned from him and is washing up the pans.

A yellow motorcar rumbles up the drive. It is glossy as an egg yolk, gleaming against the dry, pale scrub. Ettie comes to the front door to stand by Joseph. She is wringing her hands in her apron, a smudge of flour across one cheek. She squints through the glare of the late-afternoon sun.

"One, two, three, four . . ." she counts. "There are four of them?"

Joseph's heart sinks. Just visible through the dust are four bobbing heads, jolting in the open-topped car. Above the hum of the engine is the raucous babble of laughter and, unless Joseph is mistaken, the bark of a dog.

Tyres crunch to a halt. Doors are flung open and into the sunlight step four of the strangest people Joseph has ever seen. A golden-haired man emerges from the driver's seat. He is wearing an ice-blue suit and pulls cream driving gloves from his fingertips, one by one. "What a place . . ." he says as he looks around. Behind him two more men are disengaging themselves from the car. One is dressed in a saffron-yellow dressing gown. He has paired this with what look like yellow pyjamas, and his eyes are obscured by small, dark glasses. In his arms is a sleek black whippet. The third man is wearing a large, Renaissance-style blouse, a red waistcoat, a Panama hat, and—Joseph can hardly believe it—*shorts*. Like a *child*. They are a carnival of colour in this rough landscape, as out of place as tropical birds. Joseph looks down at his own sweat-stained clothes and feels a medieval peasant in comparison.

Behind the men trails a young woman. She wears ludicrous sunglasses and looks a bit like an owl.

The visitors do not raise their hands in greeting, but instead peer around the hazy landscape. These are no rumpled art students. Together they bear the unmistakable signs of health and wealth. There is an ease to their movements, a louche insouciance and something intangibly American about them, reflecting the fact that they did not recently suffer a war on their continent.

"What a place!" says the golden-haired man again. There is the crunch of dry earth under gleaming shoes as they make their way towards the house. "The name's Scott," he announces in greeting. "This is Ambrose" (saffron robe, dark glasses), "Morgan" (*shorts!*), "and Zizi" (the whippet, who wears a silk neckerchief instead of a collar). "Oh, and Peggy," Scott indicates the woman, almost as an afterthought. They shake hands with Joseph and hand their hats to Ettie.

"This is Sylvette Tartuffe," Joseph says, pulling Ettie into the sunlight, hoping the name will make the visitors pay attention.

"Not the Tartuffe we've come to see," rejoins Morgan. "Unless the great Tartuffe is a girl after all!" They laugh, and Joseph can see they are already looking over his head, hoping to catch a glimpse of the reclusive painter inside the house.

"Tata—I mean, *that* Tartuffe," stammers Joseph, "he won't be a moment." He can hear from the gurgle of pipes that Tata is in the bath, usually a long and sploshy affair. "Why don't you come through to the terrace?" he says, although the men are making their way into the house already. They have the air of being instantly at home wherever they are.

"Charming . . ." says Scott as they emerge onto the terrace. "Quaint, you know?" He speaks out of the corner of his mouth, shaping his words around a smirk. He looks rather like a cat, with narrow green eyes and small, sharp teeth. It occurs to Joseph that when he said *What a place!* he may have meant *What a hole.* Scott brushes imaginary dust from his jacket and looks for a place to drape it, eventually hanging it gingerly on the back of a chair. Morgan has seated himself already, hauling his long legs onto the table. Joseph averts his eyes from the sight of his bare knees. Ambrose has not removed his glasses, nor his robe, but settles himself into Tata's wicker chair and brings out a mother-of-pearl cigarette holder. He affixes a short black cigarette into the end and begins to smoke.

"Can I get you something to drink?" Joseph asks. He is itchy, nervous at playing the part of host in a house that is not his own. But Ettie is already coming out with a tray, balancing five gleaming glasses and a bottle of champagne.

"That'll do!" says Scott, taking the bottle from her. He aims the cork into the field and lets it rip, before handing the foaming bottle back to Ettie for her to pour into the glasses. Once she has handed them around—one for each of the visitors and one for Joseph—Morgan says, "And a saucer?"

"A saucer?"

"For Zizi." He grins. "She drinks what we drink."

Ettie says nothing but retreats into the house, returning a moment later with a shallow bowl. She lays it on the floor and Morgan empties the remaining champagne into it, which the dog falls upon with lavish familiarity.

"So," says Scott, downing half his champagne in one. "You're the great man's muse, is that right?"

Several pairs of eyes turn towards Joseph. He wishes Ettie would stay but she has already slipped into the house. "I was his model, not muse," he corrects, easing himself into a chair. "Just for one painting."

"Go on then, strike a pose!" calls Morgan, to a cackle from the others. Where Scott speaks in a languid drawl, Morgan's words are high and rapid, like a marble scuttling downstairs.

Joseph manages a weak smile, then tries to turn the conversation back around. "What brings you to France?" he asks. "Harry didn't say much in his letter."

"Ha! Old Harold Makepeace, that ass." Morgan laughs. "We met him in New York when he was trying to go down an escalator the wrong way. One of those Englishmen who have to be dragged kicking and screaming into the twentieth century."

At that moment Ettie brings out an ashtray, setting it silently in front of Ambrose just as a grey worm of ash falls from his cigarette. Joseph does not miss the slight downturn of Ambrose's sunglasses, the flick of his eyes that follow Ettie's movements as she ducks back into the house.

"Well," says Scott with a flash of that feline smile. "We're here for a little of this, a little of that." He elaborates on their travels: of how uninspiring they found Paris, how dirty Venice, how positively *dull* Switzerland at this time of year. They are here for entertainment, it is clear. They are "hunters of pleasure, gatherers of inspiration," says Morgan. They are not artists but *artistes*, as well as writers, actors, poets, and anything else they may turn their attention to. Their talents are untapped, Joseph is made to understand, just in need of the right sort of stimulation. They have dined with Picabia, the Dadaists, Man Ray. They have rampaged around Florence and breezed by Gertrude Stein's salon on the Left Bank. A visit to the great Tartuffe is but one of the many stops on their artistic pilgrimage. They are staying in the village *pension* and are off to Marseille in the morning.

"Loafers," is what Joseph's father would call them. "Wastrels of the first water." These men exude a gilded nonchalance. Scott and Morgan chatter while Ambrose smokes silently in the corner. Zizi the dog refuses the water Ettie has placed in a bowl by the door, and licks clean her saucer of champagne.

Scott tamps out cigarette after cigarette and Morgan takes some snuff from a silver box and snorts it. He passes it around the table but does not offer any to Joseph, making him feel like a child at a table of adults. He clears his throat, determined to say something that will impress them. "You know, Tartuffe's latest painting sold for—"

"I tell you what," interrupts Morgan, "this heat is something else. Calls for something a little cooler, don't you think?"

Scott smiles. "Say Joseph, do you think you could rustle up some Singapore slings?"

"Some what?"

"Singapore slings, Joseph, cocktails. It's just gin, pineapple, lime, Cointreau, Benedictine, and a dash of cherry."

"And ice!" cries Morgan.

Joseph has used all his ice on the oysters. He did not realise his guests would want cocktails, or pineapples, or a dash of cherry.

"Look, it's simple," Scott is saying. "Fresh fruit, spirits, and ice. Do you have a pineapple about you?"

"Sorry, no," Joseph says. Why is he apologising for not having a pineapple to hand? He feels brattish and resentful, forced into this situation by Harry who can't even go up an escalator the right way. No matter how much he tries to impress these people, he knows they will find him quaint and small.

Scott asks suddenly, "Is it true Tartuffe lost an eye in a fight with Cézanne?"

Joseph is caught off guard.

"Does he really drink cognac for breakfast?" counters Morgan.

"And sleep three hours a night?"

"Is it true he only paints when he's drunk?"

"That he moved down here because he had slept with all the women in Paris?"

So many voices! So much movement! Joseph is not used to this many limbs, this many words. "No," he manages to say. "No, none of that is true." His control of the situation is slipping. Someone is pacing the terrace—yes, that must be Peggy—Joseph cannot keep his eyes on all of them at once. He is anxious for Tata to arrive, but knows that he will not appear a moment before he has to. Tata will not subject himself these clamouring visitors as Joseph is being subjected now. He will not perform for anyone.

The woman named Peggy has not said a word but she is walking around, peering through the windows of the house. She has not removed her sunglasses and Joseph imagines doughy, rather piggy eyes behind them.

"Where are the paintings?" she asks abruptly.

"The paintings?"

"Masterpieces by the great Tartuffe. Surely they must be hanging about somewhere?"

"They're all in his studio," Joseph says. "The ones he's working on. It's in the stable block across the field."

"And will we be able to see them?" Her voice is clipped, not altogether friendly.

"I—I suppose so. If you'd like." Why on earth is he saying this? Why does he have such a pathetic desire to please everyone?

"I should like that very much." Peggy smiles.

The men have grown loud and boisterous. Words like *Monte Carlo, Vanderbilt,* and *Cornell* fly like darts, and Joseph has a whirling impression of lights, casinos, and noise. Ettie has placed a second bottle of champagne on the table and they have already refilled their glasses, leaving a foaming trail along the table. They have finished with Joseph and are now regaling each other with details of a night in Monaco at which, as far as he can tell, they were all present. But they roar and howl and slap the table, until a wide shadow falls across the terrace.

The men look up at this sudden eclipse. Tata is standing with his back to the setting sun, a fat cigar wedged in his mouth. He nods once, taking in the visitors. Ettie comes forward with a glass of champagne and he raises it in a toast. "*Santé.*"

"*Santé,*" the men say, sidestepping into heavily accented French. A change has come over their demeanour. They look at Tata, he above and they below, and there is a suspended moment of silence. Then Tata slaps his belly and announces he is hungry. They trail into the house, following his lead.

It is a feast worthy of the French kings of old. There are oysters fanned around slices of lemon. Artichokes splayed in individual bowls. Pomegranate seeds scattered like bloodied stars. A platter of tomatoes, neatly alternated with sickles of fennel. A lobster nestles among bushels of parsley, and sweet crescents of melon have been draped with strips of ham. Bulbous radishes loll alongside a roundel of butter, and the blue-and-cream Roquefort has already melted into the neighbouring grapes. In the centre of all of this Ettie has placed her hazelnut tart. Glossy and dark and smoky.

"Charming," declares Scott as they sit down, as if this were a mere picnic. Tata seats himself at the head of the table surrounded by the three male visitors, and the women are shunted to the other end, to the side of the room with less light and the less colourful food. Joseph hovers before placing himself in the middle of these two camps.

The men do not wait to be told to begin. They do not ask who prepared the food. They do not give thanks to Ettie, or Joseph, or God. They just eat. Saffron-cuffed hands plunge into bundles of grapes. Signet-ringed fingers scoop oyster shells. Tobacco-stained fingertips tear at artichokes and pull at fish spines. Morgan plucks a radish and throws it in the air before catching it in his mouth.

Ettie moves around the table with the wine. Joseph passes around a bread basket. He gives the oysters a wide berth this time. The guests take and grab, piling their plates with green and orange and yellow, with circles and spikes and tufts. Tata has settled himself with a pen and sketchbook on his lap, a glass of red wine to one side. He slurps down an oyster in one slippery gulp.

The room soon fills with the heat of more bodies than Joseph is used to. The air grows thick with voices and the pungent tang of food splitting apart. Lemons are squeezed, lobster joints cracked. The room becomes a blur of pluming smoke, sloshing wine, flickering candles. Laughter ricocheting up the walls, chairs tilting backwards, gold watch straps flashing. Voices rising, glasses tinkling, knives scraping.

Joseph cannot enjoy the food, so focused is he on ensuring that everyone has wine, water, bread, a clean napkin. Twice he has to rescue Ambrose's from the floor. Once he has to stamp out a glowing cigarette end on the rug.

Scott is feeding ham to Zizi, dangling it from a height. Morgan is pulling apart a peach with his fingers. "Appreciate the food, damn you!" Joseph wants to cry. He knows the labour that has gone into every dish. He knows the hours it has taken. The care in putting each colour and shape together.

Tata has turned on his charm for this evening. He observes, he sketches, but he also jokes with these raucous intruders.

They love it when he cries "Stop!" and takes one of their plates away, moving it in front of him so he can draw the half-eaten food. Ettie has to continually run to get more plates, which they find hilarious.

"What a character!" cries Scott when Tata dips a lobster claw into ink and draws with it. They think him a novelty. Joseph wants to say, "You are in the presence of the greatest painter of the age, have some respect!" but he holds his tongue. They thump their hands on the table when Tata drinks wine without removing the cigar from his mouth.

Morgan is trying to persuade Tata that he is a Dadaist at heart. "Because you, after all, you have always refused to explain your work. You do not lower yourself to say "this is what this painting means." And that is Dada! Dada is the belief that art should not—*cannot*—be explained!"

"You understand that it is a debasement!" chimes in Scott. "To explain yourself is to debase yourself!"

Joseph feels his face grow red. How can they claim that there is no point in explaining art? Why is Tata going along with this? He, Joseph, has been trying so hard to understand Tata's work, and here they are saying it is futile. Does Tata really believe them?

But no, there is a wry smile tucked inside Tata's beard. His eyes are crinkled but his expression, to one who is familiar with it, is tired and patronising. Tata is striking the pad with a stick of chalk, sketching the half-eaten feast with wild strokes. Capturing it, taking hold of it, translating it to paper.

He is using them. Joseph sees that now.

Joseph looks down the table to where poor Peggy has been shunted, expecting to see her solemnly tucking into a single radish.

But the woman is illuminated. The sunglasses have come off to reveal heavy eyebrows and bright, eager eyes. Her rather doughy features have transformed and she is talking to Ettie in rapid, fluent French about . . . what is that? Joseph busies himself with a piece of bread and tries to listen to their conversation.

"Have you ever seen a Georgia O'Keeffe?" Peggy is saying. "Of course, when I first saw her paintings I didn't even know which way *round* to hang them. But that's the point, isn't it? Isn't that *just* the point?"

"Yes!" Ettie breathes. The two women have turned from the table better to face each other, their heads close, cigarettes clasped in their hands, which move in swift circles as they talk.

"Of course," Peggy continues, "that's the first thing I do now. Whenever I buy a new painting I turn it every which way before deciding which way I like *best*. Don't you think we should do that more? Don't you think we would see so much *more* if we hung paintings upside down?"

"Yes!" exclaims Ettie in a whirl of smoke. "And you see so much more when you *feel* a painting too, with your fingers."

"Oh yes!" cries Peggy. "Texture is so important. *Tactile value.* A painting must feel alive, that's what Berenson says. Sometimes I think we should look at a painting with our *fingers* first and then our eyes. Don't you just want to run your fingers *all* over a painting when you see one?"

Ettie is about to respond, her eyes wide and earnest, when Tata booms, "More wine!" from the other end of the table. Joseph scrambles to his feet but Ettie gets there first, obediently bobbing up out of habit. She taps out her cigarette on the edge of her plate and slips from the room.

Peggy's eyes roam the walls. She alights upon the dusty Corot landscape that makes Joseph want to weep.

He tilts his head towards it. "It's a—"

"Corot," she clips. "Obviously."

"Yes, isn't it brill—"

"A bit lyrical, don't you think?"

Joseph is taken aback. Corot was one of his mother's favourite painters. "That . . . that's the forefather of naturalism, that is," he says defensively. "Without Corot there would be no Impressionism. No Cubism. No Tartuffe. No art as we know it."

Peggy shrugs. "I think he's parochial."

The room is hot and oppressive and Joseph feels small. His clothes are itchy and plain and he wants these people to leave. "Excuse me," he says.

The kitchen is a relief from the dark stuffiness of the dining room. There are fewer bodies here, less noise. Ettie is uncorking a bottle of wine, arranging a few more slices of bread in a basket. He rests his head against the cool of the wall. It is like coming up for air.

"I feel as if I've been wrung out," he says, running a hand through his hair. Every time he thinks he is rising to the conversational challenge he is pushed back again. Made to feel insignificant. *Parochial*, as Peggy would say. He is tired and longs for his bed.

"Why?" asks Ettie, and he notices that her eyes are alight. She looks not exhausted but invigorated.

"Don't you think they're sort of awful?"

"They're so . . . *much*."

"Exactly!"

"It's wonderful."

"Oh."

They look at each other. "I've never seen anyone like them before," says Ettie. "Ever. In my life. I could watch them for hours."

"But there's . . . there's nothing *to* them," says Joseph. "They're just here to drink Tata's wine, get a few stories out of him, and then leave. They don't *understand* Tata."

"And you do?"

He is quelled by this, knocked down another peg. He slides his hands into his pockets. "I'm sorry I dragged you into this, Ettie. What a night. What a mess."

Ettie walks over to him, places her hands on each of his shoulders. "It's going well," she says. Her voice is soothing. He wants nothing more than to rest his forehead against hers and make everyone else disappear. He wants to sink into her, to press his lips to hers in the cool solitude of the kitchen and let the night carry on without them. But Ettie just hands him the wine and bread, and holds open the door. Once more into the fray.

Something has changed while they were out of the room. The temperature has increased, the darkness deepened. The only light now comes from the amber glow around each candle, leaving each person's face hollow and flickering. Peggy has picked up Ettie's discarded cigarette and is dragging on it, her eyes half-closed as she surveys her companions with weary familiarity. They have become drunk, and boorish, and red in the face, but Tata is happy. He has honey stuck in his beard.

Joseph's ear is caught by their conversation. The men are engaged in what sounds like a lively debate about whether artists are entitled to sleep with their models.

"The sacred boundary!" Morgan is saying. "You must look, but never touch!"

"But how else can you truly *know* what you are painting?" counters Scott.

Even Ambrose has come alive by now, the cuff of his robe hovering dangerously close to the candles as he gesticulates. "You need an *intimate* knowledge of what you are painting," he says. "Look at Rossetti. Do you think he could have painted *Lady Lilith* if he hadn't been sleeping with her too?"

"But surely"— Tata coughs, exhaling a puff of smoke and clearing a silence into which he can eject the punch line—"all models are whores anyway?"

The four men erupt with laughter. Zizi jumps up and snatches a flicker of ham from the table. Tata thumps the arm of his chair. Amongst this commotion, there is a light tinkling from the other end of the table and Joseph glances down to see that Ettie has knocked over her wineglass. A deep red stain spreads across the tablecloth, but Ettie makes no move to clear it up. Instead she is staring at Peggy. Both women wear expressions of mangled curiosity on their faces. What has been said? What has he missed? But then Joseph's ear is snagged again by the men's conversation. Scott has turned his attention down the table and says in his sly drawl, "So what does that make you, Joseph?"

"Don't be unfair," says Morgan. "It is only women who are whores."

More laughter. More table thumping.

"Are whores something you know a lot about, Mr. Tartuffe?"

Joseph nearly chokes on his bread. Peggy has piped up from the other end of the table, eyebrows raised. Tata squints through the fug of candle and cigarette smoke as if he is only just seeing her for the first time. "I'd say I know a good deal more about whores than you do about painting, my dear."

"Quite a lot then," rebounds Peggy.

Tata is taken aback by this. He wafts away the smoke to get a better view of his opponent. "What could you possibly know about painting, my dear?"

"I am a collector."

"Oh yes, seaside sketches and picture postcards?"

Peggy bats not an eyelid and shoots back, "Not quite. It's paintings I'm interested in. That is why, in fact, I insisted we pay you a visit."

"You don't have the money, I assure you," says Tata.

"I assure you I do."

"Really, Peggy, you have to do this now?" says Scott. "We were having a conversation here."

"About *art*," says Morgan.

"About women," she insists. "And this woman wants to buy a Tartuffe painting."

"Oh push off, Peggy." Ambrose yawns. "Stop boasting."

"I'm not! I'm merely saying I came here to see some paintings with the intention of buying one."

"Nobody wants to hear it, all right, Peggy?" Scott actually slams his fist on the table.

Tata leans back, amused. "You wasted your journey, my dear."

"I'll pay any price."

"I'm not selling."

"Is that your final answer?"

"It is my only answer."

Peggy narrows her eyes. "Fine. Go back to your whores. But if you want to talk about women answer me this: Why are there so many women *in* paintings but so few doing the painting?"

There is a confused silence.

"Why . . ." Peggy takes a drag from Ettie's cigarette. "Why should women only be looked at, and never do any of the looking?"

Tata emits a bark of a laugh. "Everyone knows women are muses, not artists, my dear."

"Know? How do you *know* that?"

"Name me one woman as skilled as Delacroix!" Tata cries. "Name any woman who can paint light like Courbet. Give me the name of a woman who has painted anything of significance in this century or the last."

"But that's my point!" says Peggy. "I can't."

"Peggy, you're causing a scene," hisses Scott.

"I'm serious!" She throws her napkin at him. "Why must women lounge around in bits of gauze instead of doing any of the work?"

"Are you complaining?"

"Yes, I'm complaining! I'm trying to buy paintings but I can't find any women doing the painting. Where is the female Raphael? The female Degas? Where, I ask, is the female Tartuffe?"

"You have answered your own question," says Tata, a satisfied smirk on his face.

"It's evident," says Ambrose.

"Self-explanatory," agrees Morgan. "You said it yourself. There can be no female Tartuffe."

"If women could be as good as men then they would have done it by now," says Scott, with the air of someone declaring "Checkmate."

"They have nowhere to go," Joseph says quietly. The collective attention turns towards him like a tide. "When I was at art school there were some women, yes, but nowhere near as many as men. And the ones who were allowed to attend were only there because they had parents who were rich or liberal enough to let them go.

And once they were there it wasn't as if they were allowed to do what the rest of us did. The women had to leave the room when we did life drawing. They could paint landscapes and bowls of fruit, but no figures. No bodies, no naked limbs."

"Exactly," says Peggy. "How did you learn to draw figures, Mr. Tartuffe? You drew from the naked body. The body of a woman, a whore probably, as you say. If you are a man and you wish to learn to draw figures, you go to a life class."

"How can women hang their pictures on the wall when they aren't even allowed in the room?"

"Thank you, Joseph," says Peggy. "They have not—been—allowed—in—the—room." She punctuates each word with a tap of Ettie's cigarette on her plate. "Women have had no circle in which to exchange ideas. They have not had clubs and academies like you boys have."

"Why d'you have to do this, Peggy?" says Scott. "Always pissing on our bonfire just when things are getting good? You're so stuck in your own head you can't see the self-evident truth: women just aren't as good. Clubs and academies have nothing to do with it."

"A real artist would be able to paint without clubs or whatever you said," says Morgan. "They'd work night and day, slaving for their art if they had to. They wouldn't let anything get in their way."

"But that's exactly it!" says Peggy, her voice resounding around the room. "There are so *many* things in women's way! What time could they claim as their own? With what education would they learn? With what money or freedom could they go out into the world? You talk about women as if they can't be artists because of some inherent lack of skill but the truth is they've never been given a chance."

There is a swelling, something in the room rising and rising. The air constricting. Faces shift in and out of the candle flames. Zizi whines from the floor. Across the table, bangs, thumps, voices.

"Peggy, you're talking bunk."

"I am not!"

"You're just being provocative."

"It's ignorant, Peggy, it's ignorant!"

Voices, voices, voices. And Tata, he is laughing. He is growling. One eye is mirthful, the other angry. He is the god of light and shade and at this moment he is everything wrapped up in one. Fury. Passion. Madness. Ecstasy. He does not care about these people. Nor about this woman and her ideas. He does not care who these people are or what they're arguing about but they are in his house and they are growing loud and the evening must be his and his alone and there is only one way to end it. He pushes back his chair. Leans forward and picks up the deep brown tart in the centre of the table. He weighs it in his hand for a moment, and then he throws it in one sloppy mess against the wall. Sticky hazelnuts hit the Corot, unpeel, slide down. Shudder to the floor like rain.

The men stumble out into the night. Warm air, the flash of a bat. A distant bell sounds two in the morning.

Peggy is the last to leave and she turns at the door. Joseph thinks she is going to thank them for the evening, or perhaps apologise for her companions. But instead she looks from Joseph to Ettie and pulls a card from her purse. She hands it to Ettie. "Please give this to your uncle," she says, "if he ever changes his mind." Ettie takes the card and Joseph glances over her shoulder.

PEGGY GUGGENHEIM
Hôtel de Crillon—10 Place de la Concorde—Paris

Ettie puts the card in her pocket and closes the door.

ETTIE

Ettie ponders the card for some days. She turns it over and over in her hands before slipping it beneath the loose floor tile in her bedroom.

For the next few days Tata's studio reeks with the stench of rotting food. He has squirrelled away all the dishes from the dinner party and they slowly fester in the heat. Plump grapes turn to raisins. Ham curls into leathery scraps. Radishes pucker and apricots ooze amber juice. The studio transforms into a vast, stinking ossuary. A veil of flies descends.

Tata is ecstatic. He brings the great white canvas that has remained blank these past weeks onto his easel, and begins. His palette is a whirlpool of titanium white, asparagus green, and bright, sunflower yellow. He paints in a frenzy, gripped by a fever of inspiration. He wants to capture every stage of decay. Every skein of fur that spreads over a peach. Each bubble of teal mould that adorns the rind of a lemon. He wants to preserve the moment the way a scientist puts a pin through a butterfly.

He has even decided on the painting's name already. It will be called *The Feast*.

Ettie cleans the studio as usual, careful not to disturb the food. She looks at each dish's composition, at the placement of oyster shells and melon skins, at the way juice pools around the circumference of a plate. At the butter still smeared on the tip of a silver knife. She makes a careful note of everything. She counts the brushes Tata uses. He prefers flat ones at the moment, using broad strokes to build up the base of the painting. His palette is bold but tends towards cooler shades: indigo, violet, acid green.

"Food is the painter's greatest challenge," Tata tells Joseph over lunch one day. He has been expansive since the dinner party. Inflated by the flattering attention that he has denied himself for so long. "Not hands, as some people think. Not eyes. Food. There is more texture in food than anything else." This line goes straight into Joseph's notebook.

Ettie did not speak to Joseph after the dinner party. She wanted to reach for him, to fall into his chest with exhaustion and melt into his body. But Tata was lurking. She made sure not to make eye contact with Joseph and instead watched him carry the remains of her tart back to the kitchen, cradling the pieces as if they were shards of broken pottery.

Did Tata ruin the tart because it was something he couldn't paint? Because it was a smear of textureless brown? Or was it just because it was the nearest thing to hand, the collateral to his flailing limbs?

No. Ettie knows better by now. Tata is always selective in what he destroys. It is no coincidence that he chose to ruin the thing she had worked so hard to create.

Ettie throws down her bicycle under a tree. She brings her shirt up to her face and pads at the sweat, the breeze licking her briefly exposed stomach. She looks at the city below her, pale medieval towers hemmed in by a moss-green river.

She reaches into her satchel and brings out a peach. This hill above Avignon marks the farthest point she has ever been in her life.

She tried to run away once and once only. It was the summer she turned fourteen, when she was lonelier than she ever could have imagined. She had just reached the point where she had lived more of her life without her mother than with her. Seven years with, seven without. The tipping of the scales had alarmed her. She was on the wrong side of that divide and the gulf was only ever going to grow wider.

She had not planned her escape. She had been up all night in a frenzy of desolation, and flung herself from the house the next morning. Past the gatepost, up the donkey track, beyond the village. She did not know where she was going. She ran and she walked, following signs for the next village, then the next one, and then a town and then a city. She got as far as this hill above Avignon. She had no money. She knew nobody. And suddenly on this lonely hilltop with the vast city sprawling below her—a place bigger than she had ever seen before—she had been struck by a fierce, bewildering terror. Panic gripped her. She knew she could go no farther.

It was late when she had returned home but the front door was open. Tata was up waiting for her. His shadow slid along the wall as he rose from the armchair in which he had been sitting and stood to face her. A single candle burned.

He did not scold her. There was no storming or raging that night. He only seemed glad she had returned, and laid a wide hand on top of her head. "Go to sleep," he said. And so she had.

Ettie takes a fleshy bite of peach and nudges her foot down the hill. She makes herself take one step farther. Then another. It feels good. She has come further today than she has in twenty-seven years. She kicks off her shoes and sits down on the grass.

Her mind has been unusually tangled since the dinner party. The injection of life from outside Saint-Auguste has jolted her, shaking her thoughts from their well-worn grooves. The strange visitors brought news of people, places, and things Ettie had never heard of before. They opened her eyes one breathless word at a time. They were the sort of people she imagines her mother would have loved, had she found them in New York. Had she lived.

Ettie's life has never felt so small.

There was something Peggy said, about the female students at the Académie des Beaux-Arts in Paris. Ettie had thought she was mistaken, for there are no female students at the Académie.

"And this *protest*," Peggy was saying, "well, the women covered the buildings in banners where they had written their *slogans*, and it turned out they had made the banners from their *undergarments*—"

"But the women can't have been students," Ettie said.

Peggy cocked her head.

"Women cannot go to art school," Ettie insisted.

"Yes, they can."

"What?"

"What?"

They had looked at each other, each woman's confusion congealing into comprehension. Ettie's wineglass had slipped from her hand, spilling across the tablecloth, and she sucked on her cigarette as if it were her only source of oxygen.

"Women have been admitted to the Académie for years now," said Peggy.

It was a revelation. Tata had always told her that it was only men who were allowed to study at the prestigious art school. It was only men who could gain entry into those hallowed halls, only men who were skilled enough. And she, of course, had believed him.

Ettie had been embarrassed and silent as Peggy kept talking, and remained stunned as the evening progressed and it had become clear that, yes, women may study art if they choose. There was no fortress, no drawbridge, no battlement lined with archers. The image of the walled citadel in her mind began to crumble. Women may paint and draw, and while they may not study the nude body they can still leave the house and sit in classrooms alongside men and discuss paint and light and beauty. Even Joseph had studied with women. The thought makes her sting with envy.

Tata's lie that women could not go to art school has reverberated through her body for the past few days. There was something ominous in that lie. It was a rope tied around her ankle. A trail of snares laid in the dust. She had no way of verifying what Tata told her. There was no one she could have asked. For years, Tata was her only source of knowledge, but what reason did she have to doubt him?

She must unlearn this trick. Untie the rope from her ankle. Leap over the snares in the dust. She tries to reimagine the citadel of the Académie. The drawbridge that was open the entire time.

It was not that women were not allowed inside. It was just one woman. Ettie.

What else has her uncle lied to her about? What other traps has he laid around her to prevent her from stepping into the world? It terrifies her that she does not know what she does not know. She cannot see the ignorance that other people must sense as soon as they get near her. She thinks of Peggy's card. The address in Paris. A door has cracked open, where she did not know there was one.

She wipes the peach juice from her chin. She had not known there were women like Peggy in the world. She did not think they could exist: bold, singular, provocative. In the world of Saint-Auguste women may be housewives, cleaners, or washerwomen. Sometimes peddlers of small, useful things like tobacco and jam. They may sell fruit in the market or receive money for mending small, useful things like pillowcases and handkerchiefs. Occasionally they tend to the sick but only in the presence of a doctor who is a man. Ettie only knows one woman who got away, and her mother did not escape for long. She was delivered right back where she came from, this time in a coffin.

The days are slipping away from her. How long will she stay at the farmhouse? Will she outlive Tata or die before him, just like her mother?

"Where would you be without me?" Tata used to ask her. "What would happen to my little Ettie if I did not take care of her?" When he is in one of his harsher moods he answers this question himself. "You'd be on the street, that's where. Or with your mother, under the ground." It is important to nod obligingly in these moments, lest Tata build himself up into a fervour. "My work pays for the clothes on your back, the food on your table," he rants if not placated. "I put a roof over your head and a pillow beneath it. Where would you be without that, hmm? My art pays for everything. The least you can be is grateful."

And for a long time Ettie was grateful. She knew no other life.

But over the years a thought has wormed its way into her heart: Where would Tata be without her? She is his housekeeper and his cook. Secretary, studio hand, maid. Nurse, cleaner, washerwoman, errand girl. She cuts Tata's hair and trims his beard. She manages the household accounts. Commissions frames, sends letters, clips his nails.

Would the great Tartuffe have painted *Scallops on a Chinese Dish* if she had not gone to the market, selected each individual mollusc, prised them open, and arranged them on a platter, just so? If she had not chosen the dish, noticing how well the blue contrasted with the orange coral of the scallops? If she had not swept the studio, cleaned Tata's brushes, purchased his paints? If she had not produced food and silence when he needed it?

Where would Tata be without her?

Ettie has never been to a dentist. She does not know how a telephone works. She cannot send a telegram or put oil in a car. She has no bank account, no identity card, no knowledge of social customs or personal safety. She is ill-equipped for life beyond the village walls.

And Tata, of course, knows this.

He has ensured this.

Who would she be outside Saint-Auguste? Who would she be without Tata?

One night after she ran away there was a fumbling at her door. A hulking shape, the shadow of her uncle across the wall. He lurched towards her bed, sinking into its creaking springs, and reached a hand towards her. His whole body was shaking, and it took Ettie a moment to realise he was crying. He was drunk and sobbing at the end of her bed, his outline picked out in the moonlight.

He sniffed and made a horrible gasping sound, like a man drowning. Ettie reached out a small hand to stroke his arm. Tata shuddered, and then he lunged and put his arms around her. "Don't leave me," he whispered into her hair. "Don't ever leave me. Please. Please don't leave me." Ettie sat frozen in her bed. She was a girl, and he a broken creature. A wild animal, crying out in the night.

"Don't leave me," he whispered again. "We're safe here, you and me. We are all each other has left." Ettie let him hug her, and bent her thin arms around him like a stork embracing a bear. "I won't leave you," she whispered, her voice so faint it might have been the wind. Her promise hovered like a ghost in the room. Tata cried on, and in his pain he called her by her mother's name. "Gabrielle . . ." he cried. "Gabrielle . . ."

Ettie throws the peach stone in a wide arc down the hill. She is needed back at the house.

Tata opens one eye, his blue one. "Who did you speak to?"

"No one, Tata." Ettie clears the table without looking at him. She picks up his discarded cigar stubs, his jar of honey, his red-tinged wineglass.

"Who did you see?"

"No one."

"Where did you stop?"

"Nowhere."

A pause. "You were gone a long time."

"My bicycle chain broke."

"Three hours and twenty-seven minutes." He has closed his eyes again and is conducting the conversation with the impassive face of a carved saint.

Ettie continues her wiping.

"How long does it take to fix a bicycle chain?" She gives him no answer.

"Hmm?" He flicks an eye open. "You can't tell me? How about Joseph tells us. Joseph?" he calls, for Joseph is skulking around the end of the terrace. "Joseph, tell me how long it takes to mend a bicycle chain."

"I, uh—well, it depends on the bicycle, I suppose—"

Both Tata's eyes are open now, and he twists around to address Joseph. "Oh, it depends on the bicycle, does it? And can you tell me which bicycle has a chain that requires three hours and twenty-seven minutes to fix?"

Neither Joseph nor Ettie answers.

"Who were you talking to?" he demands.

"No one."

"Where did you go?"

"Nowhere."

He fixes her with a hard glare, then stands up, swiping the jar of honey from her hands. It smashes in a sunburst of jagged, golden pieces.

Who did you talk to? Where did you go? Why did you take so long? Who did you see? What were you doing? Why weren't you here? What are you hiding? Who were you with? Why are you lying?

Ettie has been simmering, but now she is about to explode. Today was a turning point. She has come further than she has ever come before. And she wants to go further.

She wants to run. To erupt, shimmering, into the world, to feel all its glorious textures under her fingertips. To grab it, to hold it in the palm of her hand and never let it go. She wants to taste life and bite it.

She wants to do things she is not allowed to do.

There is something she wants to feel beneath her hands, between the warmth of her fingers, against the heat of her mouth. Reverberating against her beating heart.

She wants Joseph.

JOSEPH

I burn for you.

Joseph looks at this note. It is sitting here, quite plainly, on the kitchen table, like a bomb about to explode. Did Ettie write this? It is her handwriting. Hurriedly he snatches it up. Tata was in here just now; did he see it? How could Ettie have been so careless?

"Ettie," he hisses, squeezing into the pantry where she is straining honey. He looks down at her in the cramped room and holds up the note in the dim light. "What is this?"

"A note for you."

"I can see that! But you left it on the kitchen table."

"I left it there for you to find. And you have found it."

"*Anyone* could have found it, Ettie, and by anyone I mean Tata." His heart is hurling against his ribs. Blood rampages through his ears. The note has unleashed something within him, but the electric thrill is alloyed by a sheen of fear. "Do you think Tata would allow me to stay in the house for one minute if he read? If he found out what you—what we—"

Ettie steps back from him, bumping against the shelves clinking with jars. "You think Tata could have read this?"

"It was just lying on the table!"

"Tata cannot read."

"He—what?"

"Tata cannot read."

Joseph's mouth stutters open. "But . . ."

"You never noticed?"

Joseph shakes his head. "I never . . . I didn't . . ." Images flash through his mind. He has never seen Tata write a letter. There are no books in the house. No magazines. All the shopping lists are written by Ettie. The bills, the correspondence. Tata has never read any of Joseph's articles, and on his very first day here, when Tata sat on the terrace and he handed him a telegram, Tata told him plainly: "I cannot read this."

Part of Joseph wants to laugh: How could he not have noticed? But part of him sags with a sick gulp of pity. How alienating it must be to go through the world without being able to read. To muddle along for over sixty years without being able to understand so much of life.

He looks down at Ettie. Why is she telling him this? There is something behind this strange betrayal of Tata. And—hang on a minute.

"Wait," he says. "Wait." Facts are clicking into place. He thinks again of that day on the terrace, when he introduced himself but Tata had no knowledge of his coming. When Tata did not know who he was or why he was there. "If Tata cannot read, then how did he invite me here?"

Ettie looks up at him, her eyes glinting. "He didn't."

"It was you," Joseph breathes. "You answered my letter."

He still has that piece of paper tucked in his wallet. The letter saying *Come*. It was Ettie who wrote it. Ettie who signed it with her uncle's signature.

"You never even told Tata I was coming?"

Ettie shakes her head.

"Why?"

"I knew he would say no."

"Then why did you tell me to come?"

She is very close to him. He can see the dust caught on her eyelashes. "There was something in your letter . . ." she murmurs. "Something I recognised. A longing . . ." She traces her fingertip along the cleft of his collarbone. "I wanted to know who you were."

He closes his eyes, tries to focus on her words and not the soft warmth of her finger.

"Why did you come?" she whispers, and she is so close he can feel her breath on his skin.

Joseph finds the answer on the tip of his tongue without even realising it was there. "To feel alive," he says. He had been existing in a state of numbness since his mother's death and Rupert's spectral return. It was a half-life. But then that one scribbled word had said to him: *Come.* "I came here to feel alive."

"And do you?" she whispers. Her fingertip trails along his throat. Then she reaches up onto her tiptoes and presses a soft kiss to his mouth.

Yes. In that dingy pantry surrounded by jars, in that small, dank space, pressed against Ettie, Joseph feels alive.

Each night after this kiss, this electric, sacred, clandestine kiss, Joseph lies in bed unable to sleep. There was something about this kiss. A purposefulness, as if Ettie was saying, for the first time: *This is real.* When they kissed down by the stream it had felt like a dream. Erased the next day. A footstep in the dust hastily brushed away. But this kiss was deliberate. With Ettie's hands sweeping up his shirt, his back pressing against the shelves of the pantry, their hearts a pair of steady drumbeats. This kiss was real.

Ettie, Ettie, Ettie.

It was Ettie who brought him here. Ettie who wrote the letter. Ettie who was the beginning of everything.

He cannot stop thinking about her. The curve of her back through her dress. Her finger tracing the hollow of his collar. Her breath beneath his ear. In that moment, the cupboard became the entire world.

On the third night he can bear it no longer. He feels like a man on fire.

He throws the covers off himself. It must be nearly two in the morning but he is blazingly awake. Ettie is below him in the house right now, separated only by boards and plaster. Perhaps she is awake too. He sees her as if from above, elongated on her bed, hair tousled against her pillow.

The house is dark but he feels his way out of his room, down the wooden stairs and along the flagstone corridor. He pauses outside her room. He has never been in before. He has never even knocked. His heart thunders and he waits for it to calm, for his breath to subside. He raps softly on the door.

"Ettie," he breathes, his lips touching the wood. The seconds tick by. Slowly, hardly believing he is doing it, he twists the handle. Eases the door open.

"Ettie?" he whispers into the darkness.

Nothing.

He pushes the door wider. But something is wrong. Some sense which knows when a room is empty tells him there is no one here. He steps inside. The room is still, the air thick with silence. "Ettie?" he whispers again, but he already knows that she is not here. He is about to close the door when something catches his eye. Lying on the narrow bed, illuminated by a streak of moonlight, is a scrap of paper.

Cautiously, he treads forward and picks it up. In Ettie's familiar handwriting are the words *I want you to see me.*

What does this mean? She wants him to see her, but it is deep in the middle of the night and she is not here and the house is deathly quiet.

He steps back into the corridor. It is a clue. A treasure hunt. A game.

Fear and desire swim through his body in overlapping waves. His breathing sounds so loud in the silent house. He wants to step outside, to gasp some air. And then something tugs at his memory. Another night. Another feverish desire to escape the house. A hallucinatory vision he has never been able to explain.

Something tells him where he might be able to find Ettie tonight.

The air is warm. There is no sound from the house as he shuts the front door, no lights shining in any of the windows. His only company is the crackle of insects and a warm breeze whipping up dust. He treads carefully through the long grass. A yellow moon gives just enough light to see by and he slips past the studio and the orange grove. He picks his way through a dense cluster of olive trees, the smell dark and sour. Somewhere around here is a stone building that looks like a ruin. He does not know exactly where it is for he was feverish and delirious the last time he came here. He feels his way with tentative hands and slow, uneasy steps. And then the arms of an olive tree part, and a light flickers between the leaves. A shadow looms out of the darkness. He has found it.

The outhouse has one window and he is pulled towards it, his eyes fixed on the quivering light. His heart beats faster with every step. He draws near enough to lay a hand on the crumbling wall and peer through the window where the uneven glow of a candle illuminates a scene inside.

A rough stone room. A wooden easel. Two paintings. One is the canvas Tata has just finished, *Lobster on a Silver Platter.* And the other painting is . . . *Lobster on a Silver Platter.* There are two lobsters. Two silver platters. Two slices of lemon. Two scraps of parsley.

Two identical paintings, clamped side by side.

A figure moves in the room. Ettie's back is to Joseph and she is staring at the twin canvases.

She has a paintbrush in her hand.

PART III

THE FORGER

ETTIE

The outhouse lies some distance away from the main house. It is hidden among a tangle of olive groves, beyond the neglected orange trees. Often it is shielded by sheets of dust in the wind.

Ettie takes a different route to it each night, not wanting to wear a familiar path from the house. Sometimes she skirts around the edge of the field, or sometimes she hooks down to the river and follows it upstream for a while, before looping back and treading softly through the trees. Some nights she slips along the donkey track, then steps off suddenly, creeping between the bent arms of the carobs. If the moon is bright she sticks to the shadows.

The outhouse looks like an accumulation of stones rather than a deliberate structure. Its walls are the same grey as the olive trees, so even when walking purposefully, one stumbles upon it. The door is made from wooden planks hung on rusted hinges. There is no lock but a girdle of string can be looped around a nail to stop the door from swinging open. The walls are thick and Ettie feels fortified inside, protected by two feet of stone in each direction. A wide square hole serves as the only window, open to the night.

Inside, the outhouse is a one-roomed cell. It was likely once a hay store, or where the long-displaced farmer kept his goat feed. If someone were to come across it in daylight they would not see anything of note: a dilapidated building crumbling with disuse, some hay and broken wooden pallets strewn on the floor. But Ettie has made it her home: a loose stone in one wall hides her brushes and rags. Another guards her paint tubes and a hole in the ground conceals the waxen stubs of her candles. Beneath the straw and the pallets is a sheet, and wrapped inside is a painting.

Tonight, Ettie makes her way through the olive trees. She has slipped into the studio, picked up Tata's latest canvas, and crept out again. Tata is sleeping soundly; after a bottle of red wine his mind is cushioned, his ears weak. She clutches a box of matches in her pocket.

The smell of the night is different to the day. There is a wetness to the air, a heady magic, deepening the scents of lavender and citrus. She slips the loop of string from the door of the outhouse and wraps herself inside. Finally: a space to herself. She has a stash of cigarettes hidden in a hole in the wall and she grasps for one, the opening ritual of every night.

After a few steadying breaths she clamps the cigarette between her lips and pulls loose the constellation of stones which reveals her brushes, her paints, her candles. She unwraps her painting from its sheet, pulls an old easel from the straw. The best way to simulate light, she has found, is one candle in each corner of the room to give evenness to the illumination, and another in her hand which she can raise and retract to bring more light or less. She wishes she could work in the daylight but knows she cannot. She must stick to these nighttime hours, which are hers and hers alone.

Sometimes animals join her, drawn by the candlelight. Albino lizards trickle along the walls. Moths dart into the candle flames, burning themselves out in a soft hiss. Mice burrow in dark corners and sometimes a bird will arrange itself on the windowsill, watch her for a time, then fly off into the night.

Ettie places the two paintings side by side on the easel: Tata's and hers. She squeezes a wrinkle of paint onto her palette. Twirls a brush between her fingers.

There is something addictive about conducting her life in the shadows. When nobody is looking she can do as she pleases, living in the freedom that comes when other people's eyes are turned away. She likes the night because it is so quiet. There are no sounds to interrupt her thoughts. Only the gentle rustle of leaves. She is wrapped in the silence of the darkness and loses herself in the gentle *tsh tsh tsh* of her brush.

And then, perhaps something is there or perhaps it is not, but her ears prick. There is a small crack, like a twig giving way underfoot. There is the warm rush of the wind and there, underneath, there is a sound like footsteps.

JOSEPH

In that moment, with his heart clamouring in his chest and blood rushing in his veins, with the wind blowing a warm dust onto his skin and the cry of an owl trembling across the night, Joseph realises that he has not been looking properly. He has been so focused on Tata when he should have been looking at Ettie.

Ettie who slips beneath the shadows. Ettie who watches and waits. In that moment with his hand on the wall, which is both an instant and an eternity, Joseph realises that he has been looking at the wrong person all along.

His feet stumble forward. His hand gropes for the wooden door of the outhouse and he pushes it open. The sliver of light widens. A scene comes into view: a bare stone room. An easel. A palette gleaming with paint. A cigarette smouldering on the floor. And there is Ettie, a paintbrush in her hand.

The woman he kissed turns to him. She has paint on her fingers. An apron lashed around her waist. On the easel in front of her are two lobsters, two platters, two wedges of lemon.

Two identical paintings.

"Ettie," he breathes. His voice is low, his hand on the wall to hold himself up. His head swims with the heat and the shock and the impossibility of what is before him. "What are you doing?" he whispers.

Ettie considers the easel for a moment. "Painting."

"But . . . what is this?"

"*Lobster on a Silver Platter*," she says in her calm, untroubled voice. "I painted one of them. Tata painted the other."

Joseph releases himself from the wall and takes a step forward. The two paintings are eerie. It is like looking into the faces of a pair of twins and trying to find where the difference lies. The 206 lobster's shell shines equally bright in both. The lemons are identically juicy. Even the reflections in the platter shimmer in perfect harmony. Ettie's painting is a perfect copy of Tata's.

An image flashes into his mind: *Young Man with Orange*. Another sweltering night. Ettie, here in the outhouse, standing in front of that painting before setting it on fire. And then the next morning, the same painting resting whole and unburned in the studio.

But . . . what if it was not the same painting? What if there were two paintings? Two young men. Two oranges. What if there were always two paintings? One by Tata and one by . . .

"Ettie," he says again.

"Do you see me now?" she whispers.

He nods. He sees her.

But he still cannot make sense of the scene in front of him. "What are you *doing*?" he asks. What is this strange, haunting mimicry?

"Sit down," Ettie says, and she pushes him gently onto the deep stone windowsill.

He sits.

Ettie paces back and forth a couple of times, then looks up. "I am copying Tata's work," she says. "Making a forgery."

The word "forgery" falls like a stone into the pit of Joseph's stomach. Like a criminal? His mind fills with images of shady men in underground workshops, black market alleys stuffed with stolen art and counterfeit goods. It does not fit with the calm woman standing before him. The woman who pressed herself to him in the pantry. The woman he kissed by the stream.

"What do you mean?" he manages to say. "And . . . why? Why are you doing this?"

Ettie contemplates the paintings for a moment. "To prove . . . To prove that I am as good as Tata."

Joseph exhales, leans his elbows on his knees. He had learned about forgeries in art school. He had even learned a little about forgers themselves: usually they were painters who had technical skill but whose work had been dismissed. Their forgeries were a way of mocking the art world: in one fell swoop they could prove their artistic talent and undermine the experts who had rejected them. The question of the art forger was: *If you will not accept me for who I am, then how about when I am somebody else?*

"This is all I can do," Ettie whispers, her voice thin. "It is all there is room for me to do in the world."

Joseph has heard stories about false Caravaggios. Fake Turners and Da Vincis. He has read about the forgeries discovered in museums and hanging on businessmen's walls. The world of forgery is covered in a slithery sheen of deceit; a whirlpool of lies and cunning and secrecy. All this swirls in Joseph's mind as he takes in the woman in front of him.

He shakes his head, blinks, but the two paintings are still there. This is not a hallucination. The original and the forgery sit side by side. "Which painting is the real one?" he asks.

"They are both real."

"But which one did Tata paint?"

"Can't you tell?" Joseph hears the sly curl in her voice. He has been studying Tata all this time, can he really not pick a genuine Tartuffe from a forgery?

He stands up and steps closer to the easel. Even in the flickering candlelight he can see that the two canvases are identical. They have the same freshness, the same spontaneity of line, as if the double—whichever one it is—was painted organically and not copied mark by mark. He could stare at them for years and never be able to say for certain which one is Tata's. Even the signature is identical. He lets out a laugh. Of course it is: Ettie has been copying Tata's signature for years. She has been signing off letters and contracts and cheques as if they were her own.

He straightens up and shakes his head. "I can't . . . I can't tell."

Ettie dips her paintbrush into a daub of white. She bends to the canvas nearest her and adds a tinge of reflected light to the lobster's spine.

There. There is her forgery.

"You told me you didn't know how to paint," Joseph says feebly. It is a small detail but he clutches on to it.

"I told you Tata never *taught* me how to paint," says Ettie. "That's not the same thing."

"Then how did you learn?"

"By watching. By following. I have spent my life observing. It turns out it was the perfect training."

"You're good," he says.

"I know. I couldn't get away with it if I wasn't."

He wants to laugh again. It is ridiculous how good she is. He pushes his glasses up his nose and bends closer to the paintings. She has mimicked every brushstroke. Every swirl of colour. He knows how difficult it is to copy another artist—his own attempts to replicate Tata's sketches have humbled him in that respect—but Ettie's painting has lost none of the original's vividness. It is alive.

"But why?" he asks. "Why are you doing this?" He still does not understand.

"Sit down," she says again, and Joseph resumes his position on the windowsill. Ettie reaches into her pocket and fishes out a cigarette.

"It started as an experiment . . ." she says slowly. She takes a deep inhale. "An experiment to see how good I was. Tata always forbade me from painting. He said there could only be one artist in this house and it had to be him. He spent my childhood pulling pencils out of my hand, ripping up my drawings. Making sure I could not compete with him.

"But I *needed* to paint. It is in me. *Here.*" She clamps a hand to her breast. "I used to paint in secret, at night or when he wasn't looking. It was all I wanted to do. I showed my paintings to Raimondi once . . ." A shadow twitches across her face. "He laughed at me. He told me I had no talent, no place in the world.

"But what if they were wrong?" she says with a crack in her voice. "What if I did have talent? I needed to know. To prove it somehow . . . So I took one of Tata's paintings. Just a small one, a picture of a lemon, and I tried to copy it. I wanted to see if I could get my forgery past Raimondi. I made a copy of Tata's painting and swapped it and . . . it worked. Raimondi didn't bat an eyelid. He took my lemon away and two weeks later a cheque arrived in the post. He had sold the painting, thinking it was by Tata, and someone else had bought it, thinking it was by Tata. That was it. I knew I could do it."

She stamps out her cigarette and immediately lights another one. Her hands are perfectly steady. "I wanted to try it again," she says. "To see how much I could get past them. I always let Raimondi see what Tata was working on. Let him view the works in progress. And as for Tata . . . Once he has finished a painting he cannot look at it anymore, so that was when I swapped them. I painted in secret. In my room at first and then down here. Always at night. Always alone. Tata is blind to the world beyond himself, and I used that to my advantage."

Joseph rakes a hand through his hair. It is as if a blindfold has been whipped off his eyes and the world is suddenly brighter and stranger than he thought. The paintings loom out of the darkness.

"How long have you been doing this?" he asks.

"Three years. I started copying Tata's paintings during the war and then I . . . I didn't stop." For the first time she drops her gaze and stares into the shadowy corner.

"How many have you copied?" he asks.

"Twelve paintings, two studies in charcoal. Nine pencil sketches. And now this." She indicates *Lobster on a Silver Platter*. "Every one of Tata's works that have made their way into the world in the past three years."

The cherries on the white tablecloth. The plate of anchovies Raimondi collected a few weeks ago. *Empty Room* in the Royal Academy. *Young Man with Orange* . . .

"It was you? All of that was you?"

"I found I enjoyed the trickery," Ettie says quietly. "There is a power in secrets. In knowing more than other people. As long as I covered my tracks, no one had any need to suspect anything."

"Cover your tracks?" Joseph asks.

"I had to destroy Tata's originals," she says bluntly. "If they were lying around someone would know there were two paintings."

Joseph feels an odd pang of sorrow for Tata. He is being deceived and he does not know it. "I still don't understand . . . why?" he says. "You copy Tata's work and destroy his canvases. You're good—you're astonishing—but then you give your work to Raimondi and pretend it's by Tata. Why? Don't you want some acknowledgment? Some recognition of your own?"

"Getting the paintings into the world is all the recognition I need," Ettie says. "I do this for myself. Every new painting is a test to see if I am good enough . . . To see if I am as good as him." She turns back to the lobsters on their silver platters. "To see if I am Tata's equal."

"But don't you want more than that?" presses Joseph.

Ettie takes out another cigarette, lights it. "I've thought a lot about why I do it," she says, forming each word carefully. "In part it is to confirm my suspicion that I am good enough, but there's another part of it . . . Part of me wants to hurt Tata. To fool Raimondi. I want to exact some glimmer of revenge on them. To sting them, without them knowing I am doing it." She takes a drag of her cigarette. "I feel . . . complicated towards Tata. I love him and I hate him, but mostly I feel such anger that he refuses to see me for who I am. I'm an artist. I know I am. But he will never allow me to be one. So this is my rebellion. My secret, private revenge."

Joseph can feel the fire that burns beneath her cool exterior. The anger that has been there all along, simmering beneath the surface.

"But," he says tentatively, "if you are this good, why don't you paint for yourself? Make your own art?"

At this, something inside her seems to break. "You think I haven't tried?" she whispers, her voice hoarse. "Of course I've tried. I showed my paintings to Tata as a girl and he destroyed them. I gave what I created to Raimondi and he laughed at me. I could spend years working on one painting but it would never be considered half as great as one sketch by the great Tartuffe. If I sold this painting"—she indicates the lobster—"under my own name, it would not be worth a tenth of what Tata gets. Even though it is the same painting, it is worth less if people think I painted it. I had so much more success pretending to be Tata and so that is what I did. It is the only way for me to get my art into the world." She stamps out her cigarette. "Being honest got me nowhere."

"But you have so much *skill*," insists Joseph. "You are just as good as Tata and you could use your talent to get out of here. Make a life for yourself."

"I can't," she says, and there is a sharp finality to her words. "I used to be able to paint my own work but lately I've tried and I can't. Not anymore. This . . . this is all I can do."

They stare at the identical paintings in silence together.

"Why do people care who painted this?" she says. "When they buy Tata's work, are they buying a piece of art or a piece of Tata? Why don't they want this if I painted it? What is it about my hands that renders the brushstrokes less valuable? What is it about my mind that is less interesting than Tata's? What is it about me that makes this painting less important?"

Joseph reaches a hand towards her. He is dazed by her skill, her patience, her daring. By the fragile life she has carved out for herself, which could collapse at any moment. "I can't believe you got away with it," he says. "I can't believe no one noticed."

"Most people only ever see what they want to see," Ettie says. "If Raimondi watches Tata working on a painting and then collects that same painting a few weeks later, what could be amiss? If Tata paints a picture and sees Raimondi carry it off, why would he suspect anything? I relied on other people filling in the gaps with their own assumptions. No one ever looks properly," she says. "Even you."

Joseph is stung by this; a bolt of pain like stepping on an iron nail. He was here and he never saw what was in front of him. He has been as blind to Ettie as everyone else.

Or has he?

"I did see something, though," he says. "I came here before. I saw you, here in the outhouse with *Young Man with Orange*. I saw you set it on fire. You told me I hallucinated. You told me I was drunk, or mad."

"Yes," Ettie says slowly. "Yes. I didn't know if I could trust you then . . . I didn't know if I wanted you to know . . . who I was."

"But now you do." He runs a finger along her arm. It is crusted with paint.

How strange to think that she has painted a portrait of him, though he did not know it. She came here night after night and studied his painted face in the darkness. Re-created it stroke by stroke. It is an intimate thing to do. A bubbling thrill rises up in his body, but then he remembers what else she did to his face, and the sensation bursts.

"I can't believe you burned a painting of me."

Ettie laughs. "That's the thing about making forgeries. If the original still exists then it's easy to prove the copy is a copy. So you have to destroy the original. And now I must destroy this one."

"No!" Joseph says instinctively. The lobster on the easel is a valuable work of art. An original Tartuffe!

Ettie raises an eyebrow. "Tell you what," she says. "Let's play a game." She slides both canvases from the easel. "Close your eyes."

Uneasily, Joseph does as she commands. There is a shuffling sound, a soft rustle, and then silence.

"Open your eyes."

The paintings are back on the easel. Perhaps Ettie has swapped them, perhaps she hasn't.

"Tell me which one I painted and I'll burn it," she says.

"What?"

"I am going to destroy one of these. Tell me which one."

Joseph looks from one painting to the other. She is asking him to prove his skill and disprove hers. "Ettie, I can't—"

She reaches into her pocket and brings out a box of matches. "Tell me which one."

He does not know. The paintings are identical. He cannot tell which gleam on the lobster's tail was painted by Ettie just now and which by Tata this afternoon. The lines, the colours, the impasto are all similarly alive. The paintings are each other's equals.

Ettie strikes a match. "Quickly," she hisses. He has never felt her shine so brightly. Here in the candlelit darkness, with a pinch of fire between her fingers, she is the most vivid person he has ever seen.

The flame is almost at her fingertips. "Hurry!" "I don't—I can't—that one!" he chooses wildly.

Ettie tosses the painting on the ground. She holds the match aloft, high in the air, and drops it. The painting catches instantly.

When *Lobster on a Silver Platter* has been reduced to nothing more than a pile of blackened soot, when the embers have cooled and been swept into the night by the wind, they head back to Tata's studio where Ettie places the surviving painting on the table. She checks the signature. Casts a last glance around the room. Then they slip silently back up to the house as a pearly dawn seeps across the sky.

They pause by the front door. Neither of them makes a move to go in.

"I could tell people . . ." Joseph says. "I could ruin all of this for you." It is not a threat, just a fact. "Why did you show me?"

Ettie looks up at him, her freckled face pale in the early morning light. "I want you to see me," she says. "All of me." And then she kisses him. It is warm, this kiss. Scented with ash and blue-black lavender. And it is a kiss that winds an invisible rope around them. Binding them together.

The next morning has a tense, straitjacketed feel. Joseph cannot get the image of the flickering, twitching painting out of his mind.

Raimondi will be arriving in the afternoon to take *Lobster on a Silver Platter* up to Paris. Joseph cannot bear the thought of being there. Of witnessing the moment when the painting is placed in his hands, taken away. He needs to get out of the house. To escape the heat, the claustrophobic walls. The lies that seem to suffuse the very air.

He ducks out the side door, taking off across the field and heading for the patch of sunflowers Tata likes to paint. But as he crests the hill, his breath catches in his throat. The sunflowers are gone. The summer has turned: the once-golden flowers have withered, their saffron petals shriveling to black in the heat. All that remains is a stretch of darkness. It is an eerie sight, as if the world has been poisoned.

Joseph slumps down by the edge of the blackened field. He looks back at the small square of the farmhouse.

Finally, he knows the truth. The truth about the paintings. The truth about that night in the outhouse when he thought he was going mad. The truth about Ettie. And all these truths are wrapped in a tight, suffocating lie.

What is he to do? With a twinge he knows it would be the scoop of his career to reveal that Ettie is the artist behind Tata's work. It would shoot his reputation into the stratosphere if he revealed this scandal, sending shock waves through the art world. He has been searching for a secret to crack all this time and this is it. But the next moment he feels sick for even thinking of this. A salacious article would not be worth the betrayal of Ettie's deepest secret.

He rolls his head into his hands. There is a strange thorniness to all this. Why is he writing about Tata when Ettie is the artist behind the paintings? He had thought he was here in pursuit of truth, but now he has discovered the truth he must conceal it.

He is astonished that dealers and buyers and critics could be fooled so easily. But then again, so was he.

I was here and I never saw what was in front of me.

It is as Ettie said: people only see what they want to see.

A sour unease writhes in his stomach. There are so many ways Ettie could get caught. Tata could find her. Raimondi could sniff her out. What would happen if Harry got wind of this? He would want to know everything. The how and the why. He would demand an article enumerating Ettie's crimes.

And then what? Would the police come for Ettie? Would they arrest her? Would they charge her with forgery, or theft, or arson, or some hideous cocktail of all three? The people who bought

Tata's paintings would take them down from their walls, reexamine them. They would demand their money back, saying, "This is not what we paid for."

What is it they paid for? Joseph thinks with a wry smile. The art? Or the name? It is as Ettie said when she showed him *Young Man with Orange*: *See the brushstrokes, not the hand behind them.* And now she is asking him again: *What difference does it make whose hand held the brush?*

He wrenches his head out of his hands. He must keep Ettie's secret. Seal shut his lips. Somehow work his way through the labyrinth of lies.

When they were walking up to the house last night Joseph asked Ettie, "How does this end?"

A chill had crept over Joseph at the thought of what Tata would do if he discovered that Ettie had been forging his paintings. Would he hurt her? In a wild flash he had wondered if Tata might kill her. "You have to get out of here," he whispered.

"I've tried," Ettie said. "But the world doesn't want me. Every time I try I get pushed back."

"Try again," he had said.

But Ettie did not reply.

By the time he returns to the house in the early evening, Raimondi and *Lobster on a Silver Platter* have gone. A set of tyre tracks curves away through the dust.

The sun is low in the sky and the light feels heavy. Joseph has survived the day but this secret drags behind him like a ball and chain. He wishes he had someone to confide in. He wants to write to Flora but anxiety twists his limbs into inaction. What if the letter is intercepted? What if someone in the outside world discovers Ettie's secret because of him?

He is not made for lies.

Why isn't Ettie as frozen with fear as he is? How can she be so calm in the face of this terrible, brilliant deception?

Back in his room he looks at his latest article resting in the tray of his typewriter. He has an urge to rip it into shreds; he reaches out for it, pulls it between his fingers. But then he stops himself. Breathes. He must be careful. Ettie cannot be caught because of him. He must pretend everything is as it should be.

With trembling hands he folds his article into an envelope, seals it shut, and addresses it to Harry.

ETTIE

Up with the first stirrings of dawn. Wash and dress, then down to the well in the corner of the field to haul water up for the day. Light the coals in the kitchen range, fill the small pot with coffee grounds. Collect eggs from the hens. Boil eggs, make coffee. Nibble the ends of yesterday's baguette.

Down to the studio, coffeepot in one hand, china cup in the other, boiled egg in apron pocket. Pluck an orange from the tree, peel it and set it beside the coffee and boiled egg—to the right of the paints, away from the table's edge. Line up palette and brushes. Make sure jars of turpentine and oil are full. Honey too. Sweep crumbs, leaves, dust from the studio floor. Throw wide the windows. Shoo away the beetles and flies.

Back up to the house. Clear the terrace of last night's dregs: wine bottles, glasses, an oyster shell filled with cigar ash. Ears alert for Tata. Listen to him shuffle around his room, tracing the steady route from bed to window to wardrobe to door. Soft slouch across the hallway. Crunch and slam of the front door.

A second pot of coffee, a cup for Joseph. Listen to the creak of beams as he wakes.

Pedal the old bicycle to the village to collect bread, peaches, letters. Read the letters in the shadow of an alley before returning them to their envelopes. Decide which ones to read to Tata and which to quietly throw away. Cycle home.

Glance through the open window of the studio to check on Tata's progress, then up to the house. Clean brushes, strain oil, boil water to wash rags. Drown out the noise, don't let the thoughts intrude. Slice tomatoes and fennel for lunch. Scatter peach halves with crumbly cheese and a drizzle of honey. Pluck basil from the garden. Clean the kitchen before Tata finishes painting for the morning. Lay out Tata's cigars, but keep them out of the sun. Place two wineglasses on the table, one bottle of red wine. Another on the sideboard, cork loosened but not removed. Napkins, cutlery, plates. Listen for the front door, then put food on the table as Tata sits down. Pour wine. Make small, agreeable comments throughout lunch. Do not be baited. Do not crack.

Clear the plates, pick up Tata's napkin from the ground. Bring cigars, a jar of honey, letters. Read aloud the letters, make a note of any responses. Throw the rest in the stove.

Afternoon tasks: clean up after lunch. Trim Tata's beard, clip his nails. Pump more water from the well. Tread quietly while Tata sleeps.

Go down to the studio, retrieve coffeepot and cup. Scoop egg-shells and orange peel into apron pocket. Study the painting in the light. Note the colours on the palette. Stand close, stand far away. Work out what is new, where the painting is going. Check how much of everything is left: the level of turpentine, the roundness of the paint tubes. Clean the brushes Tata has used and quickly, quietly, take them to the outhouse. Hide them in the wall. Tread softly through the olive groves. Back up to the house.

Choose shapes and colours for dinner: silver sardines, frilly lettuce, pink radishes. Soft ovals of bread. A medallion of butter. Uncork a bottle of wine. Endure the meal, sit on hands, chew nails, twist legs around each other, just get through it. Refill cigar box. Wash plates, cutlery, glasses. Chivvy the hens into their hutch. Close up the house for the night. Wait for the sounds of footsteps to retreat, for doors to shut, for a heavy silence to fall.

Wait until sleep descends on the house.

And now . . . now Ettie's day begins.

She slips through the kitchen door. Its hinges are well-oiled, swinging silently into the night. She moves like a spirit through the field, disappears into Tata's studio, emerges with a painting under her arm. If anyone were to see her she would look like a thief but she knows there is no one to spy her. She feels no eyes upon her in the velvet night.

Closing the door of the outhouse she seals herself away. Strikes a match, lights candles and, finally, a cigarette. The world slows. Her head clears.

How dull her days are. How pointless! *This is no life at all*, she thinks as she pulls out brushes and paint. She blows cigarette smoke through her nostrils as she clamps the canvas to her easel. It is a little study of apple cores. She brings out her own version, and slots it next to Tata's.

These small canvases are easy, but not as satisfying. She eyes the hay-strewn pallet in the corner, itches to get back to *The Feast*, but she must wait. Raimondi will want the apple cores first. Tata is not quite finished but she knows him well enough to read the signs. The last strokes are not far off. The final touch is always his signature in the corner: *E. Tartuffe.*

His signature. Her signature. They are the same. Even the *E* could stand for Ettie or Edouard.

Today Tata has added a set of teeth marks to the apple cores. He has painted over one of the stalks. She looks from one canvas to the other. She has to paint exactly as he does, she cannot skip to the end result. If Tata paints a patch of red and then covers it with green, she does the same. If he builds up layers of grey before turning it to white, she does this too. It is all part of the painting.

She steps back and lights another cigarette. Her greatest opponent is the sun. She rages against the coming of the light the way Tata rages against its waning. It is here in the darkness that she comes alive, living for the silent hours when everyone else is asleep.

Well, almost everyone. The sound of Joseph's footsteps has replayed in her head throughout the day. The sight of him silhouetted in the doorway. His presence in her secret, sacred space.

She would not have let Joseph in if she did not believe she could trust him. Part of her is relieved that he finally knows what she is doing. But there is also a dull part of her that twinges with unease. This deception is part of a private battle between her and Tata. Joseph's presence has muddied the waters.

Her insides twist around themselves. She blows the hair from her eyes and grips the paintbrush tighter. Concentrate. She cannot let her emotions distract her tonight.

Steal, steal, steal. Steal these thin hours to eke out a life. Snatch a handful of time from the gathering night. Create a world within the darkness.

JOSEPH

Splendid, splendid work on the latest article, my boy. It simply sings! More of this, please. Dig deeper. People are interested, Joseph. The world awaits Mr. Tartuffe's great feast.

I enclose something which you may find helpful. Make sure you put it to good use!

Harry

Joseph sits on his bed and unwraps the parcel that accompanied this note. Nestled in a box of shredded newspaper is something small, black, and shiny . . .

Harry has sent him a camera.

Joseph extracts it with the care of an archaeologist, holding it in the very tips of his fingers. This is surely a sign of Harry's confidence in him. An investment in his career. An indication of Harry's faith that he is uncovering something meaningful down here. Joseph had once used his professor's pocket camera at the Slade, and though he has tried to repress all memories of that place, he knows how to use this. He roots around in Harry's box for a roll of film, inserts it into the back, clacks the camera shut. His fingers remember what to do.

But as he turns the camera over, a rush of unease comes over him. Why does he feel guilty about unwrapping this gift? Harry wants him to capture the reality of life at the farmhouse, but he does not know that Joseph is trapped in a web of lies. He is aware of the power of the small object in his hands. He must be careful what he does with it. Once the camera's shutter is pressed, the truth is captured.

He treads downstairs and finds Ettie on the terrace. She eyes the camera with a cool curiosity. "What's that?"

"A gift from my editor."

"What are you going to do with it?" A hint of suspicion in her voice.

"Harry wants me to take photographs for my articles," says Joseph. "To show people what Tata is working on."

Ettie says nothing.

"I could take your photograph, if you like?" he offers. "Not for my article, just . . . for you."

She looks at him warily. Then she straightens up, plants her arms by her sides, and stands squarely in front of him. "All right."

Joseph raises the camera tentatively. "Aren't you going to pose?"

"No. Posing is your job." She flashes him a quick smile.

He wishes he had taken the photograph then, with Ettie's mischief clear on her face, but he wasn't fast enough. The next moment she is staring at him with her usual frankness. She meets the lens straight on, her expression determined.

He holds the camera to his stomach and takes a few steps backwards. Looks down through the viewfinder, shifts Ettie into focus, and when he can see her crisply he presses the shutter. There is a hollow click, and he has captured her. With just the nudge of a finger he has preserved this moment in time: Ettie, sunlight falling across her face, the house in shadow behind.

Tata refuses to be photographed, of course. Joseph knows well enough Tata's views on photography (an insult to fine art, nothing more than shabby mimicry, the refuge of cheats and hacks), so

Joseph takes solace in the farmhouse, in the studio, and the great expanse of landscape that has inspired Tata for so many years.

Over the next few days he finds himself arranging compositions in everything he sees. He notices barrels of sunlight shooting through the studio windows. Trails of ants crawling along the plates. The curl of hair at the nape of Ettie's neck. The camera gives him something to focus on instead of the tangled knot of his thoughts.

He wanders the village, snapping photographs of the cobbled streets, the barefoot children, the old men playing chess in the square. Word spreads that "Monsieur Adelaide from the strange house is taking photographs," and soon everybody wants a turn: "a photograph of my mother, please," "my wife," "my donkey," until Joseph is forced to lie and pretend he has run out of film. Harry has been generous, but still he must be selective in what he documents.

On his way home he stops outside Tata's studio. The door is ajar and the great man is standing with his back to the world. He is working on the huge canvas of *The Feast*. There is the long table spread with plates. There is the cutlery and the glasses. The mounds of radishes, artichoke petals, lemons. The painting is a riot of colour. A molten collage of sweetness and sharpness and heat. But there are no people. No guests are here to eat this feast. The chairs are empty. The food lies waiting. Rotting. Going to waste.

Tata adds a gleam of oil to the bulb of an artichoke, then stands back and dips his finger absentmindedly into a jar of honey. He looks alone and old and vulnerable, hunched over his work. His canvas is full of colour but empty of life. The index finger swirls through the honey, as if Tata is trying to assimilate a sweetness he knows he does not have.

Joseph angles the camera. Focuses the dial. Clicks the shutter.

ETTIE

Ettie takes the brush Tata has been using all day. It helps to use the same brush. She has studied his palette and re-created the colours he has been working with: marshy green, a tinge of sunrise orange, a cloud of winter blue.

The Feast is bigger than any painting she has ever copied before. When Tata is working on smaller canvases she can bring them into the outhouse and paint her forgery side by side. But with this latest painting, the big uneaten feast, the canvas is too large to be moved from the studio and so she must work from memory alone.

This painting, she knows, will be different.

Just as *The Feast* will be Tata's masterwork, so it will be hers.

She always tries to reenact his method of working. Her canvas is the exact dimensions of his. It always is: she orders them both. When Tata cast the first lines onto his painting she waited until day tipped into night before doing the same. Two great feasts grow in tandem, line by line, smudge of colour by smudge of colour.

She estimates Tata is halfway through *The Feast* by now. His canvas shows a long table covered with a white tablecloth. It is viewed from an angle, so the rectangle stretches away from the viewer, giving it perspective and distance. The table is laid for twelve. A few brown lines indicate chairs around the edge, but nobody sits in them. Nobody will eat this great rotting feast. Tata has painted a plate of fish bones, a bowl of lemon slices, three globe artichokes, a dish of oyster shells, a bowl of radishes and butter and, most recently, three crescent moons of melon on a porcelain plate. It is these lunar orange curves that Ettie will replicate tonight.

She has taken the plate of melon from the studio and balanced it on a crate behind her easel, the exact distance and angle of Tata's table from his. She has prepared her colours from the same tubes of paint. She has silence. She has everything she needs.

She takes a steadying lungful from her cigarette, then flicks it to the ground. It is time to begin.

She does not find it helpful to practise. Too much repetition makes her overanalyse her movements. What she needs to do is feel, and the feeling must be fresh. She holds the image of Tata's painting in her mind, lets it sink through her body, down her arm, into her hand. She holds it. The brush hovers a few inches from the canvas. She will not connect them until her hand knows what to do. She must wait but never hesitate. Be controlled but spontaneous. It is like entering into a trance. It is like a prayer.

Her breathing slows. The brush tip kisses the canvas. The pliant squish of oil sweeps in a smooth flick, and a green edge of melon rind emerges. Ettie adds orange flesh, pale seeds. Petals of colour like blossom. This is the order she thinks Tata painted in. She has inspected his canvas closely. She takes a small, dry brush and begins to blend. Not too much, for Tata's strokes are loose. The colours melt into one another the way day melts into night. Imperceptibly, inevitably. She mixes her colours straight onto the canvas, just like Tata. Everything Tata does, she does too.

Something prickles at her back. An irregular sound beats beneath the soft shush of leaves. She stills her hand and senses, rather than hears, that something heavy is coming towards her.

A long, dry peal creaks through the night. The door opens.

"Joseph!" Ettie hisses. He is alone, thank goodness, and stands tall in the shabby doorway. He looks uncertain, his shirt open to the middle, the material sticking to his chest. "Will you leave the door open for me?" he asks. "At night, when you come here. Will you let me watch?"

Ettie looks at him apprehensively. "Watch," she says. "But don't try to stop me."

Joseph nods. He takes a step farther into the outhouse. "I just want to see how you do it." He bends to look at the canvas in the flickering light. "You're working from memory?"

"There's no room for the other painting in here."

Joseph seats himself in the wide square window where he sat before. "Carry on," he says. "I promise I won't try to stop you."

Uneasily, Ettie turns her back on him. She is not used to being watched, not used to having anyone here at all. Her life in the day and her life at night are so distinct, but now one has bled into the other. Joseph has joined her nocturnal world and the boundary has become blurred. She tries to ignore the feeling of his presence, the warmth of his body, the soft ripple of his breath. She thinks she can hear the sound of his heart in the hot, dry darkness.

She closes her eyes for a moment, fills her mind with the painting, and begins again.

Night after night, Joseph joins Ettie in the outhouse. He does not speak. He does not make any sudden movements or sounds that might distract her. Tata has trained him well in this respect. Instead he watches, always behind her with his knees bunched up to his chest on the windowsill.

She grows used to his presence. Half companion, half lookout, he stays quiet and still, watching this secret painting come to life.

Sometimes he brings her food, small biscuits he has found in the kitchen or grapes from the terrace. The first time this happened Ettie did not know what to do; no one had ever served her food before. She was bemused by the strange reversal of their roles and did not know whether to scold him or kiss him. In the end she just laughed. They broke the biscuits in half and let the crumbs fall to the floor, then she turned her back on him, and he resumed his watch.

Tata adds a plate of tomatoes. Ettie adds a plate of tomatoes. Tata nestles a wineglass between the artichokes and the oysters. Ettie does the same. Day by day, night by night, on two different canvases, the same painting emerges. A crumpled napkin is added to the table. A smattering of spoons. The gawping head of a fish.

Ettie works in a fury of precision and intuition, fortified by biscuits and grapes and the soft sound of Joseph's breath. But Joseph needs sleep, and usually at four in the morning his head lolls and he trails back to the house, drawn to his bed beneath the eaves.

On each of these nights, Ettie senses a shadow at her back. A dark presence hovers—not a real person, but a memory of someone. It is this person she always expects to see when she glances back to look at Joseph. When Joseph traces his fingers along her arm it is his touch, and it is also someone else's that she feels. And though she has tried to bury the memories and the sharp, skewering pain, Joseph's presence has brought everything flooding back.

One night, Joseph makes a small cough from behind her. "Ettie?"

She does not turn around but her brush pauses.

"Ettie, I've been thinking and I . . . I still don't understand why you don't paint your own work. Why don't you try?"

Ettie doesn't reply. She is frozen, hand aloft.

"Don't you want to create your own art?"

"I can't," is all she manages to say. "I've tried and I can't."

Silence falls between them. She resumes her painting, but Joseph's question wriggles and writhes in her mind. Why doesn't she try?

After Joseph has returned to the house to sleep she puts down her brush. Takes a deep breath. Slips into Tata's studio. She returns with one of the blank canvases he has painted over. It was once a gummy impression of sticky apricot stones, but has now been slathered with white paint. Made new again.

She places it on her easel. What would she paint if she could choose anything she wanted?

She stands with her hands on her hips and stares at the blank canvas. She has not painted anything of her own in years. The impulse once came so naturally but now her hands feel like crumbling stones on the ends of her arms. How did she do it? The palette overwhelms her. Which colours should she choose? Which brush? She is so used to existing inside the careful boundaries of Tata's shadow that she does not know how to make a decision for herself.

She frowns at the canvas. Picks up a brush, then puts it down again. Fingers a crinkled tube of paint. What to create? She starts forward and then retreats. Lights a cigarette. Stubs it out. Turns the canvas upside down. Flips it around again. And then it is dawn before she knows it. The ripening sun has crept over the hills and she has created nothing. She cannot paint as she used to. She has lost it.

Joseph asked why she copied Tata's paintings instead of making her own and she told him it was a desire to prove herself. This was true.

But it was not all of the truth.

Joseph had asked her why she wouldn't leave Tata, why she couldn't run. And this truth she has buried deep. It is a truth she cannot face without feeling she might dissolve into dust.

It has been three years since she started forging Tata's paintings. Three empty years. As the first rays of sun glance off her skin she looks back at the blank canvas. If she is to paint again she must look deep inside herself. She must face the memories she has buried. She must peer into the darkness of the past and strike a match.

Ettie in a starched white cap and apron. Ettie holding a silver tray of cold instruments. Ettie washing red blood from the red cross on her uniform.

On her first day at the hospital Ettie assisted a doctor in amputating a soldier's leg below the knee. The skin was sliced with a scalpel, the rotting flesh scraped away, and the bone sawn through. She held the quivering leg steady as the doctor sawed and small shards of bone flew into the air like sparks. The next day it was decided that the leg needed to be amputated above the knee. The next day, halfway up the thigh. Each time the soldier woke up he had several inches less leg than before. On the fourth day they ran out of anesthetic.

Ettie saw men with their lower jaws hanging off. Men with half their intestines missing, the rest blackened and burned. Men with recently sewn stumps for hands and feet, the ends puckered like buttonholes. She saw the fragmented remains of men and boys lying on stretchers on the floor, crying out for water, for God, for death.

The hospital was housed in an old convent: white bricked, high ceilinged, cold as winter. It was still occupied by eight nuns and an abbess, but when the war broke out they tied white aprons over their grey tunics. Tucked nurses' caps beneath their veils. Laid wooden rosaries on top of red crosses. Their tranquil home was turned into an auxiliary hospital, far enough away from the front lines of the fighting for soldiers to recuperate safely, but well enough connected for them to be sent back to the trenches as soon as they were able to fire a rifle again. As the influx of soldiers increased the nuns called on women from the local village to help, and then the next village over, and the next one. They needed women to clean wounds, to cut bandages, to dig shrapnel from flesh with long metal tweezers. Women with no medical experience, but kind faces and willing hands. Women who wanted to help.

When Ettie read the notice in the village square on that October day in 1914, it had struck her like a bullet to the heart. She was twenty-one years old and had barely scratched the surface of life. Here was an invitation to step beyond the world she knew, and she grasped it with both hands.

The problem, of course, was Tata. She knew he would never allow her to devote more time to anyone other than him; he would never spare her from her duties, never permit her to stray farther than he could keep an eye on her. She began a careful plan of persuasion. She brought the notice home to him and, knowing he could not read it, showed him the official stamp, the urgent capitalised letters. He averted his eyes. She pretended to read the notice aloud, informing him that one person per household was required to be "involved in active war effort" (she had been proud of coming up with that phrase). They had looked at each other. Tata's face crawled with horror. "One person per household . . ." he said slowly. "Well, it had better not be me." Of course not, she agreed. He could not possibly be expected to abandon his work for something as trivial as a war. She supposed it must be her.

"Yes, yes," he agreed. "Better you than me."

Ettie felt safe in her deception. Tata spoke to no one so there was little way for him to stumble upon the truth.

Each morning she cycled to the hospital three villages over from Saint-Auguste. The smells of the farmhouse were replaced by new ones: the charred, sooty odour that came off the soldiers. The chemical tang of carbolic soap. The soil of northern France. She left Tata his breakfast in the studio, lunch covered with a cloth in the kitchen, and closed the door quietly behind her. Each evening at dusk she cycled home again. She swapped one apron for another, and made Tata his dinner. But in those blissful hours when she was out of the house she felt, for the first time, her life rubbing up against the outside world. She never told Tata what she saw in the hospital. She never spoke of the screams, or the white maggots crawling out of bloodied eye sockets. She never mentioned the gangrenous limbs or the foot which came away in her hand as she unwound its dressing. It was her own, private world, and she would not share a moment of it with him.

The hospital was unlike anywhere she had ever been before. She had never heard any language other than French, but here were soldiers whose tongues formed words in English, Flemish, Arabic. When they cried out they cried in the language of their homes. She had to learn fast, and discovered that she was a natural mimic. The first words she learned were "water," "help," and "please." Then "Stop," "sleep," and "die."

Added to her vocabulary too was a long list of medical terms: tourniquet, anaesthetic, gangrene. Sepsis, necrosis, hemorrhage. She ate up this new information. She wanted to learn as much about the wider world as she could while she was allowed to be in it.

She learned to use her hands in new ways. Sometimes she found her fingers lingering on burnt skin. She liked to feel things, the sharpness and the softness of life. Warm blood. Damp hair. Little bits of metal embedded in flesh. She was too fascinated to be repulsed. She earned a reputation for being able to attend to the most violent cases. Never once did she flinch or faint as some of the other nurses did. Never did she have to turn from a patient and steady herself against the wall, willing herself not to vomit.

She learned what a person's body looks like without arms. With no skin on the chest. With a scar splitting the face from eyebrow to jaw. She learned how much blood the human body holds, and what that blood looks like sluiced across a cold stone floor. She grew used to the smell of dirt, of urine, of chloroform.

After a few weeks she started to earn approving nods from the nuns (the "sisters," as she learned to call them). Ettie was good at following instructions. She was swift at sensing people's needs and taking care of them. It turned out she had been training all her life for this. She relaxed into the orders and the orderliness. The sisters and the other nurses did not ask about her life and she was happy not to tell them. Here she was not Ettie Tartuffe, daughter of a vanished mother, niece to a famous painter. She was just a nurse, as anonymous as all the others.

She chose a new name for herself: *Blanc*. White. A blank canvas on which she could paint her new life. Each morning she slipped on her uniform, pale and impersonal, and became Nurse Blanc. It was like the games of make-believe she used to play when she was little, wishing she could be someone else.

Ettie could barely believe she had lived a life before this. She encountered more of the world in those first few months at the hospital than she had in twenty-one years. Surrounded by death, she felt herself making a new life for herself.

The nurses were not, under any circumstances, to tell the soldiers their first names. In Ettie's third week she saw a nurse being dismissed after one of the soldiers cried out for her in his sleep. He had used her first name. Ettie saw her—Clotilde, as it was evident she was called—weeping as she was divested of cap and apron and marched summarily out of the front door. "These men need to concentrate all their efforts on getting better," Sister Blandine reprimanded everyone later in the nurses' mess room. "So do not distract them." As if growing back a limb was a matter of focus.

The pious sisters would not touch the soldiers below the waist. It was Ettie and the other village women who were called on to peel sodden trousers from the men's legs, to hold wads of cotton to bleeding groins as they plucked out pieces of shrapnel with long tweezers.

Ettie was taught to sew stitches. She found she had a steady hand.

Not all of the soldiers were able to speak when they were unloaded off the trains, so the orderlies at the station wrote diagnoses on their skin in indelible ink. Each new arrival was a puzzle to read, his skin the story of his pain.

They learned to tell how badly the war was going by the influx of admissions; the number of bodies on stretchers on the floor rather than in beds. Ettie noticed that the men got younger and younger as the war went on. She found photographs in their pockets, of women, children, sometimes other men. She laid them carefully on their bedside tables so they could see them when they woke up.

There were days, of course, when she arrived to find that men who had been breathing the night before were white and pulseless in the morning. Her eyes had stung then. But always she pressed the heels of her palms to her face and allowed herself no more than a minute, before smoothing her apron, turning to the living who needed water, clean sheets, morphine. A warm hand.

It was a mark of pride that she did not shudder or gasp at the sight of the mangled bodies that came in. She felt she owed them her stolidity. She would not let her hands tremble. She would not grimace or wince, would never avert her eyes from what she saw.

It was life that she was seeing. Life and death, inextricably bound up.

When it was quiet on the wards she used to read to the soldiers. She learned a sort of English this way, working her way through the books the men brought with them: Sherlock Holmes mysteries, Coleridge poems, and a funny old book by Edward Lear that made the men roll around in their beds with laughter, and then wheeze and cough with pain.

One of the soldiers had a copy of Tennyson's poems in his breast pocket when he was shot. It had saved his life, and as a result the small book was skewered with a bullet that stopped on page thirty-seven. He would run his fingers under the words surrounding the bullet hole and she sounded them out. As she scrubbed her hands with carbolic she whispered to herself, "She left the web, she left the loom . . . She left the web, she left the loom . . ." again and again. She knew this was poetry before she knew what it meant.

She was aware of it with only an ear for the sound and the rhythm of the words. She cycled home at night shouting into the wind, "'I am half sick of shadows,' said The Lady of Shalott."

Ettie learned to speak in this strange language of poems and songs. She learned to make the elusive "th" sound, as in "death," "mother," "thirst." There is no such sound in French. She learned what the soldiers missed most: dry gin, buttered toast, the warmth of a woman.

Some hands wandered. Some eyes slid down the carefully covered curves of Ettie's body. Some men made comments she did not understand but knew the meaning of, and she prided herself on taking no notice of them. Just as she was immune to the sight of blood and the smell of ulcers, so she was impervious to the yearnings of these men. She conducted her duties with crisp efficiency, her mouth closed but her eyes and ears sharp.

A call came down the ward one day that they had "a twitchy one." The orderlies at the station could not write a diagnosis on his skin because he was shaking so badly. "We need someone with steady hands."

Ettie did not know what she would find when she unwound the bandage wrapped around the man's head from crown to chin like an egg. It was bloodied all over and so she could not tell what part of him was damaged. His skull? His ear? His neck? She started at his throat where the cotton had been tied—several days ago by the look and the smell of it—and the man's body jerked away from her. His hands were badly burnt; the skin curled away from the flesh, which was red and raw. His fingers twitched in his lap in time with his pulse.

"We can get someone to hold him down, Nurse Blanc," came Sister Blandine's voice, but Ettie shook her head.

"No," she said. "There's no need."

The man's body crawled with tremors. They ran down his arms, his legs, reverberated through his chest. "Close your eyes," she told him, and with visible relief, he did. She began to work on the bandage, cutting through the immovable knot with scissors and unwinding it round and round his head, releasing the sticky patches, collecting the bloody and crusted muslin in a metal bowl. As she peeled the last layer she let a soft "Oh" escape her mouth. He had lost an ear.

The Man with One Ear lay in a fever of spasms for three days. Small flakes of skin came away when Ettie unwound the bandages on his burnt hands. What he ate he threw back up.

"Are you going to tell me your real name?" was the first thing he ever said to her. She was alone on the ward. It was nearly evening.

Ettie eyed him. "What makes you think this isn't my real name?"

"There's a slight hesitation before you answer when someone calls you, as if you have to remember that it's you they're talking to."

Ettie focused on picking the sticky dressing from the hole where his ear had once been. It was sealed with a glue of pus and blood. Her fingers were steady.

"I have nothing to do but lie in this bed all day," he said. "I notice things."

"What else have you noticed?" She was keen to keep him talking while she pulled fraying bits of gauze from the hole. She dabbed the wound with a piece of cotton soaked in alcohol, and he did not flinch.

"I have noticed that you look at people's injuries for a long time before deciding what to do. I've noticed that you listen to the other nurses' gossip but do not join in, that you prefer looking to talking, that you think the food here is poor, and that you understand more English than you let the soldiers know. And I've noticed that Nurse Blanc is probably not your real name."

Ettie straightened up, putting the bloodied muslin, scissors, tweezers, and balls of cotton in her bowl. "You're right," she said, screwing the top on the bottle of alcohol. "It's Ettie."

He bowed his head a little. "Amir."

That was the beginning. One name exchanged for another. One clue to who the other person was. Soon they exchanged looks, smiles, small jokes. Tokens of one life for another.

He was tall, barrel-chested. Creases around his eyes from smiling, which he did often. His beard looked wiry but in fact it was soft. He had long eyelashes like a girl's.

The doctor in charge said that his would be a long recovery. He was unlikely to be discharged back to the war; it is hard to fight when you can only hear by turning your head in one direction. His hands, badly burnt by a grenade, required dressing every twelve hours, and the ear socket was a daily fight against infection.

Despite the carbolic acid, the rubbing alcohol, and the paraffin wax, Amir always smelled of cedarwood. He had no books or photographs with him, so he spent his time listening to the sounds beyond the high convent walls, focusing with his one good ear.

"Where are you from?"

"A village not far from here. And you?"

"Algeria. Have you ever been?"

266

Ettie shook her head. She had never been anywhere.

"You should come. When the war's over, I'll show you." He said it as if it were the simplest thing in the world.

She smiled politely, and felt a twinge of guilt for secretly wishing the war would never end. She never wanted to leave this place, never wanted to go back to her old life.

"The sky is bigger than you can imagine . . ." Amir closed his eyes as she smoothed paraffin onto his raw knuckles. "The earth is so warm under your feet. There are birds with wingspans as wide as your arms. You can walk for a day and a night without seeing anyone else, if you wish. But the greatest difference is the sky . . . the sky is so vast there."

Ettie listened to him, letting her mind drift to this imagined place, which seemed to her as distant as the moon.

"You speak French very well," she commented, plucking a piece of dead skin from his hand.

His eyes flashed open. He looked at her as if trying to work out whether she was mocking him. "We all speak French there," he said slowly. "Whether we want to or not."

When he was well enough she took him for turns around the convent grounds. The nuns had been resourceful over the centuries and had planted apples and peaches, medlars and pears. There were long rows of fruit trees and walled gardens swooning with flowers. There were archways and shady corners. Undulating walkways of overlapping branches.

Amir loved the birds. He could tell any bird by its song and asked Ettie to identify the French ones he had never heard before. He picked flowers for her and tucked them behind her ear. His hands were heavily bandaged but he grimaced whenever she tried to help him. He called her Nurse Blanc in front of other people but when they were alone he called her Ettie. She liked the way it sounded in his mouth: so low and gentle.

Between bites of the nuns' peaches he asked her questions about her life, and she found she did not want to lie. She told him about Tata, about growing up in Saint-Auguste, about the day her mother left. She told him things she had never told anyone before. He could not hear in one ear so she learned to whisper in the other one. When she said she wanted to be an artist he nodded, and said that she should. As if it were as simple as that.

He was beautiful. And to Ettie, being able to touch and talk to this wounded, glorious man, was a very powerful thing.

Each day they walked farther. One afternoon they climbed a hill behind the convent. She offered him a cigarette.

"Is this a trap?" he asked. Smoking of all kinds was strictly forbidden for the patients.

"You gladly go to war but you think someone offering you a cigarette is a trap?"

He smiled and took it between two fingers. "Thank you," he said as she lit it for him. "And for your information I did not *gladly* go to war. If I had any choice I wouldn't be here at all. I wish I wasn't. I wish I were home."

Ettie was oddly stung by this. "I'm sorry you're here," she said. Her eyes flicked up to him. "But I'm glad you are."

There was a silence as they both watched the sun slipping toward the hills.

"I meant what I said"—he glanced at her—"about showing you Algeria when the war is over. If you would like, that is. We could take a ship to Oran. Or Algiers. I could show you the ruins of Timgad. We could go into the desert, if you wished."

"I've never been on a ship before," Ettie murmured, her mind overwhelmed by the syllables of these faraway places.

"I know," he said. "I guessed."

Ettie took a bite of the peach she had plucked from the nuns' garden. The world seemed so close when he talked about it. Almost within grasp.

Amir squinted one eye at her. "You are very beautiful," he said.

To be told you are beautiful by a man holding a stolen peach who looks for all the world like a god descended to earth, who has lost an ear and tells you he can show you the desert if only you wish it—Ettie had never imagined her life would contain such a moment as this, and it made her want to cry.

She threw the peach stone to the ground, stepped forward, and kissed him.

They walked in the hills. They took fruit from the gardens. They talked of the places they would go when the war was over. Amir had traveled around Algeria and Morocco. He had even been to Spain. He told her about the places where people stayed up all night singing until the sunrise. He told her about snakes that could dance and books you read from right to left. He told her what it felt like to stand on the edge of a boat as waves heaved below and fish leapt out of the water as if they were flying. He opened up the world for her as they walked through the hills, stealing covert glances back towards the convent. They found shadows in which to conceal themselves and he ran his hands through her long auburn hair, counting the colours in it. He kissed her forehead. He kissed her wrists. He kissed the inside of her elbows, her lips, the soft skin of her neck. He kissed every part of her he could.

Something was unfurling inside her. A spark, which she could either stamp out or kindle into existence. Was it love? Or just the feeling of being seen by another person?

Was that, in fact, what love was?

Ettie studied the nuns, solid and uniform as chess pieces. She watched their long skirts sweep the floor and mused on their careful celibacy, their dutiful, sexless lives, while all the while a blazing awakening was taking place inside her.

Ettie had missed the heady lusts of adolescence. She had never had a first love, or a person she could meet behind the bakery, or entwine herself with in the dark seclusion of an alley. The village boys all ran from her whenever she came near. She had received leering glances from men often enough, a stray hand, an unexpected lurch. She had squirmed beneath Raimondi's creeping fingers. But she had never desired and been desired in the same instance; she had never seen her own feelings reflected back at her, burning bright.

When their bodies finally collided it was in a field of wildflowers. They had not spoken, they just let themselves move as they wanted to move, shedding their clothes in long, instinctive strokes. The insects in the grass buzzed as they descended into it, hiding themselves in a world of green and yellow and white. Above them, birds swerved through the sky. Between them: only heat.

There was no one to hear their breath that came fast and then slow. There was nobody to witness the bowing of the grass or the clouds that tore themselves apart in the sky.

The sky was so vast that day.

Ettie had been around the village women long enough by then to know what to do afterwards. She had eavesdropped on enough conversations, had access to the right chemicals in the hospital cupboards. She knew about the rags and the sluices and the crouching over a bucket. The smell of quinine and cocoa would not raise suspicion on the wards. There were plenty of dark rooms with doors that locked.

In Amir, she was recouping all the years she had already lost, the experiences she had never had. She discovered her body and she uncovered, somewhere deep in her chest, a powerfully beating heart.

For the first time, she had a future that stretched beyond the bounds of Saint-Auguste. Amir was untying the bindings that kept her in place, one by one, releasing her into the wind.

JOSEPH

"You have stopped writing."

Tata's back is to Joseph in the studio but his ears are clearly alert. He has detected no scratching of a pen, no rustle of paper. Joseph's notebook lies open on his knees. The pages are blank.

"Why are you not writing?"

"I'm just . . . thinking, Tata. Thinking about what to write."

He had been staring out the window, his mind not on his work but turning, as it always seemed to do these days, towards Ettie. By day he watches Tata paint *The Feast* and by night he watches Ettie do the same. Two paintings inch forward in a strange, overlapping dance: one by daylight, the other in darkness.

"What is your next article about?"

"Uh . . ." Joseph glances around the room. In truth he has no idea what he will write about next. He has written barely anything since Ettie's revelation. He is paralysed by the feeling that every word he commits to paper is somehow a lie. He catches sight of the table piled high with rotting dishes. "Food," he says in a hollow voice. "I'm writing about food in your work, Tata." *The food that Ettie bought. The dishes Ettie cooked. The peaches she chose for their colour, the artichokes for their shape. The tomatoes she arranged on a plate, the knives and forks she cleaned, the table she laid.*

Tata grunts, adding a streak of sapling green to a radish stalk.

Lately, Joseph has sensed Tata drawing him closer. He likes to keep Joseph for long hours in the studio—asking for help with finding paints or cleaning brushes—and sometimes now when he is working Tata will pause, step back, and look at Joseph expectantly. As if waiting for his verdict.

"Masterful," Joseph will say, or "Just the right texture for a rotting nectarine," and Tata will nod in agreement, then turn back to his canvas.

After Joseph's latest article was published, the letters that arrive for Tata have been filled with interested requests. They are written on thicker paper. The letterheads give addresses in London, Milan, Geneva. Far beyond the bounds of Saint-Auguste, heads are turning towards Edouard Tartuffe again, eager to see what he does next.

Tata has let Joseph in and now he may as well reap the benefits: Attention. Flattery. Another set of hands at his beck and call. The shimmering promise of even greater acclaim.

Each day Tata reels Joseph in like a fish on a line.

The shakiest, most paranoid part of Joseph wonders if Tata is keeping him close so he cannot reach towards Ettie. As if by drawing Joseph's eyes to him he can ensure they will not stray.

But Tata has no idea how far Joseph and Ettie have already trespassed.

ETTIE

The bad news was Amir was getting better. The loop of bandages had come off his ear and the bloody hole was soft and puckered.

"They're going to send me back," he said, staring into the distance. They were on one of their walks in the hills behind the convent. Ettie stopped, caught her breath. She started to shake her head but he said, "Yes. I'm fit to fight. I have to go back."

"You're not fit."

"I am."

"You can't *hear.*"

"What was that?" He grinned.

But Ettie was not laughing. She had read the doctor's notes but could not bring herself to believe them. "Discharge to duty" they had said. He was going back at the end of the week.

"Stay," she whispered. "Stay, don't leave me." She grasped the front of his shirt, bunching it in her fists. "We could run away. We could hide! They'd never find us."

Amir took her shoulders in his wide hands. "We both know we cannot hide," he said, looking deep into her eyes. "They would kill me before we had gone twenty miles. And do you really think we would not draw attention? An Algerian soldier on the run with a Frenchwoman? I am here to fight, and so I must fight."

No you mustn't! she wanted to scream. *You do not have to risk your life for this stupid war!*

Standing on the hill with Amir, she understood for the first time the urge her mother had felt. The desire to run, to pursue the horizon and find out what lay beyond it. To never look back. She wished her mother had been buried in America. There was something so pitiful about the fact that, even though she was dead, she had been dragged back to Saint-Auguste. She never managed to get away.

"They are running out of people . . ." Amir murmured. He was looking out over the hills, dusty blue in the evening light. "I have to go back. They need all the men they can get. I can hear from one ear, and apparently that's enough."

Ettie had a wild desire to cut off his other ear, to keep cutting bits of him off so he could never leave.

He rested his forehead against hers. "Don't cry, my little sparrow." He slid his fingers into her long hair, pulling out the ribbon as delicately as a bone from a fish. Her tresses came loose in one tumbling wave. He ran his hands through them, gentle as a breeze.

She tucked her hand into his pocket and found his penknife. Holding up a lock of the hair he loved so much, she severed it, and gave him a coppery curl. He pressed it to his lips, then placed it carefully in his breast pocket, overlaying it with his hand. "I will end this war myself if I have to, just to come back for you," he told her.

"And you will write?"

"Every moment I am able." He kissed her forehead. "As soon as this war is over, I am coming for you and we will sail across the sea."

Every word he spoke was true. The letters came, suffused with his love. He crammed them with words she recognised from poems: "cherish," "embrace," "eternity." He drew little pictures of birds in the margins. There were no birds where he was. No trees for them to perch in. There was nothing alive at all.

The letters grew more infrequent, as she knew they must, as he drew nearer the heart of the fighting. He could not tell her where he was but every time there was an envelope for her at the hospital she opened it in a fever. His careful handwriting was perfect and even. He always addressed her as "My little sparrow."

She became obsessive. She snatched any newspaper she found, poring over the scant news they were allowed to print, searching for a clue that might tell her where he was. Enemy intelligence might miss it, but she would find the scrap of information that would tell her he was alive. Every new soldier who came to the hospital she asked for news of him. "Tall, dark eyes, one ear. His name is Amir."

"An Arab?" they would say, shaking their heads. "No, none of those in my company. But here, why don't you squeeze beside me? I need someone to keep me warm."

Her need to touch things became a compulsion. The walls, the medical instruments, her own throat. She ran her fingers along every texture she could find.

The letters still came, as full of love as before. Sometimes it was two weeks between hearing from him, then three. But always he wrote. "I am coming for you. I am coming back for you. Just a few weeks longer, my sparrow. I am nearly home."

And then one day there was a letter with a different handwriting altogether. Ettie was in the stone atrium of the convent delivering bloodied sheets to the laundry when the trundle of the post cart slowed outside. The post boy appeared holding a stack of letters. And somehow she knew, she knew before he gave it to her that there was a letter for her. She tore open the envelope, eyes racing down the scant lines inside. And then she collapsed on the floor. The earth swallowed her up. She heard nothing—no sound at all—though her mouth was screaming and her lungs were on fire. Tears streamed down her face. Her mouth was slack with saliva. Her knees bore into the ground, her forehead pressed to the cold floor.

There was roaring in her ears and she did not know if it was her voice or the sound of hell beneath her opening up and swallowing her whole.

She was aware of hands. Hands beneath her arms, hands covering her mouth, hands hauling her up. A hand snatching the letter from the floor.

"Shh," someone said. "Shh, shh."

She was dismissed that afternoon. *Can't have an unstable nurse. Can't have a madwoman disturbing the patients. Can't have a temptress on the wards.*

She could not swing her leg over her bicycle to cycle home. She could not even face the thought of going home. Where could she go? She took herself to the top of the hill where they had walked together, but it had lost its magic. No more was the air sweet with the scent of peaches. No more were the hills sun-kissed gold, but instead a lifeless brown. She was the loneliest woman in the world.

How had it happened? Rifle fire? A shell? Did he die quickly? In a trench? In a pitted crater in no man's land? Did he have someone's arms to die in, or was he all alone? She looked through the letter again but it told her nothing. Had he died because he only had one ear to hear?

Ettie sank to her knees. She used to believe that there was no good way to die. But now she knew, any way was better than this. To die in the darkness. Among the roar of guns. To die anonymously. A mere number in the war record. Far away from the country he loved, from the soil he should have returned to.

Oh yes, Ettie knew this now. Everyone dies alone.

She missed his touch. The little kisses on her forehead. His finger drawing circles around her palm. She missed the warmth of him, the smooth press of his hands, the softness of his beard. She missed the smell of cedarwood. Despite the chemicals of the hospital, he always smelled of the trees.

She could not work out what to do with her hands. Anywhere she put them they felt empty. She should have held on to him tighter.

What was achieved through his death? Did the fighting stop? Were any lives spared, did the war hurry to its close any sooner? He had not even died for his country. He had died for another: a country he had only ever seen from the depths of a trench or within the walls of a makeshift hospital. She knows what his last thoughts were of. Not her, but the sweeping plains of Algeria. The cragged mountains and the sky. *Oh, the sky*, he used to say. The sky that was bigger than she could ever imagine. Broader and bluer, as if God had stretched his arms and said, "This. This is all the sky in the world."

His last thoughts would have been of the sky. And the birds. Ascending into it.

What was she to do with her life now?

Amir had been her escape. He had given her hope that there was a place for her in the world outside Saint-Auguste. But now she had nothing. She was back in the house with Tata and his wine bottles and his paints. She peeled the skin around her nails with her teeth. She wanted to stuff her mouth with cotton, muffle the screams she knew would come. Stifle the pain. She was constantly teetering on the edge of sinking to her knees and screaming until the world ended.

For now she knew. She knew what happened when she tried to escape. She had seen the terror of the world and she had been shown what happened when she tried to touch it. She knew what happened when she stepped too far.

She sensed Amir everywhere: in the pairs of birds threading through the sky. In the jasmine flowers trembling in the wind. When she shook out her hair it was his hands she felt running through the curls.

She took a pair of scissors. Kneeling before the mirror in the disused room at the top of the house, she grabbed a bunch of her hair in her fist and cut it. She cut and cut, tears streaming down her face, soft auburn locks falling to the floor. She hacked away at her head until she was shorn. All that was left was a ragged crop like a boy's.

Her head felt lighter. She was no longer the woman Amir had loved. She was someone else, someone those terrible things had not happened to. She gathered up her hair and scattered it into the wind. Let the birds take it for their nests. Let the soft creatures of the fields bury it beneath the ground. Let the earth have it. When she ran her hand over her head it felt empty. Free.

She never told Tata about Amir. He didn't comment on her recently severed hair. But sometimes she thought he knew something, by the glint of his eye as he watched her, or the small curl at the corner of his mouth. He knew she had seen the outside world and come back changed.

She wanted to slip away, to be invisible. If anyone looked at her in the market she bowed her head, the cropped bristles of her new hair tickling her neck. She worried that if she opened her mouth all that would come out was a howl.

In her grief, she took a brush. There was nothing within her to paint anymore. She had lost the spark, but she needed to do something. She looked around Tata's studio one night and took what was in front of her, a recent painting called *Lemon in Sunlight*. How strange to think that during a war there were still lemons, still sunlight. The world still had colours in it and somehow Tata had found them. She looked at *Lemon in Sunlight* and took a plain canvas of the same size, and balanced them next to each other.

The methodical precision of copying the painting had calmed her. There was nothing to think about. Nothing to do but replicate exactly what was in front of her. She had to be focused, but this meant the raging torrent of her thoughts was quietened. Her mind was calm. The choices were already made for her on the canvas: all she had to do was surrender to the image and copy the colours and shapes. It took her two weeks of painting in the stolen night-time hours, but when she was done she had a perfect replica of Tata's painting.

That was a beginning. A new one. She could not find the inspiration to paint anything herself and so she began to copy. It was all she could do.

Life inched onwards. She was alive. Unfairly, maddeningly, she was alive. Some days she could barely believe it. Some days she wished she wasn't. But whether she willed it or not, time crept onwards, and a new life unfurled around her from one moment to the next.

Three years later, Ettie opened a letter. It was from a stranger, somewhere far away across the sea. He wanted something, and for a long time Ettie sat with the letter. She did not destroy it, nor did she read it to Tata, to whom the letter was addressed, but she kept it in her apron pocket. She brought it out at odd moments and read it again until she had memorised the sentences by heart.

She thought about the man who had sent the letter. He was a foreigner but had written in French. He wrote well but it was as if he were coming at the language from an odd angle, like he was unsure exactly to whom he was speaking. She sensed an unhappiness in him. It was an unhappiness she recognised: a desire to escape one's circumstances. It was the plaintive cry of a trapped animal, disguised as a request.

Eventually, when the crab apple trees were dropping their blossom and summer was shimmering on the horizon, Ettie replied. She wrote only one word: *Come*. And then she signed the letter with Tata's signature.

JOSEPH

August deepens like a bruise. The heat thickens. And as the days go on, Joseph's camera turns not towards Tata, as he knows it is meant to, but to Ettie.

He orders developing equipment from Paris. He remembers enough from the Slade to know what he needs: photographic paper, an enlarger, specific chemicals to develop and fix the images. And most importantly, he needs darkness. He finds a disused airing cupboard off the hall, long stripped of any linens for airing. Its empty shelves form a sort of workbench, and he can store his chemicals underneath. He takes an old curtain and pins it to the inside of the door to stop even the thinnest strands of light from creeping in. He hangs a washing line from one wall to the other to dry his images.

Tata has his studio, Ettie her outhouse, and he this cupboard.

Joseph never knows what he is going to see when his photographs develop. It is always a surprise when he pulls back the curtain and lets in the light. He stands like a gold prospector, nudging the photographs in their tray before hanging them from the washing line. There is Tata's studio. There are the paintings stacked against the wall. There is Ettie in the kitchen. Ettie wheeling her bicycle up the drive. Ettie picking lavender in the garden, the sun throwing half her face into shadow.

He sinks gratefully into these images. In the solitude of the cupboard he runs his finger over the freckles on Ettie's arms. The creases around her eyes. The dimples that pinch her cheeks when she smiles. In these photographs, he has time with her. Perfect, endless time.

One day they take a photograph by balancing the camera in the bend of an olive tree. At first Ettie stands in front of it and Joseph clicks the shutter, and then they swap places. Without winding the reel, Ettie presses the shutter again, and the images are imprinted on top of one another. When developed it will be one picture: Ettie and Joseph, side by side. The leaves will be blurry from where they have moved in the breeze, the shadows in motion. But they will be there, the two of them standing together, showered in sunlight.

There is a fragility to these days. It has been over two months since Joseph walked out of his father's house, leaving the cold walls of that grey city behind. But August is shedding its skin like a snake. Summer's end crackles in the distance. Joseph manages to type words for Harry, punching half-truths into his typewriter. He writes about Tata's vision, about his skill with the brush. He writes neat sentences about food and decay and how this feast can be thought of as *a portrait but without any people.*

But his words feel hollow. It is Ettie's hand that hovers behind the final painting. He cannot shake the sense that with every word he types he is somehow erasing her. Smothering who she really is.

Joseph avoids meeting Tata's eye these days. He is afraid that if he looks directly at him he will blurt out Ettie's secret. He hates the lying and he hates the guilt that settles over him like a skim on old milk.

He is not made for a life of deception.

Tata presses his brush to the canvas. White curls into lurid green. A skein of mould appears. He squashes the brush harder. Light.

Slickness. Oil. The juicy strings of fruit flesh. He steps back. Squeezes a worm of yellow onto his palette. Steps up to the canvas again.

Joseph is hunched over the table, trying to describe the pear that Tata is painting. The words *hazy, fluid, waxen* emerge from his pen as yellow folds into brown. *Slick, streaky, dripping* as Tata steps forward and back, the canvas gleaming with colour.

Then there is a silence, and Joseph is aware that Tata has stopped moving. He has paused, the paintbrush gripped in a tight, trembling fist. And then the old man's mouth moves and he says, "I am so hungry."

Joseph half stands. "I can fetch you an orange? Or an egg? Or—" He falters, for Tata is looking at him queerly.

"No." His voice is a croak. "I am not hungry for an egg. I am not hungry for anything I can eat . . ." He looks at the canvas clamped in the easel's mechanical grip. Cherries drip like beads of blood, tongues of ham flicker in ribbons, a rotten lemon sinks into itself. "I am hungry for something I cannot capture, something I cannot grasp . . . I am hungry for the light."

Tata reaches for the pear on the table and holds it up to the light. He rolls it in his hand, the sun's rays sliding over its contours. "The light always escapes me," he whispers.

"Of course you can capture the light," Joseph says placatingly. "You're renowned for it. You are the *master* of light."

But Tata shakes his head. "Light is the one thing that evades me . . . The one thing I cannot pin down. It torments me, the fact that I cannot—ever—grasp it." He drops the pear onto the table with a soft thud.

Months ago, Joseph would have given anything for this insight. But now all he feels is a creeping unease. A dry itch crawls across the back of his throat. A tremor of danger vibrates on the air.

"Do you know why I prefer to paint in the studio rather than out in the fields?" Tata asks. "In here I can pin down my subject. I can control everything. The staging, the arranging, the adjusting of each thing I need to the perfect angle . . . There are too many variables outside, but in here I am God. The only thing I cannot control is the light."

And there is the answer Joseph has been searching for. What drives this old man? Why has he shut himself away, banished everything else? To capture the uncatchable. To limit the world until it becomes small enough for him to command.

Tata is a man who needs to control everything within his reach.

Tata picks up the pear again, wraps his fist around it and squeezes it until the skin bursts, until chunky flesh dribbles between his knuckles and juice coats his fingers. Then he opens his hand and lets it fall, shining, to the ground.

ETTIE

The blank canvas beneath the straw taunts her. As Ettie works on her copy of Tata's great feast, the white canvas remains empty, untouched, wrapped in a burlap sack.

Some nights when Joseph has gone to bed she takes it out and sizes it up as if it were an opponent. She places the canvas on her easel. Squares her shoulders. Cracks her neck from side to side. She smokes a cigarette. Then another. Twirls a paint-encrusted brush between her fingers.

She steps forward. Raises the brush. And then nothing. It is as if she has forgotten what to do; the movements she knew so well have abandoned her, flown her body like birds startled from a tree. Her hands are useless. The brush hangs limply between her fingers.

She needs a guide. She has grown so used to the idle mimicry of copying Tata's work. Of letting her mind go blank and surrendering to the image he has already created. She is so practised at twisting herself to fit his mould she barely knows what shape she takes on her own anymore.

It is unnerving how much easier it is to be Tata than herself. She knows his habits and his desires, his needs, his movements. But hers are as unfamiliar as a stranger's. The terror she feels is the terror of failing at being herself. Because if she fails at this she has lost everything: not only who she is, but who she might be.

She closes her eyes. Takes a steady breath through her nose. What is it she wants? If she breaks open the bloody chamber of her heart, what is inside?

She wants to run. To be free. She wants love and texture and colour and movement and the vibrancy of life beyond these four walls. But why can't she grasp it?

Alone in the outhouse, she screams. Keening and loud and full of blood and rage, her voice comes from deep in her chest and for once she does not care who hears. She does not care if she wakes the whole world. She is usually so poised, so careful, but now she is wild.

She is a woman, alone in the darkness, slowly exploding.

JOSEPH

Joseph's room at the top of the house is stacked with the flotsam and jetsam of an artist's life. Coils of rope. A broken drum. Vases cloaked in dust. But behind, inside, and underneath this debris, a number of photographs have been hidden.

After he develops his photographs, Joseph sorts them into two piles: ones for Harry, and ones for himself. It is these which must be concealed. Tata may not be able to read but he could decipher these images in an instant. They must be kept safely out of sight.

Tucked inside a roll of canvas: Ettie wheeling her bicycle up the drive. She squints at Joseph, one hand shielding her brow. Long grass bends in the wind behind her. Swifts with wings like archer's bows wheel through the air.

Pinned to the underside of the desk: Ettie in the field, a bright smile on her face. She has a lavender stalk behind her ear and she is laughing because Joseph has just told her that his mother was once arrested for stealing a policeman's helmet.

Beneath an old birdcage: Ettie eating a peach, the juice running all the way down her wrist.

In the lid of Joseph's typewriter: Ettie in the doorway of the house, half in, half out. The interior is dark. The outside world is scorching white.

Slipped between the pages of *The Odyssey*, borrowed from Balliol College Library in Michaelmas term of 1914 by Rupert Adelaide, taken to the trenches of Artois and Verdun, returned soiled and stained in a medical bag printed with the insignia of the British Army: A double portrait—one image overlaid with another. The background is hazy—the smudging of leaves and grass transposed on top of each other—and the faraway hills can be seen through the figures' bodies. They are like ghosts. They are both here and not here.

This is the photograph Joseph takes out more than any other. Even though he and Ettie never stood next to each other when the photographs were taken, in this final image their hands *just* touch. It is the only picture he has of the two of them.

One evening he comes up to his bedroom to change before dinner. It has been a long day with Tata in the studio. His clothes are streaked with paint and the sour secretions that ooze from the steadily rotting food. He craves a sliver of solitude, of quietness, of cleanness.

In the cool moment before going downstairs again he sits on the edge of his bed and thumbs through the pages of *The Odyssey*. Familiar words flit past him. But the photograph is not there. He flicks through the book. Front to back. Back to front. The photograph is gone. A sheen of fear slips over him, as if someone has cracked an egg down his back. He checks beneath the bed. Nothing. Under the desk, behind the mirror, in his knapsack. The other photographs are safe but not this one. Where has it gone? Who has taken it? In a dash of blind panic he rips the covers off his bed and there, poking out from beneath his pillow, is the corner of a piece of paper. He lunges for it.

It is the photograph. It is here. He does not know how it ended up beneath his pillow but all he feels is the sweet quench of relief. He is about to return the photograph to *The Odyssey* when he notices something dashed on the back. A message.

Meet me by the stream tonight.

ETTIE

White moon, silver stars. The air is quiet and nothing moves. It is as if time has been suspended. The world is not sleeping but paused, as if the shutter of Joseph's camera has snapped this moment into stillness.

The grass is soft beneath her feet. It parts easily. Her clothes drop like a spool of thread by the river's edge. The night is warm. Pebbles slip beneath her toes. She stands in the moonlight, her pale skin luminous, up to her calves in the water. It flows around her as if she has stood there for a thousand years, a marble column in the night.

A soft rustle from the bank. She turns. Meets his eyes.

He steps down to the water's edge. Slips the buttons from his shirt and pulls it over his head. Shakes off his trousers, then his underwear. Slowly, making barely a sound, he wades across the dark water towards her.

"Joseph . . ." She whispers his name. The soft shush of his syllables. It sounds like a plea. It sounds like a prayer. It is one he answers with the cup of his hand, gently brushing the side of her face. Ever so slowly, he lifts her chin.

"Ettie," he murmurs.

Her toes curl into the silt. She leans into his palm. Her lips find his thumb and she kisses it, then his wrist, his arm, his shoulder. Gently, lightly, compulsively. He brushes the hair from her face.

Her body moves like a curtain rippling in the breeze. She closes the space between them. Joseph's fingers thread through her hair and she tilts her head back, opens her eyes to the stars, the sky. Joseph's mouth is on her neck, he is wrapping his arms around her, pressing his body to hers. The cold clasp of the water binds them to each other.

Her fingers press into the smooth muscles of his arms. Her mouth finds his and water rushes around them. Cold currents carry their secret away to somewhere unseen, beyond the river bend. A whorl of wind stirs the trees.

They fall, folding at their knees, hips, elbows, down to the grass at the water's edge. Where Joseph ends and Ettie begins she does not know. She rolls on top of him, their bodies mapping each other. Cool droplets of water become warm, pressed between their skin. Ettie looks down at Joseph, at the stars reflected in his eyes. She runs her finger over his lips.

The night will give them more hours yet. It will keep their secret, smooth it with darkness, wrap it in a silent benediction. Their bodies move together, pale limbs rippling between the shadows of the bank.

Ettie is unsure what love is—it has become muddled in her short life, confused and contaminated. If love is a doing, or if love is a being, or if love is a feeling, she does not know. She only knows that Joseph is here and something inside her is undoing. Perhaps it is breaking.

The moon trembles on the water. The clock has not yet resumed. The night is paused. Ettie thought she could seal herself off from these feelings, but love always finds a way in.

If love is about dissolving. If love is about paying attention. If love is about becoming.

Then yes, yes, yes. Ettie loves.

JOSEPH

As they walk back up to the house—clothes roughly shrugged on, hair wet, skin tingling—Joseph catches Ettie's hand. He has to say what is on his mind before they seal themselves inside again. Before the house exerts its spell of silence. Moonlight glances off the trees. His breath comes hot and fast. "Run away with me."

"What?"

"Run, Ettie. Leave this. Leave everything. Come with me."

Ettie's eyes are dark and glossy. "What are you talking about?"

For days now his mind has been plagued by an image: the two of them. Ettie painting in a studio, him on the windowsill, an open book on his lap. She wears an apron streaked with paint. He has a pen in his hand. And this studio is filled with light. Rays of sun flow through an open window. There is the gentle noise of neighbours through the walls. An unmade bed in one corner.

"We could be free," he says. "You'll paint and I'll write. We could go anywhere. We could make a life for ourselves."

He has been watching her paint the feast night by night. She works for hours at a time. Always in the darkness. There is no huffing, no snapping of paintbrushes like Tata. She enters into a trance and paints with a cool serenity, as if she and the canvas are the only things in the world. He could watch her for hours. But each night the distant church bell peals across the hills, and he is reminded that time is slipping through his fingers. He needs to escape the iron grip of this place. And so does she. "You can't do this forever," he says.

He has seen the fire in her eyes, which is stamped out whenever Tata comes near. He has seen what she can create and he resents the secrecy with which she must do it. He wishes she did not have to live like this: in the shadows, in the darkness. Ettie's talent is equal to Tata's. She is so talented everyone believes she *is* Tata. But what good is her talent if she cannot choose what to do with it?

"You need to get out of here," he says. "You are too . . . too bright, too brilliant to waste your life in that ruin. You could be free. Paint what you choose, go where you please. So come with me." The life he imagines for them throbs in his mind, in his hands, in his blood.

Ettie is staring at him. "I can't . . . I can't leave," she says. But it is not her voice that says this. It is Tata's.

"Leave him," Joseph whispers. "He's a monster."

At this Ettie flinches.

"He is! He will keep you here for the rest of your life if he can. He will never let you go." Joseph has felt the chain Tata has started to wind around his ankle and he knows there is one around Ettie's too. "Come with me," he says. "Run. And don't look back."

Ettie does not say anything for a long time. "When you left your father," she says eventually, "how did you do it?"

Joseph considers this. It feels like a lifetime ago that he slammed the door in his father's face. He packed just one bag and left his sister and brother, his childhood home, his life. But still, he knows, they are waiting for him. "I suppose I knew I could always go back."

Ettie nods. "If I leave, I'm never coming back."

Joseph threads his fingers through hers. "I promise everything will be all right. If you run, the world will not hurt you."

But at this she frowns.

"You hate him!" Joseph insists. "Leave him!"

"No, Joseph." Ettie is shaking her head. "No. If you think I hate him then you have misunderstood everything. I love Tata. How can you live with someone all your life and not love them, in some small, strange way? Of course I love him. To love is to be under someone's spell. And Tata is a master of casting that spell if he needs to. I am all Tata has in the world, and he is all I have."

"You have me!" cries Joseph. "Come with me. We'll get a studio, in Paris or London. You could paint and I could write. You could go to art school! And we could hold hands in the street. Eat dinner, just the two of us. Sleep in the same bed. Life could look like that, Ettie, it really could." He feels dizzy with the possibilities. "You could do so many extraordinary things," he says. "Whatever you want, we'll do it."

Ettie looks as if she is about to agree, say yes, run right there and then. But then she crumbles. Shakes her head.

"I want to hold your hand in the street," he says. "In the open. In daylight. I want to climb onto the roof of the church and shout to the whole world that I love you—I want to tell everyone I have ever met—because I do love you, Ettie. I love you. And I will love you like the sun loves the earth. You have your paints and I have my words. And I will use my words to love you for the rest of my days."

She closes her eyes, rests her whole body against his. He wraps his arms around her. "This life is all I have," she says faintly.

"But there's another one." He buries his face in her hair. "Out there, waiting for you. I promise."

A light comes on in the house. They both fall silent as they look to the yellow glow of Tata's bedroom window. They drop their arms from one another, and Ettie slips from him.

ETTIE

There is an old asylum, some twenty miles hence, crouching on the outskirts of a village. It generates its own borderlands, for nobody wishes to come near. It is skirted by a high wall topped with broken glass.

The asylum was where they used to send the insane and the incurable. Those who were gripped by hysteria, or sunk beneath a melancholy from which they could not emerge. Those who saw visions, those addicted to drink or opium or sins of the flesh, those who had tried to suffocate their babies. The nearby villages said it was haunted. They said it was a torture chamber. They said that on a windless night you could hear the screams for miles around.

One day the high walls of the asylum were torn down. The door was opened. It was said that the doctors had fled, the facility abandoned. But the inmates did not escape. They stayed inside.

The old walls that no longer existed kept them in.

They say on a clear night you can still see faces at the window.

Ettie sneaks out before the rest of the house is awake. She slips through the side door and walks quickly onto the donkey track. Glances once over her shoulder to make sure no one is following. The sun's first tendrils are creeping over the edge of the field. It is early and she has not slept. Her thoughts jangle against each other like a set of keys.

What if she were never to walk this track again? Who would she be without her daily routine, without the familiarity of the farmhouse and the village? Who would she be without her secrets?

Ettie stops by a bank of deep purple irises and pulls them up by the roots. She cradles them in her arms like a newborn. When she gets to Saint-Auguste she turns not towards the market, nor the tobacconist or Lafayette's workshop, but to a plot beneath the ancient village wall.

The cemetery is empty this early in the morning. Swallows wheel through the air but otherwise everything is still. Cypress trees stand like sentries on the surrounding hills. Ettie walks between the uneven headstones, grass crackling underfoot. Her mother's grave is tucked in the far corner, as if hoping to go unnoticed. She kneels down by it, brushing the dust and dirt from the sun-bleached headstone, and lays the irises across the grave.

She leans back on her heels, looks up at the horizon her mother pursued. It is the same horizon that Joseph is trying to pull her towards now. But if she went, would she just be repeating her mother's mistake? She can almost feel her mother's loneliness through the earth, knows how desperately she must have wanted to break free.

But her mother never got away. She is still here, under the earth.

Ettie closes her eyes. The pattern of escape and punishment is ingrained in her bones. Her mother ran away and died. Amir left and was killed. Whose turn is it next?

The thing about Tata is he will never leave her. He would never, could never, abandon her. He is as ill-equipped to find his way in the world as she is: he cannot cook or fend for himself. He cannot read or write. He has not ventured beyond the walls of the house for years and years. Ettie is all he has left.

It feels as if her heart is twisting inside her chest. Crushing itself, like a scrunched-up piece of paper.

What does it mean to love a monster? What does it mean to hate a place but not be able to leave?

This is the place Tata chose as a refuge all those years ago. A sanctuary to harbour his sister and her unborn child. A shelter, where they could live freely away from prying eyes.

But it has become a prison.

Joseph is so hope filled. With his messy hair and eager eyes. He believes everything to be so simple. So easy. If she were to paint Joseph she would paint him as a sea-green swirl. Uplifting sweeps. Caresses of blue. A sense of reaching higher, higher, higher. Light.

What would her life look like with Joseph at her side? She pictures the future he imagined for her. The shared bed. The held hands. The room where they work together.

But if she were to choose her own life, what would it look like?

She fiddles with one of the irises on top of the grave. Presses a velvet petal between finger and thumb.

If she were to make a life with Joseph she would want her own studio. She would want time and space for her art. She would want to fill the room with her things: her mother's dresses, her own brushes, a bowl of peaches. Paints in colours she has chosen. She wants to get up when she pleases, eat the food she likes, eat it slowly—leisurely!—as if no one is going to take it away from her. She wants to live her whole life as if no one will take it away from her. She would only cook when she felt like it, and she would eat complicated, homogenous foods. Stews, soups, jellies, and fish in cream sauces. She would make a hazelnut tart every week. She wants her life to rub up against other people's. She wants noise, she wants laughter. And she wants to paint. She wants to live in the daylight, to feel the sun on her skin as she works. She wants the knowledge that her life is hers and hers alone.

She wants freedom.

She wants a future.

She wants to be an artist.

This is the life Ettie would choose for herself. If Joseph can picture this too then yes, she can imagine a life with him.

She looks down at her mother's grave. She knows what happens when a woman yokes her life to a man. She has already spent one lifetime doing that, just as her mother did before her. She cannot squander another chance. This next life must be one she chooses.

She kisses the tips of her fingers and draws them across her mother's name.

"I'm sorry they dragged you back, *Maman*," she whispers. "They're never going to drag me back."

JOSEPH

An image swims into view. Beneath the ripples of the developing fluid a face comes into focus. A fold of limbs. A smattering of freckles. The dark button of a nipple.

Ettie sits on the bank of the stream surrounded by pebbles of light from the trees overhead, her torso folded over her legs, arms hugging her knees. Her back curves smoothly like a protective shell.

Joseph had taken this photograph as afternoon slipped into evening. They had gone down to the stream—ostensibly to wash one of the tablecloths stained with wine—and Ettie had shed her clothes and stepped into the water. She dipped her head under, and Joseph discovered that she could hold her breath for a long time down there. When she came up her eyes were bright.

He had watched her from the bank, shimmering in the late afternoon sun. When she finally rejoined him on the grass she did not put on her clothes, but sat in the dappled light, her bare skin speckled with droplets. She folded herself over her knees and turned one eye to him. He pressed the shutter, capturing that moment forever.

Joseph wants to touch Ettie's cool skin through the photograph. He wants to brush the hair from her face, run his fingers down the knuckles of her spine. He thinks with longing about what the photograph does not show. The white of her stomach. The pale sheen of her thighs. The dark nest between her legs.

He does not know what to do with this photograph. His first instinct is to burn it so no one else can see it, but at the same time he never wants to let it out of his sight. He tucks the photograph into his shirt and takes the stairs two at a time to his bedroom, brain fizzing as he thinks of a place to hide it.

He decides upon a tall Chinese vase, resplendent with jade-green dragons. It has a wide lip and a deep, curving body. He slips the photograph into the vase's opening and drops it into the bottom.

ETTIE

Ettie squares her shoulders.

Focus.

The night is warm. A lizard slithers into a hole in the wall. The blank canvas looms in front of her.

She closes her eyes.

Banish Tata. Banish fear. What's left?

To paint outward she must dig inward. She looks inside herself and for the first time in a long while she finds something glimmering. Something hopeful. Her paintings used to be torrents of darkness but now she turns towards the light. There is something she wants to grasp.

She presses her brush into the paint. Blood surges through her veins. Her lungs expand with breath and air and something bright. A movement takes hold of her. She connects her arm with her heart and lets the feeling creep into her hand. Along the brush. Onto the canvas.

It is as if she is prising open her heart and letting it bleed onto the painting.

She is unaware of time. Usually she can count every second ticking onwards but now she surrenders. Something inside her is coming alive.

It is only when dawn breaks and she raises a hand against the piercing light that she steps back. Feels the wall against her spine. Stares at what she has done.

JOSEPH

The days ripple onwards. The painted feast grows day by day in the studio, and then again by night in the outhouse. Piles of food disintegrate in the heat. Insects fling themselves against the windows. Everything is accumulating. Deepening. Trembling, as if it is about to break apart.

Each moment Joseph spends around Tata is a trial in biting his tongue. He must not look at Ettie. Must not touch her. He fears Tata will be able to read the movements of their bodies, translate the code of their carefully averted eyes. Each morning before Joseph leaves his bedroom he checks his body for marks from the night before; incriminating evidence of Ettie's mouth on his skin.

There have been some close calls recently. Tata always seems to be just behind them: suddenly appearing around a corner, or his eyes emerging from beneath his hat when Joseph had been sure they were closed. Ettie is calmer than Joseph in these moments. She adopts a breezy neutrality, her movements quick, while Joseph feels pinned like an animal caught in a snare. Tata is keeping him close, squeezing his time with Ettie into the stolen nighttime hours.

Creeping into the kitchen one night, feeling more thief than house guest, Joseph picks through the kitchen cupboards. Ettie is already down in the outhouse and he is scavenging for food he thinks she might like: late summer apricots, almonds, a croissant from the bakery in the village. He packs these into a napkin and ties the corners together like a child in a storybook. Pausing to make sure the house is silent, he slips out into the darkness. Ettie has taught him to take different routes to the outhouse each night. To weave between the trees like a shadow. To leave no traces.

He unlatches the door, pushes it open—there she is. Ettie, illuminated by soft candlelight.

But *The Feast* is not here.

Another painting rests on the easel tonight.

Joseph drops the bundle of food. His face cracks like a sunbeam and he exclaims, "It's you!"

Ettie is standing next to an easel upon which rests a small painting. It swirls with yellow and gold. Honeyed striations of colour swimming together. The canvas is a whirlpool of summer light. It is a painting to swallow you up.

Ettie glances from Joseph to the canvas and then back again. "What?" she says.

"It's you," he repeats. "The painting. It's you." He has never seen this painting before but he understands exactly what it means. "This is how I see you. Ungraspable. Like sunlight on water." He takes a step closer and pushes his glasses up his nose. "It's like the sun setting on snow. Or sparks rising from a bonfire. It's wild and dizzying and alive and it's you."

There are not enough words to describe the painting. If ever he felt clogged when writing about Tata's art he does not feel it now. But before he can say any more Ettie is kissing him. She is pushing him against the wall of the outhouse. He is pinned between the rough crags of the wall and the softness of Ettie's body. Her hands are in his hair. Her mouth is hot against his.

She had said she wanted him to see her and now he does. All of her. She is here in this painting. He lifts her up. Showers her face with kisses. Her jaw. Her neck. He wants to kiss every part of her.

Ettie squirms but she is smiling. Grinning, even. Wider than he has ever seen before.

"Ettie," he gasps, looking down at her. Her eyes are ablaze. "You have to get out of here."

ETTIE

A rectangle wrapped in brown paper, tied with string. An address written neatly on the front. Ettie slips out of the side door, hugging the parcel to her chest. She darts onto the donkey track. Glances around. Walks swiftly away from the house.

She looks down and checks the address again. Yes, it is correct. She copied it so carefully from the card hidden beneath the loose floor tile in her bedroom. Three Gs in "Guggenheim."

She walks quicker, afraid that Tata might call her back and afraid she might lose her nerve. As she nears the end of the donkey track she breaks into a run.

Her hair is stuck to her face by the time she arrives at the tobacconist, her breath coming quick. Salomé spits a cheekful of tobacco onto the floor as she enters and the two women size each other up. Ettie places the parcel between them. "I need as many stamps as it takes to get this to Paris in one piece," she says, piling a handful of coins onto the counter.

Salomé eyes her. She scoops all the coins into her palm and does not return any change. Silently affixes seven stamps to the parcel.

Ettie is about to leave when she remembers something. "May I borrow your pencil?" she asks.

Salomé slides one from behind her ear. Ettie flips the parcel over and scrawls on the back:

P,

*Hang this upside down if you like. There is no
right way up.*

E

All through dinner, Ettie thrums with adrenaline. She serves capers instead of olives. Overcooks the monkfish. Her hands shake so much when she opens a bottle of wine that Joseph has to help her.

She can barely concentrate. Night falls and she thinks that Joseph and Tata are talking about absinthe. She cannot be sure. They are only at the other end of the table but they may as well be a thousand miles away. After dinner she takes the plates to the kitchen and the china rattles in her hands.

The night deepens, bruising around the edges. Bats quiver through the air. Cicadas shush. Ettie completes her nightly rounds: kitchen, dining room, terrace. She returns a stray cork to a bottle of wine. Tidies away loose paintbrushes. She sweeps the scattered leaves from the hall where they have crept in under the door. Blows out the candles. In the rooms beyond, doors click shut. Bedsprings creak. The house becomes soft with silence.

Ettie returns to the kitchen, twirling a cigarette between her fingers. She closes the door behind her, but then something moves in the corner.

She flattens her back to the wall.

A shadow shifts. A milky eye looms out of the darkness.

Tata is seated at the kitchen table. He is in her usual chair, hulking over the table like a great bear. Her eyes adjust to the blue dim of the night and she takes a step towards him. Moonlight glances off the bottles on the shelf behind.

It is strange to see Tata in the kitchen. He rarely comes in here, as if it is too domestic, too mundane a space to contain him.

She pulls out a chair. Sits.

Neither of them speaks for several moments. Tata is running his eyes all over her, his mouth trembling as if unable to find the words he wants to say. And then all of a sudden he whispers, "Don't leave me."

Ettie's blood runs ice cold.

He knows. He has seen the yearning in her heart. He has heard a whisper through the walls, watched her when she thought she was not being watched. He is onto her.

But no, he cannot know. There is a tremor to his voice that betrays an uncertainty. He grabs her hand. "Do you remember—do you remember how we used to fish for minnows in the stream?"

Ettie stares at him. The truth is she does not remember.

"We used to go down to the stream with little nets and catch the minnows as they swam upstream. Do you remember that?"

She has no recollection of fishing—for food? For fun? Why would they do that? Perhaps Tata is lying. Or has she forgotten? Has she wiped these happy memories from her mind in her determination to make her uncle a monster? A thought troubles her: perhaps he is not so terrible after all. Perhaps she has made it all up.

"We used to put them in jars," he says. "And do you remember— remember the little bird we once found on the terrace? We nursed it back to health. The goldfinch in the cage. We used to feed it sunflower seeds through the bars. We did that, didn't we?"

Ettie is mute. She stares at her uncle as the words tumble from his mouth. Some of these memories are hers but they are not as she recalls them. Tata has chopped them up. Sewn them back together out of order.

Is he lying? Or does he believe these recollections, which bear no resemblance to her own?

"You were always such a good girl," he whispers. "You are so good to me. So very good to me."

She manages a smile, gives his hand a squeeze.

"And I . . . I have been good to you, haven't I?" His voice is pleading. "I never laid a hand on you. I was a good . . . I was good to you, yes?"

"Yes," Ettie agrees. She does not even notice the lies anymore. "Yes, Tata." They slip out of her mouth as easily as breath.

Tata's eyes crinkle, and he clasps both his hands around hers. Binding her.

"I won't leave you," she says. "I promise."

He lowers his eyes. Loosens his grip and for a moment Ettie thinks he is going to release her. Then he looks up and whispers, "She promised that too."

Ettie does not move. Her skin seems to shrink around her, hot and tight. The silence of the kitchen is deafening.

"You won't make the same mistake as her," Tata whispers. It is not a question this time.

"As who?"

Tata does not answer but Ettie feels a chill. The cold, faceless presence of Ettie's mother slips between them. Pulls up a seat at the table.

"You are safe here," Tata whispers. "I brought you both here so you could be safe."

Tata has never spoken to Ettie about the circumstances in which they came to the farmhouse. It is a story she has cobbled together through other people. If ever she asked Tata he shrugged her off with a rough grunt. If she persisted he shoved her away. If still she demanded an answer, he shouted. Sitting at the table now he looks like a wounded animal, and she is reminded of that night when she was a child and Tata stole into her room. He clasped her to him and through his sobs he called her by her mother's name. "Gabrielle . . ." he had cried. "Gabrielle . . ."

"I loved her so much," he whispers. "So much."

Ettie knows he loved his sister. He loved her and he trapped her because that is what Tata does to the people he wants to keep close. She pictures them: the two grubby siblings from the port town out west. Dancing high in the lights of Paris. And then exiled here, together in the empty nothingness.

Tata has never spoken about that time. He has never told her about the day he and his sister packed up their life in the big city. But he knows things Ettie doesn't. She understands by now that there is information he keeps from her that might lead her to pull away from him. To break free.

"Who was he?" Ettie asks in a whisper. Who was the man who broke Gabrielle in half, who planted a seed inside her that became Ettie? Who was the man who started all of this? Who were they hiding from all those years ago? "Tell me who my father was."

Tata's lips tremble and he shakes his head. There is fear in his eyes. He opens his mouth but no sound comes out. He cannot bring himself to say the name. But there is only one name Tata refuses to say. And Ettie reads it in his eyes. She sees the answer, and even if Tata's lips will not form the words, she can hear his heart beating out the words:

Paul.

Cézanne.

Ettie stumbles to her bedroom in a daze. Cézanne, Cézanne, Cézanne. Tata's old mentor. His friend. The man with the wife and son.

An answer has fallen into place. A name, where previously there had only been an empty space.

She sits on the edge of her bed. Tata's fight with Cézanne was never about art. It was about a woman. And inside that woman, a growing thing that became a person: Ettie. The physical evidence of her mother's transgression. Of Tata's greatest friend's betrayal. The embodiment of the beginning of the end.

She takes her mother's old recipe book from her bedside table. Slides from between its pages the old scrap of paper with her childhood list of names. Strikes a line through them all and writes underneath: Paul Cézanne.

A circle, finally closed.

Is the artistic talent that runs through Ettie's veins Tata's? Or Cézanne's? Or is it her mother's? The woman who was never given a chance to see what talent she held or how great she might have been.

No, thinks Ettie with a flare of defiance. Her talent is all her own. Cultivated in secret. Practised under cover of darkness. Quashed, hidden, smothered. It is no one else's but hers. Sustained by her bright, blazing self.

JOSEPH

The milk has turned. The peaches in the kitchen have split open. The flowers on the windowsill have sunk into a coffee-coloured slump. August is rampaging towards its end and mosquitoes, flies, and wasps have all invaded the house. A perpetual buzzing fills the rooms.

Joseph treads the well-worn path to Saint-Auguste. He is on a perpetual loop, like a child's toy whose wheels can only move along the set grooves of a track between farmhouse, outhouse, and village. He shuttles from kitchen to studio to market and back again. It is the same loop Ettie has been making her entire life. Over and over again. He does not know how she can stand it.

After collecting the usual letters from Salomé, after purchasing the usual bread and lemons from the market, after nodding to the familiar old men playing chess in the shade, Joseph pauses in the square. He cannot go home just yet. He needs to jolt himself from the narrow track that has become his life. The village church stands on one side of the square, frothing with hot-pink bougainvillea. He has never been inside before.

The interior is a sweet relief. Empty and cold. His first impression is of stone, still air, accents of gold. A few candles flicker in the darkness; prayers placed here by members of the village. He has been in Saint-Auguste for nearly three months. A lifetime, and the blink of an eye.

Joseph sits down on a narrow pew. He does not believe in a god but he looks upwards. The streaked light of the high windows picks out a painted altarpiece: a crescendo of limbs ascending to heaven. He is a man with no god, no community, no direction, but still the church is a sanctuary. Finally, he can be alone. There is no Tata prickling at his back, nor even Ettie's watchful eyes following his steps.

He takes out the stack of letters and finds an envelope addressed to him. The paper inside is headed with the official insignia of a hospital.

Joe,

I saw you in a dream last night. You were in the garden but you were older than I ever knew you. How did you get so old?

And I—how did I get so old?

I'm getting out, Joe. I'm going to get out of here if it kills me. How much of my life has been swallowed by this place? How much is left?

I don't know where you are, Joe, but you're not here. I think you are far away.

Good. So bloody glad you got away.

Go far, Joe. Go far.

Rupe

It is the first letter he has had from his brother in two long years. His handwriting is nothing like it used to be, but Rupert is there in the words. He is the only person who calls him Joe. He has not been called that name in so long; it is a remnant of a different life.

Inside the envelope is another letter, and this time the handwriting is familiar and even:

Sod Father (yes, Joseph! Sod Father!), I'm taking Rupert to the sea-side. We are going to feel the salty air on our faces and wriggle our toes into the wet sand and eat cherry ice cream. The doctors have given their permission.

Rupert's walking again. He needs a stick in each hand but it's better than that awful chair. He's talking more. Not to Father or Dr. Yealland, but to his nurses, and to me. Slowly, one day at a time, he reappears.

He spends hours looking at the pictures you've been sending him, tracing the lines with his fingers. Something in those pictures has jolted him awake.

Can you believe how long it's been since he was out here in the real world? Four years in the hell of the trenches and another two locked up in that hospital. I don't know what to show him first. What would you want to see if you'd been living away from the world for that long?

Well, I suppose you answered that already. Art. Sunlight. Another country.

Kisses from your sister,
Flora

Joseph stands up. He is gripped by a sudden urge to move, to flee. This is how he remembers his brother. Not as the husk in the hospital bed. Not as the sharp-angled soldier in the studio photograph. For him, Rupert is always in motion. Running, diving, swimming, grinning. Always ahead of him, looking back. His arm outstretched.

Joseph strides towards the white square of the outside world, and is hit by the thickness of the air. He misses his brother. He misses his sister. But for the first time it is not their old life he misses. It is a new one, one they have not lived yet. He does not want to miss a second of it.

He is plagued again by the image of him and Ettie in a studio. The trappings of a life lie around them where they have light, space, and time to do as they please. The days are ticking inexorably onward. Life is charging forward with the insistence of a wildfire.

He glances back at the little church as he crosses the square and spies a figure in the shadow of the entrance. The priest. He watches Joseph go and then, with a deliberate gesture of recognition, raises his hand in a wave.

ETTIE

In the darkest hour of the night, in the quietest corner of the olive grove, the artist puts down her brush. The great painting of the feast is finished, and Ettie staggers back against the wall as if thrown there. She is panting, sweat coats her body, and she stares at the canvas that glows out of the darkness. There is something terrifying about it.

The image feels alive. Perhaps it is the flickering candles in the outhouse, or the relentless pounding of her heart, but the painting seems to move. Decaying fruit crawls with mould. Wine ripples. The air shifts, as if someone has just stood up from the painted table. The scrunched napkin could just have been flung there.

The Feast is finished. But this is not the feast Tata envisaged. When Ettie began this painting she knew it would be different, and for once she has not made an exact copy of Tata's.

Where Tata's feast has twelve places at the table, Ettie has painted thirteen. She has added a bowl of peaches. They are not irregular but perfect and uniform; the sort she'd like to eat. There is one more chair than Tata painted. One more wineglass, one more plate, one more set of cutlery.

Ettie has given herself a place at the table.

She lets out a long, steadying breath. She can no longer see Tata's painting in *The Feast*. His was merely the skeleton upon which she added flesh. Painting this was like nothing she had experienced before. It took all the energy in her body, all the love and fear and desire and loss, channeled down through her arm and into her hand, which skipped over the canvas. Her brush flew across the painting, pressing passion and anguish and fury and hope into the paint. *The Feast* felt like freedom. She painted it as if in a trance. Wild, unthinking, limitless. And then, suddenly, it was finished. She dropped the paintbrush as if it had burned her. The painting spat her out, and there was nothing more she could do.

The Feast is done. She has pulled up a chair and inserted herself into the painting. Made it her own.

JOSEPH

Joseph is sitting on the terrace proofreading his latest article. The French doors are open. White curtains billow like sails. An orchestra of crickets rustle in the grass and grapes occasionally drop from the arbour above. The scene is bucolic. Ettie is out in the fields. Tata decided this morning that the final thing he needs for *The Feast* is some flowers on the table, so she is off hunting wildflowers, searching for every shape and colour she can find.

Joseph leans back and stretches. The sunlight is buttery, the terrace sandy under his feet. There is an end-of-summer mellowing in the air. The greenness of the trees is like a painted parasol, shading the scene with a cool sweetness.

From the solitude of the terrace Joseph can hear Tata bustling about inside the house. He moves with such furious sound, which strikes Joseph as ironic for a man obsessed with silence. Joseph tries to concentrate against the noise of Tata's body colliding with chairs and door frames and his laboured breath as he bangs open cupboards.

Joseph turns over a page of his notebook, and is startled to find a small cream-coloured card tucked inside. Odd. He turns it over, but all it has is a name and an address in Paris. He cannot remember where he has seen the name before but he recognises it because it is unusual: Guggenheim. Inside the house there is a crunching of floorboards, farther away now. The heavy tread of feet on the stairs and then the wrenching open of a door. Joseph raises his head, his ears suddenly alert. There is only one door at the top of the stairs.

"Ettie?" Tata is calling. "Ettie?"

"She's not here, Tata, she's—"

But the old man cannot hear him, for he continues to call from up in the attic, "Ettie? Ettie, where is that Chinese vase?"

Joseph's heart shivers to a stop. He sees what is happening like a swimmer transfixed beneath the great wall of a wave. He is pinned beneath the sound of creaking floorboards, shuffling feet, and then silence. It is a silence that draws itself out too long. There is something lurking in that silence.

A movement catches Joseph's eye. Ettie is coming up the field, her arms full of wildflowers. Lazy wafts of purple and yellow bob in the breeze. Somehow he needs to signal to her to stop, turn back. He waves his arms wildly and she pauses, tilting her head to one side. He takes a step towards her but is stilled by a sound from above. A crash, and a deep, guttural wail. It is bloodcurdling. It is the sound of a creature in pain.

Joseph can see the hand groping inside the dusty vase. Something unexpected being pulled out. A photograph between grubby fingers. In a flash Joseph sees the image of Ettie by the river. Naked, squinting, winking, beckoning. Her legs, her breasts, her eyes. The Chinese vase has yielded its secret. Tata has found the photograph.

Ettie has reached the edge of the field. She stands there, eyes wide, and as the scream from inside reaches her ears the flowers fall from her arms. Pink, orange, purple, white.

There is another roar. Joseph's mind darts to the other photographs hidden around his room: Ettie smiling. Ettie laughing. Ettie standing in the field, eyes to the horizon. There is a crunching from above. A sharp crack, and the sealed window of Joseph's bedroom, the one that has been jammed shut all this time, splinters open. Something rains down upon him.

An eye. Fingers. A fold of flesh. Hands, limbs, mouths, trees. His photographs, the secret photographs, ripped into irreparable fragments. Joseph tries to catch them, to gather them up, but the damage has been done.

Then more paper flutters down, and Joseph's heart tears itself in two. Words flit past him in the breeze: *monster, island, Penelope.* The shredded pages of Rupert's *Odyssey* fall through the air like confetti.

He glances around but Ettie has disappeared. The flowers are scattered at the edge of the field. Where has she gone? Suddenly there is a vibration from inside the house. The great body is moving, slamming down the staircase, rebounding off the walls. Tata is coming for him. He appears at the kitchen window like an eclipse. He is roaring like a man in pain. "Filthy—bitch—whore . . ." Words erupt from his mouth. "Just—like—her—mother!"

Joseph, usually inclined to running, to hiding, to shielding himself, stands his ground. For once he faces up to the terror in front of him and the terror right now is Tata, bursting through the kitchen door towards Joseph. "You!"

Then a girdle is around his neck. Tata has grabbed his shirt and it is strangling him. "What—have—you—done?" he spits, bringing Joseph close, pulling him towards his anger, his rage, to the epicentre of his madness.

"You're—choking me!" Joseph struggles.

"I let you into my house—I opened my door for you—let you watch me work—eat my food—sleep—"

"I can't—breathe—"

Tata flings him away and Joseph ricochets against the table.

"Playing games behind my back, is that it?" Tata seethes. "The two of you—in my house—under my roof. Laughing at me because old Tata would never know? Is that it?"

Heat radiates off him. Joseph can feel the anger, the humiliation, the deep, visceral betrayal reverberating from his body. "No—" he manages to throw back.

"I let you in!" Tata bellows. "I let you in and you betrayed me. You—and her. Just like . . . How could you . . . How could she . . ." He is gasping, clutching the back of a chair. "Get out," he spits. "Tell me where she is and get out." Joseph shakes his head.

"Where is she?"

"I don't know."

"Tell me."

"I don't know!"

Tata lets out a roar and Joseph knows that the roar, the rage, is not for him. It is for Ettie. Tata barrels back towards the house. Joseph grabs him by the shoulder but the old man is strong. He throws Joseph off and storms into the house, tripping over a flower pot and stumbling against the door. He is pathetic and awful and the sound that comes from him is barely human.

The darkness of the house envelops them. Tata is panting, exhausted, but he is fuelled by boiling rage as he bellows, "Sylvette! Sylvette!" He tears from room to room like a wild boar. And the words that are running through Joseph's mind are the words coming out of Tata's mouth: "Where is Ettie? Where is she? Where is she?"

But Ettie is nowhere to be found. She has slipped from their sight. Somehow she knew what was happening and she has made herself invisible, as she has always been able to do.

They have reached the front door. Tata wrenches it open and white light fills the hall. And then Tata stops still as if struck by an arrow. Slowly, his eyes filled with fear, he lifts his nose to the air. He sniffs.

And Joseph smells it too.

Something is burning.

ETTIE

In the end, it was easy.

The matches that were always in her pocket. The practised movement of her wrist. The quick sizzle. The flame appearing from nowhere.

The Feast caught instantly. The lemons and sardines, the oysters and artichokes, the tomatoes, radishes, bread, butter, wine, grapes, sunlight, shadow. Tata's masterpiece. It all went up in flames.

Creation and destruction lie side by side in Ettie's heart. She watches as large blisters appear on the canvas. Paint bubbles, melts, then darkens to a black crisp. Heat shudders in waves across the uneaten feast. Orange tongues eat at the painting until wine-glasses and melon halves and slices of ham are reduced to nothing but dry black curlicues on the studio floor. The fire swallows *The Feast* whole.

It is both violent and calming.

The Feast burns on its easel like a saint on a pyre. Smoke creeps towards the ceiling and through the open window. There is a snap like a whipcrack as the painting splits down the middle. It is broken. Ettie has broken it. Heat ripples towards her, but it is not unbearable yet. She has not finished yet.

Ettie turns to the rest of the canvases that line the studio. Quickly, feverishly, she pulls them away from the walls and piles them in the centre of the room. The crackle of the burning painting sounds like hundreds of insects. She sweeps the rotting food from the table. The fish bones, the grapes, the melon rinds. Flies hiss in dizzying circles. Plates smash. Glasses shatter. She has thrown off the last vestiges of control and is dancing to a death march of her own composition. She is untethered. She is free. She throws Tata's paintbrushes onto the pyre. They are the perfect fuel, dry as twigs. She uses his charcoal as tinder. She splashes over a bottle of turpentine, flammable as petrol. She piles everything, paintings, food, pencils, easels, brushes, paints, a jar of honey, all of it, onto the great waiting bonfire. She reaches for her matches.

She has been here so many times before, so why does she hesitate?

This time it is the end. There is no going back from what she is about to do.

Was there a moment that decided her? Or was it an accumulation of moments? Joseph's outstretched hand. Peggy's dark eyes. The card slipped into her apron pocket. A name written at the bottom of a twenty-year-old list. The moments have built up, turned over. Her life is a rolling wave which has finally crashed. The end has begun.

She has known all along where Joseph hides his photographs. She knew what lay at the bottom of the Chinese vase. And it was she who suggested this vase to Tata, for the wildflowers he wanted to paint. She saw her chance, and she snatched it.

She turns the box of matches over in her hands. Why did she need Tata to see the photographs? In the pit of her stomach, she knew that she wanted him to see her. All of her. No more hiding, no more cowering, no more bending herself out of shape to fit his vision of her. She is a woman bursting open and she wants him to feel the fire within her.

The Feast, her feast, is waiting in the outhouse. Tata will find it eventually. He can do what he likes with it. But at last he will know what she has done. He will know who she is. Her own paintings, the ones Raimondi laughed at all those years ago and the new one too, have been slipped from the back of her wardrobe. Wrapped in brown paper. They are on their way to Peggy Guggenheim in Paris. Her paintings have gone ahead, and now she will follow.

But she will not be alone. If she runs she knows Joseph will only be a hand's reach behind. They will cobble together a new life from the ashes of this one. The world is within reach, and this time she will not let it out of her grasp.

She strikes the match. Onto the bonfire she places all her pain and resentment. All her disappointments, her crumpled dreams, her frustrated wishes, and her wasted years. She puts her mother's death, her lost life with Amir, the nights of madness, the torment, the hexes, the secrets, everything, she heaps onto the waiting pyre. The bead of orange ticks down the match. The flame is coming. It is white hot. At the last moment, before it can hurt her, she throws it. The bonfire catches in one beautiful blossoming. Wood and canvas and brushes and pencils make ready kindling. The turpentine explodes in a fireball.

She watches, transfixed. Tata's paintings curl among the hungry flames. There is the familiar smell intensified a thousandfold: melting varnish, charred wood, paint evaporating into fumes. The fire grows higher and a great wall of heat buffets her. The flames reach the ceiling.

She cannot move. What is she doing? Is she about to obliterate herself along with all of Tata's work? She is trapped in a room on fire.

Suddenly there is a lungful of smoke inside her and it tastes of death. She gasps, bringing her arms to her face, covering her eyes, her mouth, her nose. She staggers towards the door—the pale sliver of life beyond the roiling heat. The cracks and crashes of destruction grow louder behind her, black smoke threatens to swallow her.

Ettie emerges, sputtering into the light. Clean air pummels her lungs and she gasps for it. She wants to inhale every particle of life she can. Gulp it down.

The soldier in the hospital had been wrong when he told her about the stranger coming to town and the man going on a journey. Those are not two stories. They are the same story.

The old farmhouse lies to one side of her. The rest of the world to the other. She throws her body forward and starts to run.

This is an ending. This is a beginning.

PART IV

THE ARTIST

LONDON, 1957

Later.

Years later.

An art gallery.

Ettie walks the empty corridors, trailing her hands along the walls. This is her favourite time, before the doors have opened. Before the footsteps and the murmurs have begun, when expectation hangs in the air. When she is alone with her work.

She walks into a wide square room. The walls are lined with canvases: years and years of her life. They have been spaced at regular intervals. Carefully positioned beneath the right light.

Ettie stops by a painting. Runs her finger along the smooth wood of its frame.

This is a large canvas, a frothing swirl of red and white. Metallic crimson streaked with light. The paint eddies and flows, the red staining the white before fleeing in rivulets. The colours ripple as if seen through water. There is something alive in this painting. Something restless in the dense glossiness of the paint and the desperate sweep of the brushstrokes.

It almost looks like a cloth soaked in blood. Washed clean.

Ettie raises her hand to the corner of the painting and traces the soft crags and waxy furrows left by her brush. She likes to know how her work feels beneath her fingertips.

People have said this is a violent painting. Some think it a religious allegory. Others a depiction of the war: the death and destruction that came for the world again. But the label on the wall says none of this. It gives only the painting's name: *A Beginning*.

When Ettie looks at this painting she can still feel the weight of Joseph's shirt in her hands. The coolness of the water, the blood flowing between her fingers. She can feel the sun on her back. The tug of the current. Her toes curling into the dank silt of the stream. The warmth of Joseph's skin.

Memories of that summer roll over her in waves. The heat, the light, the longing, and something inside her breaking open. All those moments. All those beginnings.

She looks around the walls of the gallery now. They are all here: her paintings. Her life.

Well, nearly all her paintings.

She had visited *The Feast* for the first time the previous day. It had ended up in the National Gallery in London, hung in a lofty room with silk-clad walls and leather seats. It had taken a long time for her to feel ready to face it again, but yesterday she had steeled herself. She held her breath as she climbed the wide stone steps of the gallery, gripped her raincoat over one arm as she entered the high, echoing room, and then . . . there it was. The last painting that tied her and Tata together. There was the food she had painted all those years ago: the melon slices and radishes and gently decomposing sardines. There was the smear of butter on a silver knife. There were her thirteen chairs. And there were her peaches. Ripe and plump, ready to be eaten.

She stood alone among the crowd, staring at *The Feast* like an old friend glimpsed in a strange city. Her eyes lingered on the painting. The sounds of the gallery died away. Slowly, she shifted her gaze to the plaque on the wall. There, appended to her painting was his name: *Edouard Tartuffe.*

For a moment the old panic had returned. A chill squirming in her stomach. But then she took a breath. Steadied herself. Tata's name on her work was like a rough hand laid on the top of her head, and then lifted off. A threat that became a benediction. A blessing. It was a final, twisted admission: *Your work is as good as mine.*

And as she looked back at the painting something inside her burst, like a bubble rising to the surface of the water. A pop of lightness. The knowledge that Tata had seen her. That he had known, after all, that there were two artists in that house.

Ettie wandered the wings of the National Gallery after that, reading the information accompanying other paintings. She wondered how many ghosts hovered behind the names printed in neat black type. How many invisible hands had held the brushes. Who else was hiding behind the paint?

On her way out Ettie bought a postcard in the gift shop. The woman behind the till smiled when she placed it into her hand and said, "Oh, I love this one . . . It makes me feel as if I could reach out and eat all that food myself."

Ettie smiled back. "Me too."

For all the attention Ettie has found in the world, the praise, the plaudits, the money, it is these acts of daily life which most taste like freedom on her tongue. The small exchanges with strangers. The ability to walk out of her door and go where she pleases. To sit in a room vibrating with noise and laughter. Long afternoons sat outside with no urgent feeling that she needs to return home. Food chosen for its taste rather than its shape. Her own studio.

A photograph, pinned to the wall where she paints. Two figures in a dry field. The trees visible through their bodies, the sky through their hearts. She and Joseph, fixed in black and white in that hot, distant field, their hands *just* touching. In this photograph she sees them as they once were. Young. Crackling on the edge of the world.

Ettie passes into the next room, a large white space, the first the public will see when they enter. Her name has been stenciled in high letters along the wall. A quote from an interview with her has been painted above the door:

EVERYTHING INSIDE ME IS ON THE CANVASES.
MY LIFE IS IN THE PAINT.

She pauses by a table stacked with exhibition catalogues. A photograph of her has been printed on the front. Over and over again, her face stares back at her. She picks one up, meets her own eyes. She has been photographed many times over the years but this picture was taken by the person who sees her most clearly. Who knows her by heart.

Joseph has distilled her. In this photograph she is defiant. Calm. Wholly herself.

Looking out at the world, and inviting the world to look back.

AUTHOR'S NOTE

I have taken some liberties.

This is a work of fiction, but it brushes against the real world and there are moments where I have blurred the line between the two.

Paul Cézanne was one of the most influential painters of the late nineteenth and early twentieth centuries, and he is known for his paintings of the South of France where he spent much of his life. His depiction in this novel is entirely fictional.

Vincent van Gogh, briefly referenced in this novel, was another painter drawn to the South of France and his collected letters informed much of my thinking.

Dr. Yealland, the doctor who treats Rupert after World War I, was a real person. Lewis Yealland practised his experimental electro-shock therapies on patients at the National Hospital for the Paralysed and Epileptic between 1915 and 1919. The patients were largely soldiers with "shell shock," now called PTSD. In 1918 Yealland published a book called *Hysterical Disorders of Warfare*, which I found genuinely disturbing to read. Yealland's methods included electrocution, placing lit cigarettes on patients' tongues, and putting hot plates at the back of their throats. It is an account that is stunning in its egotism and haunting in its cruelty. For further fictional portrayals of Dr. Yealland, I recommend *Regeneration* by Pat Barker.

Ernest Hemingway was not in Paris in 1920, and so would not have been in a position to fall out with my fictional troupe of artists. Hemingway spent the final years of World War I in Paris and Milan but was back in the United States during the summer of 1920, the period that this novel covers. He would return to Paris the following year and remain there for most of the 1920s.

Peggy Guggenheim arrived in Paris in 1920, aged 21. Reputedly determined to buy a painting a day, she wrote that "I soon knew where every painting in Europe could be found, and I managed to get there, even if I had to spend hours going to a little country town to see only one" (*Out of this Century: Confessions of an Art Addict*). Over the subsequent decades she became a patron of some of the greatest artists of the twentieth century and amassed one of the boldest collections of modern art in the world.

Women were first admitted to the Académie des Beaux-Arts in 1897. They were admitted to the Slade School of Fine Art from its inception in 1871, and the Slade was unusual in being "open to male and female students on precisely the same terms" (*The Magazine of Art*, vol. IV, 1883). Joseph's point that there were more men than women at the Slade and that women had to leave the room when they did life drawing reflects the more widespread practice of barring women from life classes altogether, or of only allowing them to work from draped, rather than fully nude, models. I added this detail to reflect the structural disadvantages women faced, rather than the specifics of Joseph's school at the time.

The quotation from *The Odyssey* that Joseph sends to Rupert is from Robert Fagles's 1996 translation. In reality, Joseph would most likely have read Samuel Butler's 1900 translation, but for these particular lines from Book XX of *The Odyssey*, Fagles's translation is my favourite and so this is the one I gave to Rupert and Joseph.

The hospital in the convent where Ettie meets Amir is modelled on the makeshift "base hospitals" established throughout France during World War I. The detail about writing diagnoses on the patients' skin in indelible ink comes from the records of Base Hospital No.28 in Limoges.

The abandoned asylum mentioned towards the end of the novel is based on the one in Långbro, Sweden, as described by Sven Lindqvist in his book *The Myth of Wu Tao-tzu*. Lindqvist writes, "The old exercise yard at Långbro mental hospital was shown. The walls had been pulled down. But the inmates still don't go out. They stay inside the wall that once existed." I found this a very useful metaphor for a controlling relationship.

Lastly, the only place either Ettie or Edouard Tartuffe's paintings can be found is between the pages of this book.

ACKNOWLEDGMENTS

My name is on the front of this book, but there are many more hovering invisibly behind the ink.

Thank you to my brilliant agent Eleanor Birne, who moulded this book with the gentle hands and clear-eyed instinct of an artist. I am grateful to her for always knowing what questions to ask of me, and for guiding me wherever I want to go. Thank you to the PEW Literary team: the fiercest brains in Soho and the warmest, most welcoming home for my work. I am particularly indebted to Charlotte van Wijk for spotting this nascent manuscript and pressing it into Eleanor's hands in the first place.

Jocasta Hamilton, the editor of my dreams, understood this book from the very first moment and has made it brighter, richer, and sharper with every edit. It has been nothing less than a wild and exuberant joy to be edited by her. Thank you to Charlotte Robathan, Katharine Morris, Anna-Marie Fitzgerald, Charlie Tonks, Kate Baguley, Claire Wachtel, and Juliana Nador all for getting under the skin of this story with such thoughtfulness and enthusiasm.

If you picked up this book because of its beautiful cover, it is thanks to the creative genius of Patrick Sullivan: a true artist.

My profound gratitude to Rebecca Folland, Helena Dorée, and all my international editors and translators for giving this story a home overseas. It is an immense honour to have my words translated into languages I cannot speak and books I cannot read.

To my tutor Peter Benson, who read the beginning of this novel and said, "Do not, under any circumstances, stop." Thank you to the Faber Academy for the year of wonder when I wrote this novel, and to the fellow writers I shared it with.

Thank you to Lucy McMillan-Scott for allowing me inside the mind of an actual artist, and for teaching me about light and colour and the "relentless questioning" of the painter. To Clive Lamming, who knew exactly how my characters would get around France in 1920 and how long it would take them, and was generous enough to tell me.

To Lucy Waverley, whose intuition for where the heart of a story lies helped shape this book. I am grateful for her wisdom and perceptiveness, and her deep understanding that the past is just as alive as the present. To Natasha Hastings, for the rallying words, and for telling me I could rebuild this novel when I took it apart and sat amongst the rubble. Thank you for all the hours of writing together which, word by word, made this book.

To my friends—scattered across the globe but so close to my heart—for their encouragement, enthusiasm, and for making sure I do not become a reclusive artistic hermit. To the Rijkses, my second family. Thank you for giving me somewhere warm to write this novel when I needed heat and dust and sun. Thank you for the endless support and love.

To my family, who took me to art galleries and placed pencils and pens and paintbrushes in my hands, and who never told me to go to bed if I was reading. Thank you to my mother, in particular, for her wide-open, expansive approach to art. It was she who advised me not to worry about understanding art but just to let it wash over me and take whatever I needed from it.

If there is any humour in this book it is entirely down to my father. My love of language is thanks to him, and he taught me that words are raucous and malleable and there to have fun with. Thank you for reading us stories and doing all the voices. Thank you for Asterix and Captain Najork and Gabriel García Márquez.

To Nat: the person I wrote my first stories for. Still the first person I want to tell all my stories to. I would not know how to tell a story without you. Thank you for bringing me Kate, and thank you to Kate for the books, the joy, and the understanding about building a life out of words.

To Koen, without whom nothing—not this book, nor this wonder of a life—would be possible. Thank you for believing in me before I believed in myself. Thank you for knowing me by heart.

BOOK CLUB DISCUSSION GUIDE

1. The novel is told from Joseph's and Ettie's alternating perspectives. What was the effect of experiencing the story from both of their points of view, and switching between them?

2. *The Artist and the Feast* involves lots of senses and sensuality. What smells, tastes, and feelings do you associate with this novel?

3. At the beginning of the novel Joseph is awestruck that he is allowed in Tata's house, but as time goes on the farmhouse becomes more and more claustrophobic. What is each character's relationship to the house? Is it an idyll or a prison?

4. What are the different ways that fathers or father figures are explored in the novel? Can Harry be seen as a substitute father for Joseph? Can Tata? How do you think it impacts Ettie when she finally discovers who her father is?

5. *The Artist and the Feast* opens with two epigraphs: one by John Berger and one by Celia Paul. How do these quotations relate to the story?

6. After Word War I, people were both scarred and traumatised on the one hand but eager for pleasure and abandon on the other. How does the novel explore these two ideas?

7. What role does food play in this novel? Is it enticing or repellent? Why do you think Tata keeps returning to it as a subject for his art? How do you think Ettie feels about food?

8. Ettie's mother had to choose between pursuing her own freedom or staying with her child. Do you blame her for abandoning Ettie? Why do you think she made the choice she did? Did she make an informed decision or was she tricked?

9. Art is expressed in various forms throughout the novel: in the paintings Ettie and Tata create, in the drawings Joseph secretly sends to Rupert, the poetry through which Ettie learns English, the photography Joseph uses to capture the world, and *The Odyssey,* which connects him back to his family. In what ways does art help the characters explore and express their feelings?

10. World War I was a time of great loss for Joseph and Ettie, but it also provided an opportunity for growth for Ettie. How do the characters' personal stories intersect with the worldwide tragedy of that war?

11. How do you think Tata's inability to read and write affects the way he experiences the world? And how much of Ettie's freedom is tied to being able to read and write?

12. Does knowing who painted a painting affect the ways we view, understand, and value a work of art? Should it matter?

13. What is the significance of Ettie adding an extra chair to her painting of *The Feast*?

14. In what ways are Joseph and Ettie different at the end of the novel to the beginning? How have they changed?

ENHANCE YOUR BOOK CLUB

1. Look at some paintings and discuss the invisible labour behind them. Who bought the food in a still life? Who grew the flowers and put them in a vase? Who made the clothes someone is wearing in their portrait? Who cleaned the artist's brushes?

2. Tata is very clear that he will only eat food that has colours, shapes, and textures that are worthy of his art. Try creating a meal that Tata might want to paint.

3. Choose a painting and write about it. What do you find yourself focusing on? Think about the colours, the scale, the texture. Does writing about a painting change how you feel about it?

ABOUT THE AUTHOR

Lucy Steeds is a graduate of both the Faber Academy and the London Library Emerging Writers Programme. She began writing *The Artist and the Feast* while living in France, and she currently splits her time between London and Amsterdam. She has a BA in English literature and a master's degree in world literature from the University of Oxford.